The
Fisherman's
Son

BOOKS BY MICHAEL KÖEPF

Save the Whale

Icarus (Michael Köepf and Max Crawford)

The Fisherman's Son

Michael Köepf

broadway books · new york

BROADWAY

Broadway Books titles may be purchased for business or promotional use or for special sales. For information, please write to: Special Markets Department, Bantam Doubleday Dell Publishing Group, Inc., 1540 Broadway, New York, NY 10036.

BROADWAY BOOKS and its logo, a letter B bisected on the diagonal, are trademarks of Broadway Books, a division of Bantam Doubleday Dell Publishing Group, Inc.

Library of Congress Cataloging-in-Publication Data
Köepf, Michael.
    The fisherman's son / Michael Köepf. — 1st ed.
      p. cm.
    ISBN 0-7679-0244-0
    I. Title.
    PS3561.0338F5   1998
    813'.54—dc21   98-5733
                                      CIP

FIRST EDITION

Designed by Pei Loi Koay

Title Page illustration entitled Living Water by Meinrad Craighead.
Reprinted with permission of Sheed & Ward, 115 E. Armour Blvd., Kansas City, MO 64111.

98 99 00 01 02 10 9 8 7 6 5 4 3 2 1

In Memory

Mary Morris

Heart of my sea, gone away

Man's life on earth?

Boats rowed out at dawn

And no trace left.

FROM THE JAPANESE

The
Fisherman's
Son

Chapter One

In a life raft, in the night, pushed by wind, Neil Kruger drifted on.

Spinning, the raft rose sideways on a wall of water. In blackness, he reached for a handhold. He found nothing. The raft came to the top of a sea. Wind tore at its canopy, threatening upset. He sprawled flat on the bottom of the raft as the sea fell away, lifting stomach to throat. Salt water scented with vomit washed over his legs, striking the inner wall of the raft before washing over him again. He was cold. The sea was in riot. Phosphorescent waves spilled from the tops of seas—hissing, laughing.

His hands searched for the emergency pouch. He was drifting away. The set from the southeast was strong. Another large wave came, spilling him off balance. He was on his back, water washing over him once more. He rose to his knees, cupped his hands, and bailed water through the canopy's opening. The wind blew it back into his face, stinging his eyes. He bailed more. As rain cleared his vision, he knew his brother was gone.

He searched again for the survival pouch. Found it on the wall of the raft. Neil opened it, feeling for a bailer, but the contents spilled out about his legs. He found the bailer, and bailed hard. Then more. The labor warmed, then exhausted, him.

The floor of the raft was almost clear of water. His hands searched for the remaining contents of the pouch. He found a small flashlight and snapped it on. Grabbing a nylon harness, he attached one end to the raft, the other to his body. He found the fabric sea anchor and cast it out. The raft stopped spinning. He located the parachute flares, ripped two open, and fired the first into the air. The green meteor rose, illuminating the sea all around. The sight of its power unnerved him. The flare blew away with the wind, falling back into the sea. He fired the second and waited.

No one would see. He fell back into the raft, shivering. He was smothered in storm.

Wind struck the canopy, blowing him on, away from the coast, away from the overturned hull of the Redeemer. How far was it now? One mile, two? A vision of the sinking *fishing boat came back. He felt the dark wind, saw rain and spilling seas. He saw Paul clinging to the keel. He tried to save him. He called, but his words were stolen by the voice of the wind and by men screaming beneath the sea.*

There would be no emergency transmissions. They had switched off the E-PIRB beacon just in case. They had turned off the running lights and slipped away in the night, telling no one their course. That was how the game was played. None would hear them. None would see them. He had seen the lights on the jetty. The radar screen had revealed the green glow of Half Moon Bay, the protective arms of the breakwater and Pillar Point. He had known the south reef was a chance but was sure they could make it. They had almost made it home. Almost. Before the comber broke over the reef and struck the Redeemer.

Now he was an unknown dot on a dark sea, floating away in an indifferent world. He drew his legs to his chest. He rested his head against the flotation chamber. He wanted to cry but pissed instead. A brief warmth came to his loins beneath his wet pants.

The raft again pitched sideways. Cold breaking water flooded through the canopy's opening, taking his breath away.

Frantically, he bailed again. When he stopped, he fell back against the soft fabric of the raft, feeling the ocean move beneath his body. The raft rose and fell, over and over. There was nothing he could do. He was a prisoner of the sea.

He hid his fear in memory, in the memories of another storm, long ago. Voices came. "Little men," his father said, his words carried off by the wind. "Hurry up," his mother said, "hurry up."

It was winter. His father was fishing for crabs. In the morning, there was a storm. Neil was seven years old, a child getting into a car, pushing his younger brother, Paul, to the middle of the front seat.

"Hurry up," his mother said, "hurry up," slamming the car door behind them.

His mother drove fast. The car splashed through the muddy parking lot next to the cannery. The wipers swept mud and rain from the windshield. Beyond the beach, endless ranks of high seas marched into the bay. His mother slowed the car. She had driven in silence since leaving the house.

His father had left in the night. The phone ringing on the kitchen wall had awakened all in the house. Something was wrong, maybe as wrong as the water in the bay.

The car came to a halt. Neil had never seen the sea this way before. The swells rose like mountains. They fell on the fish house at the end of the company's long wharf. Plumes of white water shot upward through the wharf's planking. Wall after wall of water engulfed the pilings. Midway along the wharf, the walls peaked, collapsing into white violence and thunder. The waves grew smaller as they came to the beach, ending in globs of foam that raced across the wet sand with the wind.

Out on the bay, three fishing boats appeared and disappeared in the steep storm seas. The boats strained at their mooring lines like wild horses rearing back on ropes. Neil had no idea where his father was. He couldn't be out on his boat. Not out on this sea—no fisherman could be out there pulling his crab pots now. But his father's boat was gone. Neil knew the outline of its cabin, its poles, the sharp angle of its bow. The bay's outer reef was breaking. Mountainous combers trailing manes of windblown spray rose up and fell into the sea. If his father had gone out beyond the reef, out into the open ocean, there was no way back.

His mother pulled him and his brother out of the car, into the wind and rain. She walked fast, down and onto the beach. Her grip on his hand was tight. It was like being led to punishment.

They came closer to the waves. He had never before been afraid of this place. In the summer, he and Paul had played on this beach while his mother waited in the sun for the boats to come in. Now the air tasted strange, strong, like a cut on his lip. The sand was littered with twisted piles of kelp, strewn about like guts from the opened bellies of monsters. Driftwood and logs lay everywhere. Seagulls stood in clusters on the upper reach of the sand, heads lowered into the howling wind.

His mother took them along the beach, through the battlefield of water and wind. The rain felt like tears on his face. He hated the way the beach was now. Where were they going? The wind, the rain, the roar of the breaking waves, the ugly masses of seaweed—he wanted it all to go away. He wanted his mother to be happy again, the beach to be the place it had been when he and Paul ran in their underwear at the water's edge or dug sand fleas out of tiny holes that blew bubbles. His mother was beautiful, resting on that summer beach waiting for his father's boat, more beautiful than the leading ladies in the musicals she loved so much. And even if it was a sin to think so, she was more beautiful than the white marble statue of the Blessed Lady at church. God wanted him to love his parents equally, but he loved his mother more. He wanted her love, her approval, more than anything else.

Suddenly, his mother stopped pulling. Her pace slowed. She stopped and looked to the end of the beach, where the sandstone cliff climbed up from the bay to the point. Neil saw what his mother saw, and he saw the tears on her face, moving sideways across her cheeks in the wind.

The fishing boat lay open on the upper reaches of

sand. Farther down, stranded in the surf, its cabin and deck turned slowly in the waves. Something had bitten the top off his father's boat and spit it into the surf. Men with crowbars and hammers climbed over his father and mother's first boat, prying things loose, hammering it apart. The *Emily K* was dead.

Two of his father's fishermen friends, Henry Cabral and Cort Heinkel, removed machinery and hardware from the boat, taking it on their shoulders to higher ground. He saw his father near the pile of junk, sorting through it. Prying metal from wood with a crowbar.

Beyond his father's broken boat, a second wreck lay impaled on the rocks below the sandstone cliff of the cove. The sea was battering this other boat into nothingness. A portion of its bow and the top of its mast protruded from the waves that licked the cliff with vicious white tongues.

At the far end of the beach, several men and a woman in a heavy coat stood near a form washed up on the sand like a large wet doll. Between his father's wreck and the doll, a broken skiff lay overturned at the edge of the surf. A splintered oar, like a dismembered arm, washed in and out in the foam.

His father saw them and waved. It was the same quick wave of recognition he had seen when his father came in from the ocean with a full load of fish. Had the storm and wreck driven his father crazy? How could he be so lighthearted while his mother stood in tears? While another fisherman lay drowned? While his boat lay in pieces at his feet?

His father came toward them, crowbar in hand, cigarette in mouth. He was a large man. He wore black Frisco jeans, a blue shirt over a turtleneck sweater, and an oil-stained yellow rain slicker over the shirt. A rain-soaked watch cap rested on his head, above narrow eyes on a face turned by the sun and sea into the color of an old baseball mitt.

"Little men," his father said, avoiding his mother's eyes.

"Ernie. Ernie," he heard his mother call above the sound of the surf.

His father dropped the crowbar in the sand and put his arms around his mother. Her sobs increased. With his mother's hair wet against his cheek, his father looked out at the churning waves.

"Emily, honey, take it easy now. It's going to be okay. Take it easy."

Gradually, his mother's crying went away. For a long time there was nothing but the sound of waves and wind.

"It's everything we had," he heard his mother say, "everything."

"We'll save what we can. Start over again. You'll see. It could have been worse," his father replied.

His mother's tears returned. "Haven't you had

enough? What more do we have to give? Let's go away. Take the boys and . . ."

He closed his ears to his mother's words, her sobs. He tried to move away, taking Paul by the hand. But his brother's feet were cemented in place as he clung to his mother's coat. A glob of blowing foam caught on his father's black pants. His father held his mother, now and then patting her on the back. He didn't understand his father. The *Emily K* was broken and dead at the edge of the waves. Why wasn't his father crying too?

His father returned to the wreck. His mother followed, saying nothing. In the distance, four men began carrying the wet doll in a blanket. The woman in the heavy coat followed. Neil tried not to watch, but an arm in a wet blue shirt hung from the blanket. The men spoke Italian as they passed, the wind scattering their words.

Henry, Cort, and his father stopped working, watched as the blanket moved by. Henry Cabral was a short Portuguese man, with a barrel-like chest. His face was handsome and dark beneath a felt fedora stained white with streaks of salt. The middle finger of his right hand was missing. He removed his hat as the blanket passed. The Italians took the blanket to a pickup truck near the cannery.

Softly, Henry told his mother what had happened. The dead fisherman was from Monterey. He had an-

9

chored his boat in the bay when the weather was calm and had gone home to his family after setting his crab gear. He had returned in the evening when the southeaster began to blow. His boat was dragging anchor out in the cove. Henry told the fisherman from Monterey that the seas were too high, the wind too strong. But the fisherman went out anyway. The fisherman and his skiff were swallowed by the waves.

The wind slackened. Neil's mother said they were going home. She took his hand again, and he took Paul's. Together, they walked back across the littered beach. They got back in the car, but his mother did not start the motor. She looked at the bay from behind the steering wheel. Finally, she turned to him and his brother.

"Neil. Paul. I want you boys to promise me something."

Neil had no idea what his mother meant. Her voice was serious, like the President's on the radio. He wondered what they had done wrong.

"I want you boys to promise. Promise that you'll never be fishermen. Do you understand? Never." Her eyes held tears.

"Yes," Neil replied, wanting desperately to make her happy again. His answer made him feel older, more important. He nudged his brother, and Paul said the same.

10   Back at the house, his mother and grandmother

argued as his grandmother prepared breakfast. It was the same fight Neil had often heard at the dinner table between his mother and his father. The war about money. It had gone on ever since his father had begun converting the old sailing boat into the *Emily K* for fishing, ever since they sold their home in town and moved out to Moss Beach, where the fog swept daily from the sea, creeping through cypress trees to engulf the sprout fields around their house.

That night, his grandmother came to tuck them in. Her hair was stringy white at the sides of her wrinkled face. She smelled of liniment and roses. She asked them if their hands and faces were clean, lest the spiders come down in the dark and lick the dirt away. She made them pray for the starving children of Europe and Ireland, pray to God to send them food. Meat and vegetables, but no fish. She had them recite an act of contrition in case they died in the night. Then she recited her sorrows. She made them promise never to be as mean to their mother as her own daughter was mean to her. She spoke of money, of the last of her savings, which had helped buy the home in Half Moon Bay, a home that had been traded for "this rickety old dump" and for his father's "crazy dream."

But his father's dream was a beautiful thing. When the boats came in, Neil would go to the dock with his mother. His father's boat looked like a swan gliding through the water. It was narrow and white, red at the waterline. He loved to see his mother's name in black letters on the bow. It made her famous. Now all her fame had vanished.

The following day they drove back to the beach. The rain and wind were gone, the sea less angry. His mother handed out sandwiches and poured hot coffee from a thermos for his father, Henry, and Cort, as they tried to salvage what they could from the *Emily K.* Eventually, his father and his fishermen friends carried jerry cans of diesel to what was left of the dream. They climbed onto the broken hull and emptied the cans.

When the fire and smoke began, Neil was excited. But as the flames reached into black clouds, he was overcome with sadness, then anger. Sadness for a burning dream, anger at the sea and wind that had made it happen. Both, for something growing between his father and his mother. From behind, a firm hand came to his shoulder. He looked up into the round, reddish face of Cort Heinkel. A dirty flat cap was pulled low over Cort's eyes. The stub of a wet unlit cigar protruded from the side of his mouth.

"We work hard, play hard, den all to hell we go, kid. Stand back, or you're a barbecued fish." Cort's words were thick with a German accent. There was a smile on his face, a smile in the face of a terrible thing.

"How could Jesus let this happen?" Neil blurted out.

Cort's hand fell away. Cort looked down at him, serious. "Better not think that stuff, boy. She does what she wants. Jesus took his huntsmen off the sea lickety-split. All twelve of those apostles, soon as he found them. He knew what was what."

Neil moved away. He didn't understand his father's fishermen friends. He had never heard anything like that at mass. His grandmother told him that the devil lured fishermen to the sea, where he washed and scrubbed their souls, making the ocean unbearable to drink.

He did not know why, but his father and the fishermen lived apart from other men. They belonged to no organizations or clubs in town. They never went to school on parents' night. Their talk was full of things Neil could not understand. He often thought of his father and the fishermen as priests in a secret church. They were like the black-garbed men who came and went at the rectory next to church in town, secretive men who lived apart and shared mysteries hidden from others. He was fascinated yet fearful of this world of men. It was a place where he was certain he would never go, and now he had promised he would not.

Neil walked back to his mother. His father and his mother stood close but apart, watching the flames. His father held Paul in his arms. Neil went to his

13

mother's side. She took no notice. A sudden shift of the wind sent a cloud of smoke over them. His mother turned to walk away.

"Let's go," she said, without looking back.

His father followed. His mother's grief was gone from her face. But Neil felt that something invisible had replaced it. She wore a mask. Looking at her, Neil sensed he must never tell his father of the promise he had made.

A fist of wind struck the raft, lifting an edge. Neil rolled to the high side, and the raft fell back. A glow of light flashed over the sea. A rumble of thunder followed from far away. The storm was turning.

Near dawn, the clouds opened for a minute. He saw cold stars. A light flashed far in, then was gone. Point Montara? A car on the coast road? He was drifting fast, up and into the shipping lanes. His best chance was a ship. If the clouds and rain lifted from the sea, it was a good chance. A ship bound in or out of the Golden Gate would spot him, and he would be saved. With light he'd have a chance. He hung on, bracing himself against the flotation chamber, waiting for dawn. Counting time with each rising sea, each hang and twist, each sideways fall. His mind drifted too. Back to a safer sea of remembrance.

The beach came again. The same beach in the northwest end of Half Moon Bay below Pillar Point where his father *and mother's dream was murdered by the storm. He was on the beach three years later. He was older, stronger.*

A fishing boat was in trouble: the *Norland,* Ott Bergstrom's boat. It had been driven into the surf line by another fierce southeaster attacking the bay through its exposed southern entrance. After three days, the storm had blown itself out. The sun was shining. The *Norland* lay grounded midway through the surf. Waves erupted with explosions of white over the stricken vessel. A crowd of people watched from the beach, Neil and his mother among them. Three men could be seen working in brief bursts of activity on the *Norland*'s sloping deck. With each blow of white water they ducked behind the tilted cabin, seeking shelter. His father was one of the men. Ott Bergstrom and Cort Heinkel were the other figures clinging to the lee side of the cabin.

His father had been fishing crab with Ott and Cort on the *Norland.* The crab season had been good. As the weeks went by, the *Norland* had unloaded crate after crate of the crabs. But things had gone bad.

For three nights and days, his father, Ott, and Cort had fought to keep the boat off the beach, out in the raging bay. Now they had lost.

They had been at sea pulling crab pots when the southeaster struck. There was no time to attempt a run for the city and the protection of San Francisco Bay. The breaking bar outside the Golden Gate would have rolled them under. Somehow, they made it back in to Half Moon Bay, maneuvering through the outer reefs, white with monstrous combers. But there was no way off the boat—the seas were cresting and breaking all along the fish dock.

His father, Ott, and Cort made fast to the *Norland*'s mooring amidst hills of water pushed by wind. They dumped their crab crates overboard and ran their engine ahead to lessen drag on the mooring. Their skiff, tied to the *Norland*'s stern, quickly sank. The men cut it loose to prevent it from fouling the boat's propeller. It lay on the beach, crushed by the surf.

Each night, Neil went with his mother to the raging beach. They parked facing the sea with other cars containing wives and children of fishermen. Henry Cabral on the *Evon* and Carmelo Denari on the *Cefula* were out on the bay. Each had a deckhand, a young boy hired from town. All were stranded like his father. Through the dark, rainy night, the women on the beach kept the motors in the cars running. They left their headlights on. Neil caught glimpses of the white hulls rising and falling between waves out on the bay. He was old enough to know that the lights were on for another reason: They helped the imprisoned men on the bay judge their position in relation to the beach. The closer the boats dragged mooring toward the watching eyes of the headlights, the closer they came to disaster in the raging line of surf.

By the second night, the women stood shifts in one car at a time. Neil stayed with them, perched on the edge of the front seat, peering out the windshield.

He saw faint mast lights swinging wildly, appearing and disappearing in rain and mountainous seas. He imagined the men on the boats between black mountains of water, trapped in the tiny prisons of the boats' cabins.

Inside the warm car, the women were cheerful. He thought they didn't understand. It was like a party, not a vigilant watch for tragedy. He remembered the limp doll on the beach. His father and the other fishermen could be spit up like broken toys.

Henry Cabral's wife, Annie, a woman whose round face always seemed to be smiling, sat in the back seat with Bernice Bergstrom, a large lady with a pointed nose and red cheeks. They wore kerchiefs and shared a steaming thermos bottle of coffee laced with bourbon. Neil sat in front between his mother and Bethel, Cort Heinkel's wife. Bethel was tall and thin, with dark eyes and long hair that spilled out from beneath the kerchief tied tight to her head. She spoke differently than his mother or the other women, like a cow-boy's girlfriend in the movies. At home, his grand-mother called Bethel "bar trash," but he wasn't sure what she meant.

The women joked about the men. They did not seem scared. They talked about movies, the *Hit Parade,* other women in Half Moon Bay. While they gossiped, his father could be drowned. To escape their laughter, Neil leaned closer to the windshield, closer to the slap of the wipers.

After a while, Bethel's fingers pinched him on the cheek.

"Hey, little sailor, Daddy's okay. They're doing fine out there. Rub-a-dub-dub, three men in a tub, sweetheart."

He turned and glared with anger. This was not a party. He was scared to say it. Bethel read the anger in his face.

"Whoa, take it easy." She leaned closer and whispered in his ear. The smell of strong coffee, bourbon, and strange perfume came to his nose. "Psst, I'm worried too, but do you want to scare your mother to death?" Bethel pulled back and winked.

He understood.

By dawn of the third day, the storm vigil was over. The men had lost. Their fuel ran out. Without an engine, the strain on the mooring was too great. First light found the *Norland* aground in the surf.

But the boat still had a chance. The storm was

blown out. The sky was clear, the air calm. The *Norland* rested halfway through the surf line. An attempt would be made to save it before the waves battered it to pieces.

Beyond the breakers, fellow fishermen maneuvered their boats: Henry Cabral on the *Evon,* Carmelo Denari on the *Cefula.* Henry was attempting to float a line through the surf, attached to a cluster of crab buoys. If the men on the *Norland* caught the line, they could use it to haul in a heavy hawser. The hawser, once attached to the *Norland,* would help bring its bow around into the surf, keep it from being pushed farther and farther up and onto the beach. At high tide and towing in tandem, the *Evon* and the *Cefula* would attempt to pull the *Norland* free.

The *Evon* maneuvered close to the beach. Henry Cabral stood on the flying bridge. His deckhand was on the stern. They were dangerously close to the breaking crests. Henry waved, signaling his deckhand to toss the buoys. The pickup line attached to the buoys paid out from the stern into the white surf. Driven by the breaking waves, the line drifted in toward the *Norland.*

Suddenly, a large swell rolled in from beyond the *Evon,* rising up from the bay, dark green, cresting white. People on the beach cried out. The *Evon* was in danger of being thrown to the beach with the *Norland.* White smoke shot from the *Evon*'s exhaust stack as

Henry made for deeper water. The green monster of water came to the *Evon,* taking her up and up, bow to the sky, threatening to throw her over onto her own deck. On the flying bridge, Henry Cabral stood like a jockey leaning forward in stirrups, while the deckhand hung on for his life in the aft stay cables, legs kicking air. The little fishing boat came to the crest, balancing like a toy, with its propeller exposed and spinning. The monster broke and fell with a roar, but the *Evon* twisted sideways, falling off to seaward. The crowd on the beach cheered. Neil's mouth was without sound, for seconds later the wall of white water smothered the *Norland* in an explosion of white. As the white wall passed ever smaller to the sand, somehow, the men on deck were still holding on beneath the cabin.

The *Evon*'s escape from the green wall pulled the pickup line away from the *Norland.* The buoys and line drifted wide of the grounded vessel. Like people at a football game, the crowd on the beach waved and shouted for the *Evon* to adjust position. Soon, however, the crowd pointed to something else in the surf. A man. A man swimming toward the crab buoys. Each advancing line of white water covered the swimmer's head, but he kept reappearing on the surface of foam, arms stroking forward. Back on the *Norland,* Ott Bergstrom and Cort Heinkel were still crouched at the side of the cabin. Neil's heart raced. The head, the stroking arms in the water were his father's.

"Go get it, Ernie," a man yelled from the crowd.

His father came to the cluster of buoys, grabbed them, and held on as several waves passed over his head. He pushed the buoys under his body and began swimming back toward the *Norland*. Twice, he was washed off the buoys. Twice, he remounted and swam on.

The swimmer reached the *Norland*. Neil's heart swelled with pride as the crowd cheered again. Ott and Cort reached for the buoys, then pulled his father out of the sea, up and over the *Norland*'s gunnel, awash with white water. His father was beyond the power and force of the sea itself.

Later, the tide lowered. The *Norland*, in waist-deep surf, lay on her starboard beam. A hawser stretched from her bow out through the surf to the *Evon* and the *Cefula* tied in tandem, idling seaward, waiting for the tug-of-war with the *Norland* when the tide came in.

While his mother spoke to another woman, a man from the crowd handed Neil a bottle of whiskey. "Hey, boy, run this out to your old man and his pals," the man commanded.

He knew if he moved quickly his mother would have no chance to call him back.

Holding the bottle high over his head, he splashed into the water at a dead run. The cold made him want to turn back. But the men on the boat had seen him. They waved him on. The water came chest high. A wave splashed his face. His head ached, the salt burned his throat. He came to the side of the *Norland*. His father, Ott, and Cort were laughing down at him from the crazy, sideways deck. Wet clothing clung to their bodies. Big arms reached down. Neil slipped. His head went underwater, but he held on to the bottle. The arms found him, took him, swung him up into the air, out of the sea.

"Attaboy," his father said.

The men drank from the bottle. Wet and shivering, Neil had never felt more important in his life. He had come to the edge of another world, a world where children did not go.

But satisfaction soon washed away as cold filled his body. He looked back to the beach. His mother stood apart from the other people, close to the water's edge, hands in her pockets, watching. Watching him. He knew what she was thinking. He had gone too far.

Chapter Two

A s dawn came, the raft rose vertical on a sea. His stomach felt hollow. Half-way up, he knew it was a freak, an event of the ocean. Several seas overtaking one another, swelling up like a mountain. He fell to one side of the raft. His fingers dug in. The raft was turning over. His legs were in air as he heard the sound of falling water above, hollow and loud. When it hit, all turned to silence. He felt the raft tumbling over. He was in the canopy, then back on the floor. In the canopy once more, then floating in water. The raft turned yet again, and he was being swept away, but the *harness held and his fingers caught the edge of the canopy's opening. The wave passed, and he knew he was safe.*

When he finished bailing, light was full upon the ocean. But the rain came again, and the clouds did not lift. The wind lay down by half, but visibility did not improve. Was he below the islands? Inside the islands? Between the islands and the point? At the top of a swell, he thought he saw a buoy to the inside. But crab season was over. It could have been a seabird, or a lost winter trap. If he came to a lost trap he could grab it, tie on to the buoy, and use it as an anchor. Wait for the weather to clear and somebody to see him. But he saw nothing, save rain on gray sea and cresting white swells. A dark thought rose beneath the raft, circling: He was outside the fishing grounds. Outside the islands and the shipping lanes. Drifting on, out into the open and seldom transgressed deep.

He forced his mind away, taking stock in the rolling raft. He gathered and stowed the contents of the emergency pouch. Foot pump, sponge, two packets of food, two sachets of water, a folding knife, first aid kit, fishing kit, signal mirror, leak stopper, spare batteries for the flashlight, seasickness tabs, and two plastic paddles, easily assembled. He could make it.

He drank half a sachet of water, sealed it, and secured it back in the pouch. He put the signal mirror to his face. Quickly took it away. He could make it. He would. He had made his choice, and now he chose to live.

． ． ．

Light came fully to the sea. Hours passed. The clouds drove by. The seas came on. Lifting him. Lowering him. Like life's events. Trivial and large. Passing by.

The rain stopped. He searched the sea. He turned the mirror to the sky, but there would be no reflection in the sunless gray. Rain came again. He bailed some more. Wiped the bottom of the raft with the sponge. Squeezed it out into the sea. Waited some more.

He'd met his mothership in the night. Wished he had not. Wished. He should not have listened, should not have trusted those men his brother met. They were not fishermen.

"We should see these guys," Paul said.

"Why not?" he heard himself reply.

Later, hundreds of sea miles later, it all came to a choice. He could still smell the blood, washed from the deck with the saltwater hose. Sweet, metallic, forbidding, washed away and diluted in the ocean.

Neil Kruger closed his eyes. Once more, he saw the form clinging to the keel. His brother. Once more, he heard the yellowfish crying out beneath the sea.

He opened his eyes and pushed it away, trying to remember other things he had forgotten. Anything to rescue him from where he was.

He put his face against the flotation chamber, his ear to the fabric. He heard things resonating, coming up through

25

the sea. The thought of death came. Last thoughts. A final thought. What would it be? Was there a choice? Take what's there? The last thing we think? That moment before death. How long could that memory be? As long as life itself? Then nothing? Nothing at all. A rock cast into the depths, sinking into darkness.

He made it go away. He made himself a boy once more.

Down in the pilings beneath the dock he saw rubber-lip perch swimming in long strands of seaweed, moving back and forth in the swells like billowing hair on women. He and Paul wanted those fish with their spade-shaped copper bodies and their lips tinged with purple. Barnacle eaters. They had strings of kingfish, jack mackerels, ugly skates. But no matter how many hooks and leaders they lost in the pilings and seaweed, they could not catch the rubber lips. So visible, so serene, so close below.

A day was passing. The wind did not increase. Nor did it decrease. The seas came closer together, but the height of the swells and their snarling white crests were lessening. Far away, the storm was beginning to change. Hope was floating on the sea. The storm would pass. It would clear. He would be seen. He was waiting.

By late afternoon, the raft was softer. He took the air pump and attached it to the fitting. He pumped it between his hands. The effort was exhausting, but he wanted to live. Later, he rested, drifting, until his thoughts and the motion of the sea were one.

He and Paul were fishing on Patroni's dock, waiting for the boats to come in, while their mother worked at the foot of the dock, in the cannery. They were waiting for his father. But the memory was clouded by another. What was it? Intense, but already forgotten. He was helpless.

Night came. The sea took him on through the dark. Possibility was withdrawn. His heart beat faster against the cold.

He closed his eyes, attempting to calm himself. The raft rose and fell. The heartbeat of the sea. Rising and falling, again and again, until he remembered the first time he felt it.

Neil, get up. Neil." His mother's voice was a whisper, her fingers touching his shoulder. He heard his name once more. Was the house on fire? But his mother was not waking his brother, in the bunk above. Light from the hallway shone upon the hands on the clock, next to the little statue of the Blessed Lady atop the dresser. It was two o'clock in the morning.

"Neil, come on. Your father needs you. You have to go on the boat."

His mother was joking. His dream had taken another bad turn, but as he came fully awake he saw that it hadn't. His mother pointed to pants, shirt, and a sweatshirt, arms and legs of cloth dangling lifeless on the chair next to his bed. She pressed two pairs of socks into his hands. How could this be?

His mother moved away, out through the bedroom door and into the lighted hallway. He saw her silhouette, her pregnant stomach large beneath her robe. He was betrayed. She made him promise on that morning years ago. Made him promise, and now she was giving him over to his father.

"Emily, what's wrong?"

His grandmother's voice came in the dark, passing through his bedroom, toward the hall. She moved from her cold back-porch room, layered in flannel nightgowns, gowns that made her look like a ghost. Her arthritic gait was uneven. She came to the wash of hall light, and he saw that her teeth were out, cheeks hollowed. He pushed his covers down and slowly swung his feet to the cold floor.

"Go back to bed, Mom." His mother's tone was hushed and irritated. "He has to go with his father."

His grandmother's face turned toward Neil, then back to his mother.

"Jesus, Mary, and Joseph—the boat, Emily? Are you crazy? The boy's twelve."

"It's only for the day. They'll be in tonight," his mother answered.

He wanted them to stop. His brother was stirring

above. He could do it. He prayed his grandmother would go back to bed.

But she would not let up. "For the love of God, Emily. It's not right. He's—"

"Shut up. Go back to bed. Don't tell me how to run my family. I've got enough to worry about. Bills. The new baby. You telling me what to do in the middle of the night. The fish are running, and his father needs him. We need the money."

His mother's voice was firm, final, at the edge of cruelty.

His grandmother turned away and came back through his room. He pulled his sweatshirt over his head to hide from her muffled sobs. His grandmother wrapped him in her arms, pulling him into her old woman's scent, running her cold fingers across the side of his face. She made the sign of the cross over his forehead, then kissed it. A tear struck his nose, trailing down to his lip. Her thin arms let him go, and a taste of salt came to his tongue.

He went downstairs to the kitchen, rubbing his eyes. Without looking at him, his mother made coffee and hot chocolate, standing over the stove. He loved her so much. He would do whatever she wanted him to do. He knew that in her heart she did not want him to go.

His father came down the stairs and into the kitchen, pulling on his canvas jacket. He stood at the 29 stove, warming his hands at the burners. His father poured a cup of coffee, turned his back to the stove, and cradled the cup in his thick fingers. His watch cap was on his head. His woolen sweater protruded at his neck. He was wearing his black rubber boots. His father was ready for the sea.

Neil sipped his chocolate. His mother and father exchanged words of function. Neil was grateful. The winter's crab season had been poor. His mother and father fought, mostly about money. But salmon season brought money, and temporary peace.

Now something on the boat was broken, something called the automatic pilot. His father could lose a day's fishing to repair it. Neil understood that he was to be the broken thing's replacement.

His father said nothing as he drove the pickup down to the wharf. Neil was cold. He thought of the ocean. He did not want to go to that empty, cold place. He said a silent Hail Mary: "Pray for us sinners now and at the hour of our death. Amen."

He thought of war. He was a soldier going to battle. He imagined Billy Bergstrom, Ott Bergstrom's son, sick from polio. He saw him in his wheelchair, hovering above the headlights as his father drove on. Was this how sickness and disaster came, suddenly in the night?

His father parked the pickup next to the fish cannery. Neil followed him out onto the dock. Below, in the pitch dark, waves hissed and broke through the pilings of the pier. The air was cold and wet. It smelled of seaweed and barnacles and the salt scent of blood.

Neil had never come to the wharf at night. When the fish were running, the fish house at the end of the dock was often crowded with happy and friendly people from town. Neil thought of Chamarita, the Portuguese celebration, which came to Half Moon Bay each year. During Chamarita, a beautiful make-believe queen, dressed like a bride, carried her crown of silver dollars down Main Street to church and placed it on the altar in thanks for the food that sailors in history brought to starving people on islands far away. When he had come to the wharf in daylight with his mother and brother, he had seen piles of salmon higher than his head on the fish house floor. They were beautiful, bright and silver like the color of money in the queen's own crown, angels from a fish heaven his father and the other fishermen kidnapped from the sea. But now it was night, the wharf no longer happy and friendly.

His father came to the metal skiff ladder that dropped down into the blackness of the bay. Neil heard the power of the sea's swells moaning through the ladder's lower rungs.

His father pulled on the rope to his skiff, anchored off from the dock. Neil heard the skiff bang on the ladder below. He was terrified to descend the ladder, swinging like a pendulum in the sea's swells. His father looked up at the stars. The palest of light shone on his face.

"Wind's coming."

Was he talking to himself? There was no wind. The night air was cold and still.

"What wind?" he asked.

"Look," his father said. "There in the stars. They're twinkling. Wind. It's up there. Dock is damp. Before the day is over, it's coming down."

His father never told him what he was thinking. Why now? Was it a lesson he must remember?

His father knelt, swung his legs over the edge of the dock, and descended the ladder to the dark water.

"Okay." His father's voice came up from the darkness, calling for Neil to descend. Though petrified, he swung his legs over the edge, onto the cold rungs of the swinging pendulum. The ladder vibrated as he climbed down to the sea. At the last second, a swell brought the skiff up to him. "Jump," his father called, and he did so, finding it easier to overcome terror than to disappoint his father.

They were away. He sat, facing his father, in the stern of the skiff. The skiff rose and fell on the swells to the sounds of his father's breathing and the oar blades' slicing into the water. The oar strokes made dim eddies of light in the sea. Neil's stomach felt hollow as the skiff slid down the back side of each oncoming swell. His mouth was dry. He said another silent prayer. Maybe it was a dream, and soon he would awaken in his warm bed at home. But the prayer did no good. He touched his fingers to the water as the sea slid by. It was cold. He had come to a place where dreams and prayer did not work.

His father's hands swept close to his face with each stroke of the oars. The skiff moved out into the bay, toward hundreds of scattered lights. The fish were running, and boats from far away were anchored beneath mast lights. The lights moved up and down on the swells, mingling with the stars in the moonless sky. Neil saw the Milky Way and thought of mast lights on a larger ocean.

The cold intensified. As his father's arms took him over the water, he felt as if he was beginning a journey from which he might never return. He crossed his arms on his chest, placing his shaking hands under his armpits. He'd never see his mother again, his brother, his grandmother. His father would row forever, on and on through the dark night, past each star in the sky, taking him farther and farther from home. So far and long away that they would be forgotten, and rowing on still farther, he would forget his way home.

"Cold, honey?" His father's voice rescued him from himself, even though he hated it when his father called him by that baby's name. "Here, put your hands on the oars. Push when I pull. A little work will warm you up. Your teeth are tap dancing."

Neil waited for his father's backstroke on the oars. He placed his hands on the round wood below his father's warm hands and tried to push to help, but instead his father's first pull took his arms forward with such strength that he was pulled from his seat. After several strokes, he understood the timing. He pushed hard to add to his father's pull. His father's power was coursing through the oars into him, and as the cold left his body something else flowed in, something he did not understand. It was like the protecting love of his mother, but different, something he wanted, a place he wanted to go, a place only his father could take him.

They came to the *Maria B,* the family's fishing boat, asleep on its mooring. It rose and fell in the dark swells, a water phantom in the pale light of the stars. Sounds of water lapped at its hull. The flying bridge atop the cabin looked like an empty pulpit. The boat's long outrigger fishing poles resembled wings on some great sleeping seabird.

They climbed on board at the stern. The wet deck moved beneath his feet. All about him on the bay, cabin and running lights were coming on. Motors were starting. Anchor winches pulled chain. The fishing boats were waking up.

His father led him to the cabin. He switched on a light, lit a gas burner under a coffeepot, and told Neil to stay put. His father went back to the engine room. The boat awoke, the engine running with a low vibration. Neil's stomach was hollow.

His father went to the bow and tied the skiff to the mooring line. He unhooked the mooring from the bow cleat, and falling chain splashed into the water. The boat was free.

Ghostlike, the *Maria B* moved slowly past the remaining boats at anchor. Standing at the helm, his father switched off the light, and the cabin was dark save for the blue flame of the stove. After the boat cleared the outer edge of the anchorage, the engine speed increased. They joined a line of mast and stern lights headed for the sea buoy that would point them through the outer reef. The boats were close together. To the right, luminous white water showed on the reef, like a mouth opening and closing in the dark. Sure of his course through the reef, his father took no notice of the breaking water as he lit a cigarette. The match illuminated his face, watching ahead, and the smell of coffee mixed with smoke in the dark.

The boat rolled harder as they passed farther out into the bay. Neil felt nauseated. His father switched on the shortwave radio, and voices in English and Italian mixed with static came to flood the cabin above the drone of the engine. They were serious voices, 35 laughing voices, complaining voices. Voices that spoke of machinery, course settings, fish prices. Voices with hidden meaning. The voices spoke of the dawn to come and the possibility of wind. Always wind.

His father called Henry Cabral on the radio. Their conversation was brief.

"Good sailing and good fishing," his father said, placing the mike back on its hook. He was answered in turn by Cort Heinkel, Ott Bergstrom, and Carmelo Denari. The Half Moon Bay boats were moving out onto the sea as one. The men were beginning to hunt.

The boat rolled harder. Neil's head was spinning. He wanted to vomit but fought against it lest his father think less of him. They came to the blinking light on the buoy. His father turned the boat out to sea, and it rolled hard. Neil braced himself. He heard the moan from the buoy as they passed. The wake of the boat glowed white with luminescence. Mast lights ahead were fanning out beneath the stars. His throat burned with an acid taste.

"Neil, lookit here," his father said, drawing him out of his pain. "Look at the compass. The spot of binnacle light on the compass card. See the numbers?"

He moved next to his father. He saw the compass and the light.

"Watch," his father said. He took Neil's hands

and placed them on the helm. His father moved behind him, large hands still on the wheel.

"Turn the wheel to keep that spot of light on the course. The right numbers. One hundred and sixty-five degrees. See it? The heading. If the numbers swing left, turn right. If they go right, turn left. That's all. Keep your eye on the game. On the bow. Port and starboard. Each side of the boat. That's it. After a while, you'll see the flash from the Pigeon Point light up ahead. Keep the bow on the light. Here now, take the wheel."

Neil was terrified. He couldn't steer a fishing boat on the open black sea. His father was mad. Neil was doing all that he could to stand upright on the pitching cabin deck. Now his father expected him to take the helm, to steer the boat through the dark. His grandmother was right.

His father's hands left the helm. The roll of the boat became worse. His father's instructions were too simple, his voice too matter-of-fact, as if Neil had been told to walk to the grocery store to get a loaf of bread for his mother.

He searched for the courage to cry out in protest, but the numbers spun away on the compass. He turned hard. The numbers passed back the other way. The wheel and the boat's rudder had a will of their own.

"Easy there," his father said.

He turned again, but not so hard. The numbers came back, this time lingering in the pencil of light.

"Good," his father said, slipping into his slicker and yellow bib pants. He opened the cabin door.

"You got it," his father said.

The cabin door slid shut. Neil was alone. He wanted to cry, wanted his father to come back. But he had gone to the stern, down into the pit to bait hundreds of hooks. Neil looked back once and saw his father beneath the deck light on the boom, head down to his work, oblivious to the danger they were in.

Neil's sickness was gone—terror came in its place. The numbers on the card moved left. He turned hard, fingers pressing into the wooden spokes of the helm. The numbers came back, went away again, drifting from the light. The stern pitched high in a following sea. The engine raced as they slid down a roller-coaster swell. He was out of control. He was going to turn the boat upside down in the black sea. His mouth and his father's would fill with salt water. His mother would be sorry for giving him over to his foolish, trusting father. They'd search the beaches for his body. His friends at school would miss him. His teacher would erase his name from the roll written on the blackboard. He turned the wheel hard. His mother would drown in her own tears. But the numbers came back to the light. He steadied the helm, recaptured the course, and struggled on through the dark. If fear wouldn't save him, necessity would.

A minute later, hours later, a lifetime later, Neil looked up from the war between the binnacle light and the numbers and saw the first faint flash of the lighthouse miles ahead. To his left, the outline of distant hills above the coastline was appearing in the dawn's glow. The boats that had been sailing close by were now spread far apart, separated by a sea which had divided itself into lines of low hills running to the horizon. By night, the sea was frightening, but now at first light its visible immensity made him feel so small that fear itself seemed inconsequential.

As light came upon the sea, his father returned to the cabin, and Neil was released from jail. His fingers were stiff and his arms sore, but his heart soared with accomplishment. He had done it: He had not turned the boat over. He had not taken them into the beach or run into another fishing boat. He expected praise.

His father once more talked to his friends on the radio, but he did not mention his brave son. His father turned on the Fathometer. He poured coffee, studied a chart, lit another cigarette, changed course, ate a doughnut, all with one hand on the wheel.

"Get some sleep," his father said finally, pointing down into the fo'c'sle. The anticipated praise did not

39

come. Neil climbed down a short ladder to his father's damp bunk. Closing his eyes, he sank into a dreamless sleep.

A strange, humming music was resonating through the hull when Neil awoke—discordant music, like wind blowing through telephone wires. The engine was slower, quieter. Bilgewater sloshed slowly back and forth within the stomach of the boat. He did not know how long he had slept, but he sensed the boat was fishing. He swung his legs over the edge of the bunk and climbed back into the cabin.

The ocean was green. The sun, above the shoreline to the east, reflected off the water with a brilliance he could not face. The distant land looked small, insignificant compared to the sea all around. The violence of the boat's night movements was gone. The boat moved on the water at a walker's pace, rising and falling on oncoming hills of water. The boat was a cork; he was an ant riding upon it.

The vessel's outrigger poles extended out over the water like arms. Thin wires, attached to large springs, hung down and back from the poles disappearing into the sea. The strange music came again as a pole rolled toward the sky. Neil placed his hand on the thick base of a pole and felt a vibration. It was the source of the sound that had awakened him. The poles and wires turned the boat into a musical instrument, and the depths were playing an eerie song.

Neil made his way to the stern, timing his movements with the swells of the seesawing deck. His father stood in the pit with his back toward him, leaning over the stern, intent upon the water boiling up behind the boat. His father's hands reached out, holding a leader stretched taut toward the swirl of water at the stern.

The movements of his father's hands were calculated, delicate, like those of a stalking cat. Something precious was on the end of the line. His father's body bent further at the waist. The leader was pulling him. It slipped across his father's fingers, popping tiny beads of water. His father was flying a kite, playing it carefully, but the string did not lead up into the sky— it led down into the sea.

His father's leg and boot made adjustments on a metal wheel behind him in the forward part of the pit. He was steering the boat backward, balancing himself, arms out, one leg back. His father looked like an Oriental dancer, not a fisherman.

A following sea came, higher than the rest, higher than the top of their cabin. A flash of silver moved beneath the approaching wall of water. Neil saw the fish like a painting hung on a wall—its body twisted one way, then another. The swell passed. His father drew the fish closer. Its tail beat steady, swimming against his father's strength and the pull of the boat. His father moved one hand carefully over the other, drawing the fish closer. The taut leader sliced the surface. Neil saw the fish's red gills moving beneath the green water, the hook in its jaw. He saw its eye come up from the depths. An eye without fear.

His father wrapped the leader around one hand. Without taking his eye off the fish, he reached backward to the deck for a gaff. He brought it out over the water, turning it hook end up, poised above the fish. His father's leader hand came up. A splash of the fish's tail broke the surface. The fish's blue head rose. His father clubbed downward, and a hollow *thonk* came as the bat struck the head of the fish. It rolled to its side, convulsing, slapping water to the sky. His father struck again, this time with the hook. His father's body bent over the stern, both hands on the bat, pulling hard. The salmon came from the sea flying through the air, its head impaled on the gaff hook, its writhing body glittering in the morning sun. His father flung the fish hard to a bin. Water, fish scales, and drops of blood flew through the air. The fish's tail beat upon the deck. His father ripped the hook from the salmon's jaw with the gaff. The fish lay in the bin, shuddering its life away.

Neil's heart was pounding. He looked at his father. His father looked at him. A smile came to his father's face. His head nodded in a gesture of finality. "New pair of shoes," he said, before turning away to rebait the leader.

A taste of fish blood came to Neil's mouth. He wiped it away with the back of his hand.

The morning wore on. More fish came to the lines, his father working and killing without rest. Neil was sorry for the fish, clubbed and pulled over the stern, yet his heart beat faster as the flashes of silver came up from the depths. His father played each salmon carefully toward the stern by the long leaders. It was a deadly game. Each fish brought to the bin was a point for the boat. Each one that twisted and spit out the hook was a point for the fish.

The fishing gear was complex. He asked his father questions. If he wasn't busy, he replied.

"Lots of questions, little man," his father complained with a smile.

Neil didn't care. His father owed him for his work in the dark. But the answers came in one word or one sentence only.

Neil studied the rigging of the boat and the fishing gear carefully. It seemed as complicated as any problem at school. On each side of the trolling pit, three metal spools with short handles were attached to the deck. His father called the metal spools "gurdies." They were powered beneath the deck by chains and shafts connected to the boat's engine. The gurdies held thin trolling cables that were spooled out or in, up and over pulleys suspended above each side of the boat on curved pieces of pipe resembling question marks, as high as Neil's head. The cables were pulled down into the sea by lead cannonballs. The cables were threaded through porcelain insulators that took them out on the ends of lines hanging down from the outriggers. Brass beads, six inches apart, were attached to the trolling cable at intervals of three fathoms. His father attached the fishing leaders by metal snaps to the brass beads. To control the depths of the lines, his father attached brass rings on nylon cord between the beads to catch the insulators on the way down, swinging the lines away from the boat to the poles. The poles dipped to the sea and rose to the sky with every roll of the deck.

His father had names for the lines that hung from the poles. The lines hanging closest to the boat by double springs his father called the "bow lines." The lines that hung from the tip of the poles were the "main lines," and those attached inside the mains, which trailed far behind the boat, his father called "dog lines," because the floats that held them back from the stern followed the boat like a dog trailing its master. Halfway up the poles, chains hung into the sea. These chains were attached to flat pieces of finned metal that rose and fell beneath the surface like small metallic sharks. His father called them "flopper-stoppers," and they slowed the roll of the boat.

His father worked without pause: operating the gurdies, playing fish, steering the boat, checking the compass, running the lines, watching the poles, adjusting the depths of the cables, and keeping an eye to the sea all around. His father was a symphonic conductor of fishing.

Sometimes, the long leaders came up without fish. His father pulled them in, removed bait mangled from missed strikes, and snapped on new baited hooks from hundreds arranged in metal trays in front of the pit, like bullets on ammunition belts.

His father used other lures to trick the salmon too. Shiny metal lures called "spoons" and wooden ones called "plugs." The plugs had glass eyes and wiggled through the water. Neil's favorites were the "hootchy-kootchies," attached on short leaders behind large blades of curved metal called "flashers." The "hootchies" hid sharp hooks under colorful plastic hula skirts that resembled tiny octopi and squid. The flashers made circles in the water, and the hootchy-kootchies danced behind them. Neil wondered whether these lures looked like food, or did they resemble banners in an underwater carnival, enticing the fish to one last deadly ride? He tried to imagine the intricate arrangement of cable, leader, and lures moving through the depths, all controlled by his father in the trolling pit. His father was a sea spider, passing his intricate web through the depths.

By midmorning, the sea had changed from green to blue. The swells had grown larger, wider, but Neil was more accustomed to their effect on his body. One bin in the stern was full of salmon—it looked like an open pirate's chest of silver coin. His father placed sacks over the treasure and told him to water down the sacks with a hose that ran water continuously from a pump connected to the engine.

The fishing boats that had scattered over the sea at dawn were now closer together. They trolled up and down in a wide lane of boats above the school of salmon. Neil thought of farmers' tractors plowing back and forth across the land.

At times, other boats passed close by, appearing at the tops of swells, disappearing in their troughs. Fishermen in the stern, exposed waist up in the pits, looked like hand puppets in constant motion. Half Moon Bay boats passed. Cort Heinkel on the *Marina,* Henry Cabral on the *Evon,* Ott Bergstrom on the *Norland,* Carmelo Denari on the *Cefula.* His father waved. The puppets in the pits waved back, flashing numbers with their fingers and making gestures with arms and hands that Neil did not understand.

Now that the boats were more concentrated, his father told him to go to the flying bridge atop the cabin and "watch ahead." Carefully, Neil climbed up and over the trunk portion of the cabin and ascended a short ladder to the bridge. He sat down on a plank behind the flying bridge wheel. The view was exhilarating. High in his wooden saddle, he was riding a horse upon the sea. The ocean was a vast plain, punctuated with hills and gullies of water. The other boats were wild Indians.

Neil looked down into the water passing under the bow as the boat trolled on. The surface of the sea was as smooth as skin. Occasionally, brown jellyfish as large as basketballs passed by, trailing purple tentacles into the depths.

After a while, the boat passed through a tide rip of foam, bits of seaweed, empty cardboard bait cartons, driftwood, and tiny white birds pecking at the sea. The pecking birds flew up as the boat approached.

Later, he heard the noise of wind approaching from the stern. But there was no wind. He looked up. The air was filled with short-winged birds, coming from nowhere and everywhere at once. Thousands of birds. They skimmed the tops of swells, soaring up and diving down like confused squadrons of tiny jet planes, miraculously missing the poles and cables of the boat. The birds passed off the bow. They veered, pitched up, and dove straight into the water in puffs of white spray, before disappearing beneath the sea. "Sooty shearwaters," his father named them later.

A line of graceful pelicans appeared, wings beating

in slow-motion unison low on the water. One by one, they rose up, folding wings to bodies, and fell headfirst into the sea, close to where the short-winged birds had disappeared. The boat caught up to the pelicans. They paddled away from the bow, yellow sacs beneath their beaks dripping orange water. The jet-plane birds popped back to the surface all around the boat, silvery fish dangling from their stubby beaks. The sea, the very sky itself, was alive with layers of life in pursuit.

They passed through the squawking birds while his father brought several salmon in a row to the deck. As he did so, a disturbance of white water appeared off the bow. Suddenly, the spout of a whale exploded. The sun made a rainbow of its breath. The animal rose, water spilling from its black mass. Orange and sparkling silver drained from its mouth. Neil's heart beat fast. The whale was coming straight for their bow. He looked to his father, who was playing a fish on a leader. "Look out!" Neil cried. The whale was going to collide with the boat or tangle in its lines.

His father saw the whale but turned back to the fish. The whale dove toward the boat, disappearing beneath a broad tail encrusted with barnacles, black on top, white on the bottom. Neil was sure of an underwater collision. The poles would be torn off and pulled down into the sea.

"It's diving under the boat!" he called. His father heard him but again went back to his work, as if the whale were nothing more than a harmless stranger passing on a crowded street.

The whale vanished below, coming up once more minutes later, far to the stern.

Time passed with the swells. Neil watched the poles and lines like his father, calling out "Fish!" as he saw the telltale dips of poletips and pull of the springs. He felt less sorry for the fish. Like his father, he was fishing too. Like the men on the other boats. Like the birds from the sky. Like the whale that fed through the depths.

The sun rose higher into the sky. The fish came less frequently, then not at all. His father turned the boat—a difficult maneuver, for he had to take care not to tangle the faster-moving lines, on the outside of the turn, with the slower-moving lines on the inside.

They trolled back to the birds. They were no longer diving but swam in groups on the surface and flapped away across the water, too bloated to take flight.

The air was cool, but the back of Neil's neck warmed in the ascending sun.

His father took off his slicker jacket; he put on rubber gloves and sharpened a long knife. He took the salmon by their tails and slit open their long white bellies. Reaching in, he pulled out the guts and tossed them into the sea. Quickly, his knife went to the fish's heads trimming away the gills. Seagulls appeared. The birds dove for the tossed entrails and had tug-of-war fights for possession of guts stretched between their beaks.

Neil left the flying bridge, went to the pilothouse, and ate for the first time that day—several doughnuts and a Pepsi—secretly proud to be able to eat in the face of the carnage he had seen at the stern.

He heated water and fixed a cup of instant coffee for his father. He took it to the stern, where the gulls continued to screech and fight. His father took the cup in his bloody-gloved hands.

"Attaboy," his father said, before drinking down the coffee and turning back to his work.

Neil sat on a hatch cover and watched his father slice open the fish. Something next to a fish bin caught his eye: something small and pink on the wet deck. He picked it up.

It was a heart. The heart was beating! He centered it in the palm of his hand, feeling its pulse against his flesh. How could it live, severed from the body of the fish? The beat slowed. Stopped. He touched it with a finger. It beat again! He cast the heart into the sea. Before it struck the surface, a flying gull caught it in midair and flew away.

He looked at his father, slicing another belly. The half-empty coffee cup resting on the rear hatch cover was now smeared with blood. He imagined his father's heart beating within his strong body. Neil felt his own heart alive within his chest. He thought of the altar at church, the statue of Jesus with his exposed immaculate heart dripping painted blood, radiating rays of golden light. The priest often spoke of a "divine mystery," words Neil never understood. Was it found in hearts? Did the soul hide there? Did God take our hearts from our bodies when we died, just as his father cut them from the fish?

Neil looked again at the hovering, trailing gulls, and thought of angels. He looked again at the vast ocean into which his father flung the hearts. His father had brought him to a strange and terrible place.

Neil spent the rest of the fishing day seated on the flying bridge. The excitement of the morning gave way to the monotony of afternoon. The color of the sea changed again, this time from blue to tea brown. The water was lifeless, save for an occasional searching gull. The fishing boats spread out again—searching. Their sterns were empty of fishermen. The noise on the radio increased.

By midafternoon, his father, trolling on, kept the boat on a single course, back up the coast toward Half Moon Bay.

Neil grew tired. The steady drone of the engine, the low song of the trolling cables, the hypnotic roll of the deck, the sun overhead, all merged into a dream, a dream his mother had woken him from a hundred years earlier. Never before had he felt so alone with his own thoughts. He saw again the diving whale and diving birds. Down they went, deep beneath the fishing boats, where schools of silver salmon swam through suspended ornaments of jellyfish. And deeper still, down into darkness, down to secrets of the sea that even his father did not know.

A puff of chill air on his face woke him from his reverie. In the stern, his father was looking to the west.

The ocean's skin began to wrinkle. Soon he felt the breeze solid on his face, intensifying as the boat rose to the tops of swells. Was this the wind his father had said would descend from the stars? His father brought the fishing lines and lures to the boat, swinging the cannonball weights into their resting places. He coiled leaders into the stern and covered them with wet sacks. His office of death was closed.

His father left the trolling pit and pulled the flopper-stoppers to the deck.

"Let's go," he called, beckoning Neil down from the flying bridge, back to the cabin.

Soon they were running full speed into an increasing wind. Spray washed the front windows of the boat's cabin. The hull pounded hard into oncoming walls of water, the wind hummed low through the rigging. Ropes slapped against the mast like clapping hands. Water dripped from the roof of the cabin. Yet again, the sea had changed into a different world.

The once glassy swells turned white on top. On the

crackling radio, the fishermen called them "sheep." His father spoke to Henry, who said the "cows" would soon be coming too. An Italian voice came to the radio: "When the coast is clear, I'll be home, honey dear." The voice laughed. There was something in the wind, something that made the fishermen silly and nervous at the same time.

All around them, the fishing boats beat into the wind, racing for home. The *Evon* and the *Cefula* followed behind. The *Norland* ran abreast outside, in the glare of the descending sun. As they dipped into the sea, spray flew from the fishing boats' bows, exploding over their cabins, driven back by the wind as the sun lowered in the west. Neil thought of shooting stars and comets. His father told him that the sun was pushing the wind. He didn't understand, but the sight of the fishing boats drenched in spray, with smoke laid back from their stacks, made his heart beat faster.

A boat passed close and inside, its cabin shiny and wet, water draining from its decks. A voice came on the radio. "Faster, Ernie. Faster, *mein* huntsman," Cort Heinkel called.

The boats that had run out beneath the stars into the night were racing back the other way. But Neil's terror in the dark, when he had stood alone at the wheel and the binnacle light, was gone. He had changed as quickly as the sea.

Two hours later, he braced himself as the wind and

waves struck the boat harder. But as each wash of spray drained from the cabin, he could see the outline of Pillar Point more clearly ahead. His father stood tireless at the wheel. His arms and legs were strong— the sea could not knock them off course. They were going home, but they were not going home. He was outward bound, he didn't know where. He was on a journey that had begun in the dark beneath the stars, when his father told him to place his hands next to his on the oars.

Neil looked shoreward and saw the beach before Half Moon Bay passing, the houses and buildings beyond. He saw the bell tower of Our Lady of the Pillar Church, to which the beautiful queen took her crown of money each spring and where he had made his recent confirmation, when he kissed the ring of the bishop, his mother and grandmother looking on in their finest Sunday clothes. His confirmation made him a soldier of Christ. Now he was with the fishermen. He was a soldier of the sea.

Chapter Three

Dawn came again. He ate a packet of rations. Pumped the raft. Moved his arms, moved his legs. Tried to stay warm. He finished the remainder of the first sachet of water. The sea and wind were as the day before. Gray sky, scuttling patches of rain, southerly seas cresting white, close together. He drifted on. Time turned treacherous, then stopped, then reversed, then sped ahead again, each second a minute, each minute an hour. Night came.

·   ·   ·

He heard voices in the dark. Other things too. Men scream-
ing above him, trapped and dying.

"See, that's what we like. Local knowledge," Whatever-
his-name said. "Smith," he was called that day. A boyish
look. Lots of smiles. All-American. Everything sinister is
innocent. The other one, "Taylor," wasn't so innocent.
Deliberate, hidden cards. He had a look right to the eyes,
like a blue shark, no turning away at the last moment.

These were men who changed their names at will—such
were the people in Paul's life. His brother prowled underwa-
ter reefs as an abalone diver by day, swam the swirling
currents of bars by night, demanding respect in the eyes of
lesser men. Bars at the edge of the sea, littered with the
tidal wash of the land—stranded liars and dreamers. The
same bars where a few brave men celebrated arrival from
the sea in abandoned escape, and anticipated departure in
the quiet bottom of a glass. That's where Paul met them, in
a place of unwritten deals, where things happened at the
edge of the sea's possibilities.

"What about these guys?" Neil asked Paul.

"What about them?" Paul answered. "Can't hurt to see
what they want. All right?"

Smith and Taylor wanted to make them rich. The four of
them got in a car and drove south of town along Highway
One, down the coast, checking things out. Beaches, coves,
old dog holes Henry Cabral had talked about, places where
they unloaded booze in the old days, when the pro-highs, the
government men, were watching the wharf.

Smith and Taylor had a story. They were pilots. Cartagena, Buenaventura. No cocaine—heavy stuff, too heavy. They said they had pancaked their last load five hundred yards after takeoff. What did Neil know? What did Paul know? It was a story.

Smith and Taylor said they had changed their business plans. No more airplanes. Heavy loads were moved by ships. They had new connections in Thonburi and Bangkok. Tons. A big operation with lots of fishing boats along the coast.

"Everyone's doing it. You'd be surprised to know," Taylor said.

Smith nodded, beaming, pretending he'd like to tell more than he could. "A slick operation. Nothing can go wrong," he said.

But things go wrong. Worse than wrong.

They got their local knowledge: a little cove south of the Pigeon Point light, above Año Nuevo. It was a straight shot in to five fathoms, no visibility from the highway, a low break on the beach, a farmer's gate and a dirt road through an artichoke field, right down to the sand. The off-loaders would take care of all that. In the dark, nobody would see a thing.

Neil let the memory go, feeling the raft tug against the drag of the sea anchor. He had to be ready in case a ship passed in the night. He switched the flashlight on and took another flare, then switched off the light to save the batteries. Held the flare tight—he had to be ready. The wind blew him on.

How far had he come? Where would he be at dawn? He estimated his drift. Up and out. Bodega, Salt Point, somewhere like that. At first light, Point Arena? Maybe. The storm might abate, the wind shift northwest. It would blow him back the way he had come. Blow him home.

Rain fell in the dark. He was cold and thirsty, yet he had to save water. He took off his shirt and removed his undershirt. He put his shirt back on and reached outside, soaking his undershirt on the wet canopy, wrung it out, then repeated the process, twisting the cloth above his lips with his head held back.

Hope rode the apex of each oncoming sea. Despair followed, wallowing in its trough. The vision came again. His brother on the overturned boat going down. What could he do? He willed himself against it. It would make him mad. He sat back, closing his eyes. Waited for the boy to come again, take his hand, and lead him over the waters. Take him home.

O*s pequeños pescadores,"* Henry Cabral said, looking up, greeting them with a smile as he and Paul came to the backyard. Portagee talk. They didn't understand.

The wind was blowing and the boats were in. His

father and his fishermen friends were working on gear outside his father's workshop, behind the house. They were making things to kill fish.

Weeks had passed since the night his mother had woken him to go out with his father. It was a Sunday. Neil, Paul, their mother, and their grandmother had returned from mass in the Chapel-by-the-Sea in Moss Beach, a small satellite church of Our Lady of the Pillar in Half Moon Bay. When Neil and Paul got out of the car, they had started toward the fishermen, but their mother had called them back and made them go into the house to change their Sunday clothes.

Neil was desperate to make time start again, and he prayed that the fishermen could help him do it. Church slowed time to a crawl, moving it backward until he felt like one of the plaster statues of saints standing lifeless about the walls.

Paul was different: His brother was a muscular and compact ten-year-old, a shortened version of their father. An underbite gave his square face a bulldog appearance. In his black and white altar boy's habit, he had something to do, like an actor on a stage. Paul told his mother and grandmother that he wanted to be a priest. Neil knew he was lying. At school, Paul listened to the same dirty jokes as Neil, and he giggled about breasts in their bedroom at night. Paul's saintliness was a ploy, a harbor of refuge used in their petty squabbles. Paul would run to their mother and grandmother with exaggerated tears.

But at church, on the altar, his brother, with his hair slicked back with Wildroot Cream Oil, was beyond good, closer to God hiding and swirling in the wine that he poured into the priest's chalice.

During mass, his mother sang next to Mrs. Riley, whose feet pumped away as she played the organ. His mother's voice was beautiful. When she sang "Ave Maria," old women in the pews wiped tears from their eyes. His mother's voice was magnificent and good, as good as the hearts inside the plaster saints, as good as angels flying unseen all about the sky. After mass, the parishioners and the priest mingling at the door would compliment her. Neil, too, sometimes felt good assigned to the more mundane job of passing the collection box on the end of a stick, and this goodness pleased his mother. She and her boys were something they were not all the rest of the week.

But most of the time, goodness was boring. When time stopped and Neil gazed into the eyes of the dead saints, he heard the distant sound of breaking surf above the mumbled prayers of the priest. He thought of his father and the fishermen and the sea, of fishing boats running out under the stars, of severed, beating hearts and seagulls fighting over entrails in a place he could hardly think was good—miraculous, yes, but never good.

Since that night when he went with his father, his mother's attitude toward Neil had changed. She spoke to him less, scolded him more, looked at him differently, even though it was she who had released him from his promise and sent him with his father. And when his father asked if he wanted to "go on the boat" once school was out, his mother said nothing.

While Neil and Paul changed clothes, their grandmother looked out the window across the backyard to his father and his friends. "Bums," she said. But when she went to the kitchen, Neil and Paul headed to the yard to see what the fishermen were doing.

"Os pequeños pescadores," Henry Cabral said, looking up, greeting them with a smile. Portagee talk. They didn't understand.

His father sat on a fish box, measuring and cutting lengths of leader from a spool of monofilament, spreading his arms wide like a priest exalting his parishioners. Cort Heinkel, smoking a cigar, sat with Henry on another box. They were polishing brass spoons taken from a bucket of soapy water. When the spoons turned shiny bright, they hung them by their hook ends on the wire mesh of crab pots stacked high for the summer. Nearby, clothes on the clothesline flapped in the wind, mingling with the words of the men. Carmelo Denari sat on an overturned bucket, attaching hooks with pliers to thin bands of metal. Carmelo's face was the color of brown sugar beneath

61

a large corduroy cap that had dangling flaps. Nearby, at the welding table, Ott Bergstrom hammered rust from metal.

Paul stared at Henry's hand, the one with the missing finger. As Henry polished, the lure began to shine in the sun.

"What happened there?" Paul said, pointing to Henry Cabral's missing finger.

Henry's eyebrow went up. He stopped polishing and looked at Paul. He rubbed the stump of his missing digit.

"It's an old story, boy," Henry replied. "Happened a long time ago. Sometimes when I rub it, it makes me remember things. Feels like it's still there. Here, wanna touch it?"

Henry stuck out his thick hand to Paul, who jumped back, shaking his head. But Paul was undaunted.

"Rub it and tell me a story," Paul commanded.

Cort nudged Henry in the ribs. Henry looked at their father, who raised his shoulders and went on working. Anything Henry said was okay with him.

Henry pointed to the grass. Neil and Paul sat down in the weeds, with their backs to the crab traps. The wire cages smelled of rotting barnacles and starfish.

"Jesus, better get the hell out of here, kids," Ott Bergstrom called as he struck again at the welding table. "Once he cuts loose, he never shuts up. He's never told a story he couldn't tell again. And again."

Ott was a huge man. Neil's father called him a "square head." Like Cort, Ott wore a faded white stevedore's cap, but he had big ears that stuck out. The crown of his large nose was flaked with peeling skin. His voice was loud, always at the edge of a shout; his words were often angry, like the sea on a windy day.

"By *Gott*, let the man talk, Ott," Cort called to Ott. "Let the boys hear what they won't learn in school."

Henry rubbed his finger for effect; he picked up another lure and started polishing. "First you got to know about my father before you can understand about the finger," Henry said, looking up from the spoon and into their eyes.

Without a word, Neil and Paul nodded in unison.

"My old man came over from the islands," Henry began. "Came from the Azores with his brother Euzi and their two wives to Half Moon Bay to kill and boil *baleia*, whales that he said came each winter swimming down to Mexico, 'from the north of the world like fat pigs.'

"They lived in a fish camp on the cliffs above Pigeon Point. There was abalone on the beach, venison in the hills. A winter garden of horse beans. My father said the women had the 'good eyes.' They watched the sea for the whale's 'white breath.' They had longboats then, with lanteen sails. They worked from the beach with harpoons and rifle bombs. One year, he told me, they struck and killed thirty-four animals. The wind and current took five, and nine more sank when the bombs went too deep, exploding their lungs. But twenty were brought in that season, to flense and boil into oil. He said one bull alone gave ninety barrels.

"But in time the whaling went bad, and my uncle Euzi was lost. His boat struck a large cow that took him and two more—what the old man called his *companheiros de mar*—far to sea, into a fog bank that hid a black wind. My old man's boat couldn't keep up. He called for his brother to cut loose, but the last he saw was my uncle waving, happy with the strike, setting his sail to put more drag on the cow as they went into the fog. Nothing was found."

Neil felt a chill from the wind flapping. He saw a happy fisherman disappearing forever into mist. It was a bad story, but it was also good—so much better than church.

Henry Cabral continued.

"Pretty soon the white breath on the sea was gone too. My father said that with my uncle's death, the sea off Pigeon had become *veneno*—poisoned. He brought the family to Half Moon Bay and built a new fish camp on the beach beneath what he called 'the lady's arm'—Pillar Point. But by then the whales were all over. He turned to lingcod, which the women split, salted, dried, and packed in barrels. When they started putting motors in the boats, he went for salmon. But the Italians bought all the fish, and if you were not related, you starved in those days. He sold fish off the end of a horse wagon up and down the streets of town and out to the ranches, and sometimes all the way into Chinatown in the city, up and over Pedro Mountain. His load was cooled by wet seaweed. That's how he lived. That's how he fed his family. That's how come I lose my finger."

Henry stopped polishing. He held up his stub-fingered hand once more for Paul to see. Neil felt his brother twisting nervously beside him in the grass as Henry pulled back his hand.

"I was a kid, not much older than you, a kid fishing the Farallon Islands with the old man, to help out the family. A rock cod spine struck my finger. I go to shake him off the hook, and the next thing I know, I'm wearing a fish on my hand. The fish's poison went deep, and the top of my finger swelled up like a lemon. The old man said the poison would go to my heart before he could get me in to a doctor. He poured a big slug of grappa down my throat and wrapped the finger off with leader linen. He started telling stories about the family, lots of things I never heard. A good story, a sad story, and while I was caught up in it all, he took my hand in his hand, pressed it gently to the gunnel, and took off my finger with one slice of a fillet knife. Jesus! That took my thoughts away. I saw the finger fall down into the ocean and sink out of sight."

Paul had a sick look on his face. Neil knew how he felt. What kind of men cut off their children's fingers? He never wanted to find out.

Henry Cabral was silent for a moment. Neil's father and the other fishermen kept up the pace of their work. Neil imagined a finger sinking down into the dark depths.

"Old Tony," said Cort Heinkel, breaking the silence. "That old huntsman was like a father to me, but he lets me keep all my fingers. Fished me right off the beach. He was one tough old Portagee, Henry, *mein Gott*.

"Your father made a joke about that finger. Said he should have saved it. Said he should have put it on a hook rather than give it away free to the lingcod."

T*he fishermen were laughing, but the laughter stopped as the raft was hit by a gust of wind, bigger than the others. He felt himself turning, sliding off balance. Would the wind catch the bottom of the raft and blow him over? But the raft sank to the bottom of the next swell, regaining equilibrium.*

He took the flashlight and switched it on and off again

and again, toward the windy blackness of the sea. He watched for a long time, but his was the only light, a light that grew dimmer and dimmer. To save the batteries, he stowed the light and rolled tighter for warmth.

He woke with a start. The dream was brief. He and Paul were boys again, holding tight to each other in the raft. He loved his brother, even though he was a pain in the ass. In the dream, they looked at their hands. Their fingers were missing! The fishermen were there too, laughing, holding knives and laughing. Their fingers were sinking, deeper and deeper, like fat worms amidst feeding fish.

Later, he imagined a school of such fish beneath the raft, swimming this way and that, like an old fisherman's words. Words he should have remembered. Words he heard once more.

Henry Cabral hung a polished spoon in the crab traps. They jingled in the wind like chimes. He took another and began another tale.

"Now. I'll tell you something else," he said.

"Jeez, he's all wound up now, boys," Ott said, breaking in with laughter. But the other fishermen were silent, and Henry continued.

"Summer of '24," Henry Cabral said, looking

down at the spoon he polished in the hand with the stub finger. "Dark night. No moon. Million stars. I ran the *Elizabeth* then. My first boat. Cort's running the old man's boat, the *Ponta Delgada*. No running lights. I see the glow of Cort's stern wash up ahead and follow him close. Right, Cort?" Henry said, looking at him.

"That's right, Hen. Close enough to be in love. We were the young dogs then. Young huntsmen. And we were up to no good. That's about the time I fall for Bethel. Old man Patroni just brought her in from Texas. Skinny thing. They called her 'Dance.' *Gott* damn, those Wops give me the hard time, even though we made the big money for them."

Neil looked at Carmelo. So did Paul. They knew "Wop" was a bad word—insulting to Carmelo. But Carmelo went on working the hooks in his hand, like it didn't matter.

Cort continued his own story, interrupting Henry's. "One night I spend all my money on Bethel, and they take me by the shirt and throw me out into the street. Those *Schweinehunds* say the Okie whore is a better fisherman than me. A better fisherman than I could ever hope, 'cause all I had was a little hook in my hand, and she had the whole ocean between her legs. *Ach!* What's a man to do? Pissed me good. But that was my story, Hen. You tell yours."

Cort lit a fresh cigar. A puff of blue smoke came from his mouth, swirling around his nose and his tiny blue eyes.

Unseen, Paul nudged Neil and Neil nudged back. They were excited. These were not kids' stories.

Henry went on. "Up and down we go in the easy swells, through the night, headed for what my old man called the *noite de pesca*—night fish. Easy money. He didn't like me doing that too much. It was only easy money if the pro-highs were not out in their cutter with the one-pounder on the bow.

"But that night everything's fine. I sat on the board in front of the wheel, engine to my back. Old-style cabin. Wide open to the stern. Everything is old style. Flashlight battery for the binnacle light, pocket watch, chart, and a lead line to measure the bottom if the fog comes down. No radios then. A single-cylinder Hicks beating like a strong heart behind my back, warming me up.

"Me and Cort worked on those engines all winter. We put on big carburetors and bolted lead to their flywheels to make them spin faster. We sailed through the water like bonito. Of course, loaded down with the booze on the return trip, we ran much slower. But like I say, everything was good. No fog to hide the steamers, hands as dry as a banker's. The old man didn't trust those bootleggers, but the whiskey money from the Italians was good. I already paid off the boat. I promised Annie that in two more runs we would have enough to start a house. Yes, but when everything is good at sea, something is wrong. . . ."

Henry Cabral's voice trailed off. As Neil and Paul listened, Henry hung a shiny spoon by its hook to a row of lures hanging from woven wire net on the traps. He took another from the bucket, pausing to rub the stump of his missing finger.

"The ocean talks," Henry said, putting more paste on a rag, moving it in circles over the metal in his hand.

Neil felt uneasy. His father and the other men kept working and said nothing. Was this a secret of fishermen? How could the ocean talk? A gust of wind sent a sudden slap of fabric through the sheets and shirts on the clothesline. Neil thought he saw a curtain move in a window in the back of the house. Was his grandmother watching? His grandmother said fishermen were godless and worse than crazy. Was this what she meant? Did his father and the fishermen never go to church because the ocean was their religion? God and his angels flew high above the sea in heaven. The devil lived deep in the earth, but did he sneak out? Could he swim up through the sea and speak?

"We were out one hour from the point," Henry continued, taking Neil from his dark thoughts. "Astern, the lights from town were disappearing. I

70

don't know why, but cold came to my heart. My hands felt stiff. I took them off the wheel and rubbed them together. I felt pain again in the finger that's gone. See, I heard my father's voice in the ocean that night while Cort and I ran out to the mothership. A kid should always listen to his father."

They were listening, hard, even though Henry Cabral was not their father.

"The old man said that there was no such thing as *dinheiro fácil,* the easy money. His words whispered from the dark water. I thought the old man was wrong. 'Fish. That's the only business of fishermen,' my father said. 'Leave the rock crabs to the land. Let them think just a stupid Portagee *pescador,* a fool stuck in his little boat like a prisoner in his cell. It makes the rock crabs feel free. But their thoughts of freedom are like the kiss of a whore. The rock crabs are men with bosses, and the boss can step on them whenever he wants, crushing dreams out of their thin shells. There is no *confiança,* no trust, between the rock crabs. There are far too many of them to be free. They blow bubbles of words from their faces and tear off each other's legs for dinner.'

"Jesus, he told me and Cort some crazy things, and they were all coming back that night. He once told us a tale from the old country. God hid the souls of the dead in the deepest part of the sea so that none of their ghosts would disturb the living on the land. On

Judgment Day, God would call upon fishermen to haul all the lost souls up in their nets. The fishermen took the deal. But they had to keep their mouths shut, and harden themselves if they heard the cries of waiting souls begging to be thrown a hook to pull them out of the sea. To help keep this secret, God made fishermen appear simple to the living of the land. Because who would think to ask an ignorant fisherman where God hides his dead? And for keeping his secret, God gave fishermen all the fish in the sea to do with as they pleased."

Henry's words were interrupted by Ott Bergstrom, banging several times on the welding table. Neil felt the wind on his face. He was listening to a story hatched by the devil. This was not what he heard from the priests in church. He knew he should leave, take his brother and go, but he didn't.

Henry Cabral hung a spoon, took another, and kept talking. The rhythm of his words set the pace of Neil's father's and the other fishermen's labors.

"When the old man died, Cort and me found him. Dead mending a sardine net. He had fallen from a wooden stool in the yard, one hand holding tight to a roll of twine, the other on the mesh pulled over his face like a blanket. Running out that night, I saw him again just like we found him. That's when my missing finger started hurting and I started to think: My life is on a scale. One side my life, one side memory. Lots of things my father did, lots of things he told me. I can't explain it right. But he was always trying to show me some balance.

"Before he died, he warned me in his own way not to run for those bootleggers. As we ran out to the mothership that night, he was telling me again. I heard his words, whispers coming together like a single school of fish swimming in the same direction. He was showing me his life, making me remember, so I would not sail wrong in mine."

Henry's story swam one way, then it swam another. Neil listened carefully. Ott turned metal and struck again. Carmelo spit. His father lit a cigarette and went back to his work.

"My father said, 'The ocean always feeds us. Stay away from the *tubarões*—the sharks. Money is blood to them,' he said. 'They trust no one. Leave them to their money. Trust the few who go to the water. The ocean makes men even and their hearts open. The *puta tubarões* swim alone, even when they are together. Put a hand out for their money, and they take off your arm.' "

"Yah, but you guys did all right," Ott Bergstrom said, interrupting. "I bet you and Cort still got cans of money buried in your backyards."

"*Ja,* and that's why we're sitting here polishing our diamond rings," Cort shot back, dismissing Ott with a wave of his hand.

73

Carmelo laughed quietly, shaking his head. Neil's father smiled and measured another leader. Neil wondered if his father had such stories, stories of *his* father. If he did, Neil had never heard them.

Henry's story had awakened something inside, a hunger he could not name. Neil tried to picture Henry's father, and though he could not see him, he felt him strongly. He looked at his own father once more. Would he ever speak of his father as Henry now spoke of his? What could he say? Neil did not know his father.

But Neil also felt uneasy, as if he were being lured on. His grandmother had warned him of gypsies catching and stealing children. He had never seen a gypsy, and prayed he never would. Henry's story felt dangerous, like bait on a hook. Henry, his father, Carmelo, Ott, and Cort—all were fishermen. Neil's soul could be caught in invisible hooks, traps, and nets.

Henry looked up to the windy sky. Neil followed his stare and saw small clouds scuttling by. Henry looked down and spoke again.

"Every spring the old man picked wildflowers and took them outside the point to throw in the sea, in memory of my lost uncle Euzi. He first took me with him when I was ten or eleven, just before I took the poison from the rock cod spine. He never said much at all, a few words, then he throws the flowers in the water. All Portuguese, like he was talking to his brother. I was thinking about all this stuff the night Cort and me were running out to the ship for a load of booze. I heard my father's words coming back from the sea."

"You were spooked. Afraid your asses would get caught by the pro-highs," Ott Bergstrom said, interrupting again.

"No. It wasn't like that, Ott," Henry answered. "Like I said, things were good. The weather was good. The night was dark, with an easy swell from the northwest. The pro-highs were all drinking coffee, tied up in the city, drawing their easy government money. Mr. Patroni had a way of knowing all that. What was bothering me was back on the beach.

"See, the day before, something strange happened. I'm walking out on Patroni's dock to fuel up for the run, and I see these two guys eyeing me.

" 'Hey, Portagee—Dago—whatever you are. Come here, kid,' the first guy says. The insulting one was tall, tweed cap flopped down over his ear. His eyes said nothing, but his mouth had a small smile that showed a cruel heart. 'Your old man a fisherman?' he says. 'He catchee lots of fishee? How about your sister? Any fresha fishee around here, wopa doodle dandy?'

" 'Lay off, Fred,' the second guy says. 'Hey, boy,' he goes on, 'don't mind this guy. He's a real swell for the ladies. No offense, kid, but say, what we'd like to do, pal, is hire a boat. A boat that will take us fishing. Pay top money. Your old man got a boat?'

"The second man was short. He had a brown hat with a satin headband set with a feather clip. Very sharp. These men had no fishing poles. Their clothes were good, their hands white and smooth. First I think maybe they're pro-highs or cops. But they weren't. They were rock crabs, men whose talk was like the spit of bubbles on a crab's face.

" 'I'm a fisherman, not a kid,' I tell them. 'I got my own boat, and I don't take scissor-bells out.'

" 'Jesus Christ on a running board, your own boat? How old are you, kid?' the second man says.

"I tell him I'm nineteen.

" 'Well, that's great, kid,' the second guy says. 'Takes a lot of dough-re-mi to own one of those Dago pisspots out there in the bay, don't it? You must of caught lots of fish to own your own boat at nineteen.'

"I tell them I'm not Italian. I'm Portuguese.

"The first guy comes up. Real close. My stomach feels hollow. Already I've told 'em more than I should.

" 'Maybe you do other things than catch lots of fishee with your boat, little Portagee. Like maybe take nighttime boat rides far out to sea?'

"This guy comes close to my face. I say nothing.

" 'Gee,' he says, 'you ain't gonna dummy up on

me, are you, kid? You know what I'm talking about, don't you, little Portagee?'

"He taps me on the shoulder, hard. It hurts. I'm scared.

" 'See,' he says, 'me and my friend here would like to pick up a case or two of the real McCoy. Know what I mean? For our fishing trip, just in case the fish ain't biting. An' from the looks of this so-called fishing village, more than fish bite around here. I mean, we only see five or six fishing boats in the whole goddamn harbor, kid. Six fishing boats don't need three docks stretching out into the bay. And look at that: four great big so-called Italian-French restaurants with upstairs hotels, all in this foggy out-of-the-way ice hole in the middle of artichoke fields. C'mon, kid, I'm sure you can help us out.' "

"So what did you do, Hen?" Neil's father questioned.

Paul was bouncing on his knees. He had to take a piss, but he was glued to the story.

"I clammed up, Ernie. Told them nothing," Henry answered. "If I told those two guys anything, Mr. Patroni's sharks would have run a razor across my throat, chopped me up, and put me in a ring net for crab bait. I walked away, with the floppy hat laughing after me. Walked off the dock and up the road, and when I was sure their eyes no longer followed me, I went quick to the Patroni House.

"Inside, I go past the empty tables, straight through the double doors into the kitchen, where an old man was rolling ravioli with floured white hands. I go through the pantry and through a door down a long hallway, to the secret door into the saloon. I enter. The sharks at the card table look up and turn back to their game. The air is full of smoke—Toscani cigars. The bartender sees who I am and nods me toward the stairs. I go up the steps, rehearsing in my head what I'm gonna say. Upstairs, I take off my hat and knock on Mr. Patroni's door. Down the hall, a whore coughs and sticks her head out a door, then disappears again.

" '*Avanti,* ' a voice calls out through the door. I go in. Mr. Patroni sat like an octopus in his hole. He's bald and wearing a T-shirt in a cold room. He's pouring milk into a bowl for a cat waiting next to his desk.

"I put my hat behind my back and step closer. He didn't look up. All I see is the top of his head. It was like looking at a man without a mouth or eyes. The legs of the desk were carved into angels with folded wings, and it held several sharpened rods stuck with stacks of paper.

" 'See, young man,' he says, without looking up. 'You're lucky your father taught you how to fish. You see this goddamn mess all over my desk, the garbage pile of money that comes and goes with everybody wanting to lick from the same bowl?'

"Mr. Patroni looked up. My heart beat faster. His small eyes were blank, like a fish or a wolf eel that eats all the crabs from a trap. I was in a place I did not want to be, a place my father warned me not to go.

" 'So what do you want, my young fisherman?' he said.

"As fast as I could, I told him about the men on the dock and their questions.

" 'Ever see them before?'

" 'No,' I said.

"His eyes look me up and down. He turns away. Pets the cat.

" 'Good. Like you say. You never seen them before, and chances are you'll never see them again.'

"But that was the thing. It didn't seem so fine. That afternoon, when Cort and me were fueling up under the dock for the night run, I saw one of Mr. Patroni's sharks looking down, watching me."

Neil met his brother's eyes. They both knew the old Patroni House, across the highway from the bay, a two-story wooden ship stranded between a brussels sprout field and a dusty parking lot overgrown with weeds. The structure was abandoned; its windows were broken. It belonged to Joe Patroni, the cannery owner.

Henry was quiet for a moment, thinking, before going on.

"So everything is good as we're running out, but

everything is not good. Around midnight, we run over a school of sardines, and I don't hear the old man's whispers no more. I put the two men on the dock out of my head and start watching for the mothership. The water is like glowing milk as we cross over the school of fish, so bright I can make out the name *Marina* painted on Cort's stern, dead ahead on my bow. Five minutes later, the sea goes black again. But soon we cross another school, a half hour wide, stretching up to the northwest to where the stars meet the sea. Miles of sardines. Enough to feed the salmon, crabs, and rock cod until the end of the world.

"We cross the twelve-mile limit. Cort adjusts course to the southeast, and pretty soon I see the lights from the *Stadaconna,* anchored deep in fifty-five fathoms. Old lumber schooner, wide of beam, converted to an Alaskan packer and now a booze runner out of Vancouver. The *Stadaconna* stays right there until empty, then they sail her back for another load. In fog, it was hard to find her. They rang a bell three times every five minutes, and if the current set heavy, we could be way off. Had to shut down the engine, listen, and go again. But that night it was easy in the windless swell. Not like six months before, when a city boat went alongside in a big sea and the high, double-planked hull of the *Stadaconna* rolled down on her, catching the city boat on the gunnel and taking her under. Me and Cort seen the city boat turn keel over. The guy never got out. Right, Cort?"

"That sure is, huntsman. Back then is just like now. You don't watch the game, and bingo! Slime eels swim up your ass for breakfast."

Cort laughed alone at his own joke, his cigar tilted up. Neil found his accent hard to follow, and what was funny about a man drowning?

Henry ignored Cort.

"Anyhow, Cort goes in to the mothership first. Loads up and drops away, waiting for me. I get the bow, spring, and stern lines snug to the ship. They drop the string over, and I snap on the bag of Mr. Patroni's money. It flies out of my hand like a bird, and the five-gallon tins swing out in the cargo net.

"Pretty soon me and Cort are running open throttle back to the beach, loaded down with thirty cans of booze on each boat. One hour from the mothership, I see stars outlining Pedro Mountain, where the night sky meets the land, then the dark outline of Pillar Point reaching out with her arm to take us in from the water once more. Take us in with the easy money.

"The sun is still below the hills, but first light is on the water when we come to the dock and pull under the hoist. We unload the boats, and I climb up the ladder to get my money from Mr. Patroni's sharks, but they want me to drive the truck over the hill. A shark says the regular driver is hung over. It was a favor from Mr. Patroni, he says. 'A favor for a little bird that chirped in his ear.' Fifty bucks more. I already had seventy-five for the run. That was a lot of money in those days. I'm tired, but I agree to go.

"I drove the Studebaker off the dock over to Eugene Pardini's barn, and two Filipinos load crates of artichokes onto the back end to hide the cans tarped down under the forward end of the bed. Then off I go, thinking about easy money.

"I'm headed down Highway One and cross over the wooden bridge at Frenchman's Creek toward town. That's when I see the car in the side mirror, way back. I figure the sharks are shadowing me for protection, and I forget about it. I rub my eyes, watch the road ahead and the rows of artichokes passing by in the fields.

"When I look again in the mirror, the car is gone. Jesus! It's right next to me, in the opposite lane. I almost choke on my next breath. A pistol is aimed right at me out the passenger-side window. The barrel is moving back and forth, motioning me to the side of the road. The floppy hat is smiling.

" 'Big load of fish, huh, kid?' the floppy hat says when he comes back to the cab. He orders me to get out and leave the motor running, marches me around the back end of the truck, and tells me to face away. I heard my father's words rushing back to his stupid son. I felt like a fish on a hook pulled up to the side of the boat. I was dead. Would I hear the sound of the gun? Past the fields I could see the morning ocean in the distance. The last thing I would see.

"But instead of a shot, I hear the truck pulling away.

"I was walking toward town when the sharks came up.

" 'Get in, kid,' one of them says. Then he leans out the window and spits. 'The old man thought you might need a lift.'

"The back door of the sedan swings open, and I'm scared all over again. There are four men in the car, and they tell me to get in between the two guys in the back. The shark giving orders held a double-barrel shotgun—*Fucile di lupo,* those guys called them. He sat on one side of me, and the other guy beside me had a military Springfield held upright between his legs. The shark with the shotgun lit a Toscani. The sedan took off.

" 'Didn't have to put up much of a struggle, huh?' The shark with the shotgun said, blowing smoke toward the driver. 'Lucky kid.'

"We passed the edge of town and started around the curves along Pilarcitos Creek, up and up toward the mountain house. No one says a word. I also notice that even though they were chasing hijacks, they weren't driving very fast. That's because it was all 83 over before we caught up with those guys. It was like someone had poured ice water down my back when I saw it out the windshield. The hijacked truck must have been creeping up the grade in compound. Mr. Patroni's sharks were waiting on the long curve cut between embankments near the top of the mountain-house road. They shot from the side so as not to hit the cans in the back. A bullet went through the floppy hat's ear, and as we stopped, two bushwhackers were pulling him from the cab of the truck. They dragged him to the side of the road next to a ditch and stood over him with their rifles resting on their stocks. They had smiles on their faces like they were out deer hunting. One guy was laughing.

"The man with the shotgun next to me orders our driver to drive around this mess. We go on, and real quick I see the hijack car, the one that pulled me over. It's crashed into the embankment beyond the truck. A shark smoking a cigarette sits on the car's running board with a Thompson across his knees. We stop. The second hijack is out in the middle of the road, curled on his side right on the pavement. I see his foot moving back and forth. The shark next to me tells me to get out and wait by the car. He walks up to the hijack in the road and stands over him with the shotgun. He says something to the downed man. Jesus Christ, then the guy with the shotgun points back at me. His finger is like a pistol. My head is pounding, my heart is coming out of my mouth like the tongue of a rock cod pulled up from deep water. The wounded hijack brings his head up. His face is full of pain. He's looking right at me. He puts his head back on the pavement. Again, the shark with the shotgun says something to him. For a long time everything is frozen: The grass in the nearby field. A bird on a strand of barbed wire at the edge of the road. My blood.

"Then the hijack slowly moves his head back and forth on the pavement. No, his head is saying. Then the shark standing over him shoots his face off."

Henry was quiet.

A sigh of wind moved through the woven wire on the crab traps at his back. The polished spoons tinkled. Paul stopped piss-bouncing. Neil and Paul had heard something they should not have, something that frightened, something dark and bad, but exciting. It would steal their souls if they took it into their hearts.

Neil and Paul sat like statues as their father continued to measure leader. Henry and Cort polished spoons. Ott pounded some more at the welding table. Carmelo attached another hook to metal. Neil read nothing in the mask of the men's faces. A tale of death and the work at hand: It all seemed one.

Henry Cabral hung another spoon. "You know, with that shot, everything I heard my father say, running out on the night ocean, came flooding back. I was finished with these guys. They had no trust in each other. I looked at the ditch at the side of the road. A trickle of spring water ran down it to willows in a canyon far below. My eyes followed the stream to the ocean in the far distance. I saw what I knew. I was finished with the land."

Chapter Four

3 7 degrees north, 125 degrees west.
He'd been there before—outside the Pioneer Seamount, unseen Matterhorn of
the deep. On its slope, an old fisherman rests in his cabin,
eyes of water gazing into blackness, skeletal hand on rotting
helm, steering steady ahead into dark eternity. All that
fisherman knew, all he felt, was carried away in deep, cold
current. Neil knew that man, huntsman below.

On the night sea, the chill of that current welled up and
found him, eddied past and flowed away. That dead man
was a fisherman just as he was a fisherman. They measured

their lives in fish. Lost at sea? Buried in the depths? Nobody cared. Each taste of fish was a piece of their hearts.

They ran up and down in position for two days, pretending to fish where there was nothing to catch. On the second day, a container ship passed. He and Paul worked the stern of the Redeemer *like actors on a watery stage. The sea was sterile blue, the sky without birds. There was no feed, there were no fish, but their big catch would come in the night.*

After sunset of the second day, the message came on the sideband radio. Paul stepped the frequencies in reply, a banal chatter of code, filled with meaning. The mothership would reach their position that night, a last stop on its long offshore progression. She was unloading as she went, serving money from her hold to waiting fishing boats from San Diego to San Francisco. They were the last.

"That's the plan," Taylor said. "The crew will be gone. One here, one there. When it's your turn, when we get up to you, me and Smith will be the only ones left. Then we run to the coast with our nuts in our throats."

"What about the ship?" Neil asked.

"Don't worry about the ship." Smith laughed. "We'll take care of that."

Neil didn't worry about it, but he should have worried about it. Instead, all he could think of was the run back in, thirty hours straight to the cove south of Pigeon Point. At night, his face would be pasted to the radar, watching for converging blips. By day, he would be looking for white cutters with orange stripes at the bow. If they were spotted, they had one chance: Sink the Redeemer *before the coast guard reached them. The hacksaw was taped to the seacock. Lies had been rehearsed. Sink the boat that fed him—a choice quick and final. No going back. Consequence without remorse.*

Neil was sure they would make it to the coast. He always did in the past—his father had shown him the way.

The cold current took his body once more. He thought of the old fisherman trapped in his boat on the bottom of the sea. He shook his head to make the image drift away. He rubbed warmth into his arms and slapped his legs until pain came to reassure him he was still alive. He wished for daylight. When it came, he opened the second water sachet and second ration bag. He watched for ships. There were no ships. Nothing.

The wind moderated. Patches of blue broke through racing clouds, and the white waves diminished. He still could not see the coastline. The sea about the raft was streaked with foam that converged in a broad white line—a rip, the confluence of two rivers in the sea. One, pushed by the storm racing up the coast, moved faster than the other, which was driven by wind hundreds of miles away. He saw bits of garbage in the rift: A branch white with barnacles. Plastic bottles faded from the sun. A lightbulb. A broken plank.

He had learned to search for these rips long ago, to anticipate their hidden prizes. It was where the salmon hid.　89

Pistol, honey," his father commanded.

Neil stood in the trolling pit behind his father and took the long-barrel twenty-two revolver from the sheepskin holster on the aft hatch cover. His father reached behind his back. Neil put the gun in his up-turned palm. His father's fingers wrapped around the grip, and he aimed the barrel into the boiling water.

His father brought the fish toward the boat, and his movements slowed. Wrapping the leader around his right hand and aiming with his left, he leaned over the stern. The fish was huge, golden bronze beneath the surface of the plankton-rich water. Its tail beat steady and strong. A flasher oscillated in front of its head: A pink hootchy was impaled in its jaw.

His father brought the fish's head to the surface, aiming the pistol. But at the last moment the fish shook its head, bent toward its tail, and ran.

"Spooked," his father called, twisting free from the leader before it cut the flesh of his hand.

"Take the gun," he said sternly.

His father looked at the leader, attached to surgical tubing secured to the stern—his "killer line." It was stretched to the thinness of a pencil. The powerful salmon was sounding. Its beating heart would not die.

The pumping on the tubing slowed. His father put hands to the leader, carefully leading the fish back to the stern, adjusting his arms and body to the roll of the boat.

Minutes passed. Once more, his father led the fish gently to the stern. The leader sliced the surface of the water like a knife. Again, his father's open hand reached back and Neil placed the gun in his fingers. A team. His father was a surgeon of death, Neil a nurse handing sinister instruments on demand. Neil hated the pistol. The shot to the fish's head was unfair. Earlier, he had told his father what he thought. His father had given him a strange look, then he had smiled and turned the palms of his hands to the sky, opening his arms to the surrounding sea.

"Fair? What's fair in this world?" his father had said.

He had not understood.

His father aimed the pistol, gently leading the fish's head up to the surface. One second more, and the shot would come—the fish would be theirs.

Neil saw it first, rising up through the murky water under the boil of the stern. He saw the trailing whiskers on its crinkled snout, the bulbous head and black eyes, yellow incisors in its great open mouth. He saw a trace of finger bones beneath the pale skin of a flipper.

"Look out," Neil called to his father, but it was too late.

His father's body bent to the sea. His hand,

wrapped in leader, was pulled to the water as the sea lion took the fish. Neil grabbed his father's shirt as he began to be pulled from the boat. His father tried to twist the leader from his hand, but the initial shock cinched it down. Blood appeared on his fingers, and his boots came off the grating in the trolling pit as his body balanced over the gunnel above the wash of the prop.

"Knife!" his father called, reaching back with his free hand.

But before Neil could do anything, his father twisted free and fell back into the boat.

Seconds later, the lion rose from the sea in an explosion of pink water—it was an immense bull. The huge salmon was still hooked hard in its mouth. The sea lion looked like a dog with a silvery bone, blood washing from its jaws. Its cold eyes seemed to be beaming with cunning satisfaction. His father regained his footing, took the pistol in his bloodied hand, and fired twice. Jets of water splashed short of the animal's head. The killer line stretched. Flasher and lure tore from the salmon's jaw, sending a chrome blur through the air.

"Duck!" his father called, pushing Neil down into the pit.

When they got to their feet, the flasher was hanging inside the trolling pit, its straightened hook embedded in the cap rail close to their bodies. The sea lion and the fish were gone. Pink foam and silver scales marked the sea where they had disappeared.

"Get the rifle," his father said, disregarding his bleeding hand.

Neil returned from the cabin with the carbine. His father took it, charged the bolt, and scanned the sea behind the stern. Drops of blood fell from his fingers, but his face was placid, revealing neither pain nor anger. A long minute passed. Then, far beyond, the sea lion rose, shaking its head and ripping out the salmon's guts in its mouth. Gulls swooped down, fluttering near the sea's surface, snatching at the entrails. His father aimed but did not fire—beyond his range, the monster had outsmarted him.

All that had happened in midmorning. By one o'clock, the fish were off the bite. His father had wrapped the leader slice on his hand with white tape, and Neil left him in the pit, went to the cabin to make lunch. The wheel in the cabin turned one way, then another, as if moved by a phantom sailor. But it was just the autopilot, searching out the boat's course, the very same autopilot whose malfunction had first brought him to sea.

Ahead on the port beam Neil saw the southeast Farallon Island being assaulted by boiling surf. The island rose from the ocean like the tip of a mountain covered in snow. But this snow was from seabirds that inhabited the island's bleak moonscape. Seagulls, cormorants, murres, birds without name. Unlike birds of the land, the seabirds uttered cries that were harsh and cruel, like the rocks and sea on which they lived. At the island's highest point, a stubby lighthouse blinked its message of danger under an overcast sky. The Farallon Islands were killers of ships, rocky sentinels set in a foggy sea twenty-five miles west-southwest of the Golden Gate. Joyous mariners anticipating rest sometimes ended their lives there, scant miles from home.

The Half Moon Bay boats and the rest of the fishing fleet had been fishing the islands for days. Before leaving Half Moon Bay, his father had blown chipped ice into the hold from a machine and hose on the end of the wharf. At night after anchoring, close by the southeast Farallon, Neil and his father would climb down into the belly of the boat to lay the day's catch head to tail in bin-board compartments, filling their gutted stomachs with ice, putting them to sleep under a snowy blanket.

The Farallons were not like the open waters off Half Moon Bay, where the boats trailed their leads and cables over a flat, deep bottom. Here, reef, rock, and pinnacle lurked. Everywhere, the chart was marked with the symbols of wrecks: a single line crossed three times by shorter strokes. His father was constantly engaged in an underwater chess game with the bottom of the sea. It made him edgy and irritable as he checked chart, compass, and Fathometer to keep the fishing lines from being checkmated by a submerged rook or queen of the deep.

In his thirteenth summer, Neil felt like a prisoner. The boat was small, the ocean vast, and there was nowhere to go except into the sea of his mind. His father made no attempt to understand him. The operation of the boat and fishing gear was everything, and conversation was reduced to function. The boat was not a vessel of forgiveness. His father's motto was "One mistake is the last mistake." If Neil erred, punishment came in a silent glare. Each hour, each day, his childhood floated further and further behind the stern. At first, he had been excited to go with the fishermen, as excited as the day on the beach when he had splashed through the surf. But now Neil was their captive.

His second brother, Philip, had been born late in that same summer his mother first woke him to go to the boat. But the fishermen had their second bad crab season in a row, and after Philip's birth his mother took a job at the Patroni and Sons cannery. Henry Cabral said San Francisco Bay had become a sewer. The crabs could not spawn the way they used to. Neil's grandmother took care of Paul and Philip, and when summer came again, his mother said his father needed help on the boat. "There are bills to pay," she had said. He felt sentenced to the sea for money. The promise he and Paul had made the morning of the wreck was never mentioned again, and if she remembered it, she had hidden it away. When he went with his father on the boat, a silent bond between Neil and his mother felt severed forever. And when she went to the cannery to work, something was lost between his father and his mother, some silent, private promise broken.

The Patronis owned the wharf and the cannery. On windy mornings, when the sea was rough, the fishermen sat in Hazel's coffee shop in Princeton, fishing with spoons in their coffee cups. Sometimes, Neil heard talk about old man Patroni, dead for years, as their words mingled with cigarette smoke and the smell of grilling bacon. They talked of buried money, of dead men in unmarked graves, of things not legal, things that men had to do for money. It was the same kind of talk Neil and Paul had first heard from Henry Cabral.

One day Neil and Paul snuck into the old Patroni House, hoping to find treasure. The restaurant had been closed for years, its facade staring unpainted out to the sea. Inside, there was a dim, dusty bar, broken chairs, collapsed tables. The air smelled of mildew and ghosts. Neil and Paul crept through a dead kitchen, where now only pinch bugs and spiders fed. They climbed a narrow, dark stairway, looking at each other, knowing that this was the stairway Henry Cabral had climbed with his hat in his hand.

They came to a long hallway with doors, one of which was open, revealing the desk Henry had spoken of, the one with angels on its legs, its surface empty now save for dust and the web track of a spider. A handless clock lay dead on the floor. The room was still. Wallpaper was peeling everywhere. The room was deathly silent, but Neil imagined conversation and the forgotten schemes of men. A sudden noise came from an open door at the side of the room. A blur of wings took flight through an open plank in the wall, fluttering, flapping, escaping to air. Neil and Paul raced for the stairs, never to return. In bed that night, they speculated on the wings—pigeons or bats, they couldn't be sure. But before Neil slept he thought of time.

The cannery that bore the Patroni name was a hellish place, a black metal castle of tanks, pipes, and chimneys spewing steam and stench into gray sky. After school one day, Neil and Paul slipped through an open bay door of the cannery to see where their mother worked. They hid behind stacked cases of cans. The air reeked of fish. Pipes hissed. Metal scraped against metal. Men in black boots pushed carts of uncooked salmon into long cylindrical pressure cookers. Doors clanged behind the carts. Later, the doors reopened. Eyeballs came tumbling out, a low avalanche rolling across the wet cement floor like scattering marbles—eyeballs that once had seen the deep secrets of the ocean.

Beyond the cookers, his mother stood with other women. They wore black rubber aprons and white hats. Cooked fish moved past them on conveyor belts. Annie Cabral was there. So was Ott Bergstrom's wife and Bethel. The women plucked flesh from the moving carcasses and placed it in shiny metal cans that moved like a metal river on tracks above the conveyor belt. Bone, tails, skin, and heads tumbled from the end of another belt, into a bin. This bin fed a large metal pipe that ran from the cannery to the end of the wharf. Water pumping through the pipe returned the remains of the fish to the sea. The beautiful salmon he had seen coming up from the ocean, twisting and fighting on the end of his father's leaders, became pink sewage discoloring the water of Half Moon Bay.

His mother worked in an awful place, standing for hours in a steamy stench, plucking clean the bones of fish. She said she wanted Neil and Paul to get ahead in the world. "Get a good, steady job. Go someplace." Was it someplace like this one, where the silver angels of the sea were squished into little cans? A place where the same thing happened over and over again? His father's cold world seemed better than this.

Soon, however, his mother did get ahead—off the fish line and into the office. She became a bookkeeper for the cannery's owner, Joe Patroni, a stocky, cigar-smoking man. Now she seemed content to let his grandmother do the cooking, cleaning, and attending to baby Philip. But Neil sensed resentment on his father's part. His parents grew further apart. His mother resembled the land, his father the sea.

Neil would never be like his father. She may have forgotten it, but Neil's promise to his mother was forever. But who *would* he be? The fishermen were strange and different. Not the "Ozzie and Harriet" men he had seen on television, not the "I Love Lucy" men, the kind fool men, the men in suits who drove Chevrolets home to rows of perfect homes in perfect towns with wives who turned them into jokes. Neil sensed that his father was a sort of man his mother did not want him and Paul to be. A fisherman was not the way to "go someplace," but what kind of man should he be?

"Neil!" His father's call came sharp and serious above the engine and the turn of the pilot.

Neil left the cabin and went back on deck. His father stood atop the aft hatch, rifle in hand.

"Watch the boats. Stay out of the pit," his father ordered. His eyes were searching the sea behind the boat, beyond the dog-line floats. On the deck, the head half of a salmon lay shredded and bloody.

"He's back. Following us," his father said, anger in his voice.

Neil scanned the ocean all around the boat. Suddenly, the dark head returned, far behind the dog-line floats, eating the guts and heart from another fish. His father aimed, but the lion was still out of range. He put the rifle down and climbed back into the pit, pushing both dog-line gurdies into gear, drawing the trailing lines to the boat. Had he given up? Would he stack the gear and leave the sea to its thief?

The dog lines came to the stern. His father unsnapped the floats, coiled the leaders on board, and swung the cannonball leads from the sea. He climbed from the pit, picked up the rifle, and stood again on the hatch. A hollow feeling came to Neil's stomach. He understood. They were not leaving. His father was drawing the animal closer to the boat, making it search the remaining bow and main lines.

A half hour passed. His father was a statue with a rifle.

Then it came, a snap high in the air, the main-line spring pulling back at the tip of the starboard outrigger. The stays to the pole danced as if the trolling cable had struck the rocky bottom. The rifle went to his father's shoulder. Another long minute passed. Suddenly, water erupted dead behind the stern. The head of the lion, a salmon in its mouth, broke surface in pink turbulence. As the deck rose on a swell, a thin geyser of water erupted in front of the dark head, the animal's jaws opening wide as the bullet skipped into its face. The salmon fell from its mouth. A second and then a third shot hit the animal's neck and ear. A red jet streamed from its head. The sea lion's eyes opened wide in surprise as it tried to dive. A fourth shot came. The beast thrashed, spinning off across the surface of the sea like a torpedo streaming blood, up and over swells until it slowed beyond the stern, where it eventually changed to a lifeless thing, rising and falling in a circle of red.

His father stepped off the hatch cover, put the rifle down, and lit a cigarette. Moving back to the pit, he reset the dog lines. There was neither satisfaction nor remorse on his face. Neil took the rifle back to the cabin. The gun felt loathsome to his hands. His father was a killer.

When he returned to the pit, Neil was silent for a long time, remembering the shock on the sea lion's face, the blood streaming from its body.

"Maybe you didn't have to kill it," he blurted, before he could talk himself out of saying anything.

"What?" his father said.

"Couldn't you have fired warning shots. Fired close to chase it away?"

His father looked at him. His eyes were narrow slits

beneath his blue baseball cap. Neil expected anger, but it did not come. The cigarette rolled slowly back and forth between his lips.

"Why fish? Why eat?" his father calmly replied, smiling, taking the cigarette from his mouth. "Nothing's both ways. It dies, we eat. That's the way it is. That's the way it always will be. There's nothing in between. Nothing new under the sun."

His father smiled. His father was wrong, but Neil kept his tongue. His father noticed his silence, and the smile left his face. Pointing to the sea all around, he said, "This is real; no one can change it."

Neil didn't understand, but there was no use arguing with his father. The boat trolled on. His father reset the dog lines and sat back on the edge of the pit to light another cigarette. His eyes searched back and forth over the sea and up to the tips of the poles. Functional silence was restored. Neil, too, scanned the sea, watching the poles, waiting. Waiting for some understanding of "real" to come, like a fish caught on a line and revealed when hauled to the surface.

That evening, they ran into the anchoring grounds close under the rocky southeast Farallon. His father set the anchor close to the washing rocks. The island offered scant protection from the swells, but it would give some shelter from the wind, should it come in the night. Soon the anchorage became a village of anchored fishing boats. The Half Moon Bay vessels lay close to one another in the watery town.

Before dark fell completely on the sea, Neil and his father went to the pit to clean the rest of the day's catch. Nearby, several sea lions bellowed menacingly on the wave-washed rocks.

"Why don't you shoot them too," Neil said, pointing to the rocks with his cleaning knife.

His father looked at the sea lions, then at him, and laughed.

"Wouldn't be fair," his father said, turning back to his work.

His father was crazy. Early that day, nothing in the world was fair. He killed the sea lion that took the fish, but killing these wouldn't be fair? Neil searched for rebuttal, but nothing came. His father's mind was a treacherous reef.

Silently, they cleaned the remaining fish, opening their white bellies, slicing out gills. Neil felt cold as he washed blood from his hands with the deck hose. He thought of his mother, grandmother, and brothers, distant on the land. They seemed as images sinking beneath a surface. He saw again the symbols on his father's charts marking wrecks. Was *his* soul now marked?

A blue shark came swimming slowly through the fish guts that sank behind the stern. Its pectoral fins were like wings on a soaring bird, its undulating tail hypnotic beneath the sea. The shark opened and closed its mouth, gliding effortlessly through the blood, ingesting a sinking crescent of gills. It was beautiful. The sea's devil was an angel from below, an angel from the sunken ships, an angel from the murdered sea lion, an angel that swam up from the ocean's earthly blanket, an angel of his own heart.

That night, Neil lay in his sleeping bag in the dark confinement of the fo'c'sle, gazing upward at the stars that shone through the foredeck skylight. Bilgewater sloshed in time to the roll of the anchored boat. Across the narrow companionway of the fo'c'sle, his father slept beneath waves of snores. Their narrow bunks were beneath the surface of the sea, separated from the depths by the thin wood of the hull.

When the snores subsided, underwater sounds came from the ocean. There was the noise of the anchor chain, lifting and falling on the rocks far below. Strange sounds came too, crackling sounds, whistle sounds, moans, screeches from far away. The boat was an ear. A story came, a story told in the backyard near his father's workshop, Henry Cabral's story of *his* father. God hiding the dead in the sea. Was it true or just an old man's lie? Would God cast his nets down on Judgment Day? Was it real?

Neil listened to the sounds of the sea. A dark thought came. What if God left the dead souls in the sea forever, the souls of all who ever lived and died? What if God was a fisherman like his father, full of cunning method? A solitary fisherman in the vastness of his universal sea. What if He lured living things from the sea, tricked living things to their death? What if God left them? Forgot them? Who would know? Only fishermen would know, and they had promised not to tell.

His father's snoring began anew. The thought washed away with the lap of water outside the hull. Neil drifted away, down into the sounds and a dream of the sea.

aylight was upon the sea, gray and without warmth through the low clouds. The swells bore on monotonously, lifting and lowering. A whitecap slopped against the raft and over the canopy, and a tiny jellyfish—small, transparent, dead—sloshed into the bottom of the raft. Neil scooped it into his hand and felt its jellied lightness on his skin. He examined its threadlike tentacles, barely visible. He was holding time. Transparent, weightless, broken time, washed from the sea on which he floated.

Neil woke to his father's alarm clock. The stench of blood and diesel fuel in the bilge mixed with the smell of sulfur as his father lit his first cigarette of the day.

He fought nausea from the unseen smoke. In the rolling confinement of the fo'c'sle, only one of them could stand at a time. Silently, his father dressed first. The red dot from his cigarette dimly lit his face. A determined face, without joy and without fear. A face ready for another day at sea.

His father ascended the short ladder up into the cabin, started the engine, turned on the radio, and fixed a cup of instant coffee. Neil, in turn, slipped into his cold, moist pants and boots. Each morning began wordlessly the same. They were robots, the sea and boat their master.

Neil went to the bow to await his father's command to switch on the motor that activated the anchor winch. Scattered stars still lingered against the dawn. His father called, and Neil started the winch. As the cable and chain spooled up from the depths, Neil looked shoreward. A faint glow of morning sky silhouetted the fading jeweled lights of San Francisco, twenty-five miles to the east. He saw the distant outline of the towers of the Golden Gate Bridge, a child's model far across the morning sea. He was a viewer from another time, watching a far civilization awake.

Leaving the anchorage, his father put the boat on a course southeastward toward the lightship. Neil went to the stern and baited cold herring from the icy buckets brought up from the hold. A half hour later, the engine slowed. His father came on deck, threw the flopper-stoppers into the sea, and joined him in the pit as the first rays of sun came to the ocean, imbuing its surface with wavelets of orange.

At first light, the fishing fleet lay scattered over the swells, still searching for yesterday's fish. To the south, a freighter ran inbound to the city. Offshore, their Farallon bedroom had once more become a distant peak protruding from the sea. Together, wordlessly, Neil and his father set the gear for the first tack.

The trolling cables hung down into the sea, but no salmon came to the gear. His father looked from pole to pole. Neil saw his mind searching, calculating current, wind, water. Casting the deck bucket overboard, his father put his hand in the water to test the temperature of the sea, rubbing his fingers together as if there were some answer, some revelation of where the salmon had gone.

"Hake!" The word came with disgust. "Pull the gear," his father ordered.

As each leader came, bronze fish with big heads, bulging eyes, and needlelike teeth twisted on the leader's end. Neil had seen them before. Once, he had left one on deck in the sun. Within an hour, its flesh had melted from its body, leaving nothing but skin.

Neil and his father shook hake from every hook. The lines were besieged by seagoing rats. His father beat the leaders against the transom to dislodge the hake. A long line of floating white bellies appeared off the stern, like stepping-stones on the water's surface. Neil remembered his thoughts of the night before: souls deceived and left in the sea.

With the lines back on board, they ran north until they came to a cluster of boats tacking uphill. Neil saw Carmelo Denari on the *Cefula,* working in the stern with his son, Nicki, who now helped him on the boat. Nicki was Neil's age. He slept with his father in the fo'c'sle, worked with him, ate with him, just as Neil did with *his* father. What did *Nicki* think? Was *he* a prisoner too? Neil wanted to ask Nicki rather than just imagine it, but they were separated by the sea. On their port side, Cort Heinkel waved from his stern, pointing down into the water. Neil's father slowed the boat, and they reset the gear.

The hake robbed them of the morning bite. Only four fish came to the deck after they reset the gears. Hours of nothing passed. The sun rose high overhead, ushering in the time of day when fish came seldom to the lines. The fleet scattered. On the radio, the Italians jabbered incessantly. His father kept the boat on a steady northwest course. The sun felt good on Neil's body. He went to the cabin to eat. To starboard, a long black tanker in ballast, with a white wake in its teeth, lumbered through the fishing fleet, outward bound from the Gate. Neil could see the upper tips of its huge propeller slapping the sea. On the stern, a man dumped garbage into a flock of careening gulls.

In the far distance, dead on the bow, Neil saw the outline of Point Reyes, a promontory of cliff three miles long, rising to six hundred feet on its seaward edge. The Half Moon Bay boats often anchored there. The point was a rock castle guarding Drake's Bay, ancient refuge of Spanish galleons, as well as a famous English pirate. From Pigeon Point through the gulf of the Farallons, all this sea was now familiar to Neil—it was his kingdom of water. The fishermen were knights and he was a knight errant, confined to a boat, with imagination his only escape.

Sometimes, he saw in Point Reyes the outline of a sleeping woman, her resting head pointed out to the sea. Often in the afternoon, a mist appeared at the lady's head like long strands of hair falling into the ocean, where it magically vanished. It was a warning, a warning from the sleeping woman that wind was coming. If she was right, and wind came, the longer the boats lingered near the Farallons, the harder it was to reach sanctuary behind the point's ramparts. If the sleeping woman's warning went unheeded, she punished the fishing boats with growing seas and whitecaps as they beat to her for protection.

But that day, as Neil watched the sleeping lady, something was different. Gray hair was forming on her head, but her hair falling down to the sea did not disappear. Instead, it formed into a thick, billowing blanket on the surface of the ocean, higher and higher until the lady herself vanished. Neil looked to the stern. His father was also gazing north. The gray became a wall, and the wall came to them, smothering all in its cold embrace.

The fog clung to the sea. It was a fog the fishermen called "soup." Neil could see only a few feet beyond the bow. It imprisoned the eyes, magnifying the unknown. Neil returned to the pit.

"Watch the game; we're in the steamer lanes here," his father said.

Neil did not need to be told. He had heard the fishermen talk, heard about the boats that had been run down by a sudden wall of steel coming swift out of the fog. Men run down and left to die.

Neil looked ahead into the gray nothingness for a form that might destroy them. The minimal words he and his father sometimes exchanged now ceased altogether. The fog stole their ability to speak; thought itself became conversation. Swells rolled from the mist, lifting and lowering the boat, passing silently, disappearing once more into the fog.

The boat trolled on. The air was cold and wet. The fog made them weightless spirits on a ghost vessel. They were on a sea of sameness, sailing to nowhere, having come from nothing. The fishing fleet was all around them, yet nowhere to be seen. Across the water came the sounds of engine and deck speakers, invisible boats passing close by. Neil and his father were blind men feeling their way through a watery maze. A boat tacking across or down their course could mean disaster. Neil thought of the outward-bound tanker he had seen before the fog swallowed them. A ship could strike without warning, cutting them in two, demolishing them in its prop, spewing them out in its wake. He listened anxiously for horns, the shaft rumble of a ship, the slap of a gigantic propeller upon the sea.

But Neil saw nothing—imagination alone pierced the veil. At first, he hated how his brain sailed away from his body, conjuring danger and death. Then he welcomed it. Detachment was his friend. He was not where he seemed to be—he was somewhere else, looking in, hidden in the fog. Whatever happened, it was not really him. He had become someone he was not, peering through a mist. He began to understand something about his father and his father's friends. A secret of fishermen in a sea of danger.

The fog brought the fish back on the bite, and they hooked several in a row. The dog-line floats behind the boat were lost in the mist. His father drew them in, shortening their radius of turn, making the boat more maneuverable in the hidden fleet of fishing boats.

His father put the boat about, and they tacked downhill. Salmon after salmon came to the leaders. His father worked the port lines, and Neil worked the starboard. Earlier that season, his father had taught Neil how to run the gear and carefully play the salmon to the boat. Neil thrilled to the pull of the fish on his fingers. He held life and death in his hands. He and his father became a coordinated team playing the fish to the boat, driving gaff hooks into the salmons' heads, swinging their struggling bodies onto the deck. And as they killed, between each heartbeat, between each breath, their eyes stole glances into the emptiness ahead.

The fog brought silence to the deck speaker. A fishing boat came ghostlike from the fog on the starboard quarter. His father adjusted course. The passing boat disappeared as if it had never existed.

·   ·   ·

Time passed, each tense minute absorbed in smothering, damp gray. Without horizon, the sea and the sky were one. Father and son labored on in a dangerous dream. At one point, Neil thought he heard the moan of a ship's horn far away, then nothing.

When the voices returned to the deck speaker, he thought little of it. The radio was his father's business. But soon he listened.

The Italians were speaking in English. "Lighta ship, lighta ship," they said, followed by the words "coasta guard, coasta guard," over and over again.

His father sent him to the cabin to switch to the coast guard emergency channel. A troubled voice came. Neil understood right away.

"Mayday, mayday, mayday," the voice said, quick and high-pitched. "This is hospital ship *Benevolence,*" the radio went on, "bearing one-oh-two degrees, east of San Francisco lightship. I repeat . . ." The same message came again, followed by garbled static and several voices speaking at once.

His father came beside him in the cabin. He switched on the radio direction finder.

"Pull the gear," his father said. There was urgency in his voice.

Neil went to the stern as the engine increased rpms. The first leader on the main line had a fish on it. The fish rose out of the water, skipping over the surface with the acceleration of the boat.

His father returned to the stern. "Cut it loose," he said, handing Neil a cleaning knife, before putting another gurdie in gear. Neil held the leader with the fish in one hand, disbelieving what he had heard, hesitating. His father reached over with another knife, slicing the leader and fish away.

"Goddamn it, cut 'em all loose," he shouted.

Within minutes, the flopper-stoppers were on board, and they were running full speed to the east through thick fog. His father pulled the outriggers into the mast and returned to the cabin. He called Henry Cabral and Cort Heinkel on the radio. They spoke briefly, exactly, without wasting words, comparing direction-finder shots on the distress signal. His father sent him to the flying bridge to watch ahead. The fog turned to dripping rain on his face as the *Maria B* raced through the gray curtain, pushed by the swells on her stern.

Cort Heinkel's voice came to the deck speaker. "East-southeast of the ship. The ship, she's under, *mein* huntsmen."

Neil could not hear his father's side of the conversation. "No, Ernie, no. Henry and me, we must be inside you. Ott, he's someplace close on our stern. Carmelo too. Turn down more. Down the hill."

A voice came from the coast guard, calling all fishing vessels. The *Maria B* heeled hard to starboard as his father corrected course. The whine of the engine increased further. Neil's heart beat faster. His father was racing the boat. If danger came out of the fog, there would be no time to turn away.

On they ran, into the mist, parting the sea in a wake of white, on and on into nothing.

Suddenly, Neil saw it. He stomped hard on the roof of the cabin to warn his father below. The surface, racing toward them out of the fog, was black. His father did not slow the boat. Seconds later, the sea turned to oil. A suffocating stench came. The bow wake disappeared. The stern boiled brown instead of white. Debris came in the ooze. Steel barrels, planks, crates. All covered in black.

They broke again into clear water. On their starboard, a fishing boat emerged from the mist—a Monterey—followed by another, then another on its stern, and two more boats behind. They were city boats, Italians, running full speed in tandem. A man leaned out of the open cabin door on the lead boat and raised his arms high in the air, as if beseeching the fog itself for answer. Looking down, Neil saw his father step out of the cabin to return the Italian's signal. His father cupped both hands to his ears, repeating the gesture, making sure the Italian saw him. His father's hands came from his head. He gestured downward, his hands flat toward the surface of the sea, repeating the sequence of signals twice more. The fisherman on the Monterey answered, mimicking his father's movements.

Back in the cabin, his father slowed the engine, then stopped it as the boat came out of gear. Italian words came quick from the deck speaker. The city boats slowed in unison, gliding forward with their engines cut off. Men emerged from the Montereys, standing still on their bows, listening, ghost figures in the fog. His father also went to the bow, put his hands to his ears, and listened for clues from the invisible sea.

Nothing came, save the sounds of scattered seabirds hidden in the gray. A minute passed. Nothing. Nothing, except the lap of sea against the hull as the boat wallowed in the swells.

A sound came, once, then there was silence. After a minute, it came again, something nearly human, like a baby crying, choking in a far room of a house. His father heard it, pointing the direction. "Bearing?" he called up to Neil. Neil looked at the bridge compass. "North," he said to his father. By now, his father and the Italians were all gesturing in slow motion in the same direction.

His father returned to the cabin. The engine came back to life, and the boat lurched as the propeller bit the sea, rudder hard over to the north.

A single orange life jacket floated out of the fog. Then a green tarpaulin came like a gigantic leaf below the surface. After that, rope, lightbulbs, wooden boxes of produce, cans, clothing, blankets, scattered boards. The boat was racing through a floating dump. The sea went clear once more.

From his vantage point on the flying bridge, Neil saw something white on the sea's surface, emerging from the fog as the boat raced on, something washed by wavelets bobbing ahead. Neil stomped his boot, certain that it was a person. His father slowed the engine. Neil climbed down from the flying bridge and hurried to the bow and took the boat hook from the deck. The white thing came on. He turned to his father, who was framed in the cabin window, holding the wheel. His father leaned out the cabin door, watching the surface of the sea.

Pale legs spread out from the nurse's uniform. One foot was bare, and the other was covered by a black shoe. She was facedown in the water, her arms spread, as if embracing the sea she gazed upon below. Neil swung the boat hook over the bow and braced himself. He looked back to his father, waiting for the boat to come out of gear. His father drew his body back into the cabin. Behind the cabin window, his father shook his head. The engine increased in speed.

The woman passed close under the bow. The wake passed through her body. Her hair moved as if blowing in the wind; her arms gestured as if waving to unseen friends in the deep. The white form passed into the fog on the stern, and Neil saw her no more. He wanted to turn back. Take the dead woman from the sea. But his father sailed on.

Later, much later, the sounds of cars came from the sky. High above in the fog, cars crossing the Golden Gate Bridge. Cars with people who did not know the cargo his father brought from the sea, far below in the waning light. The rescue was over. His father was listening his way in, with survivors on board. Night was coming. Neil heard the foghorns on the south and north towers, but the Golden Gate was invisible. His father stood at the flying bridge's wheel, listening to the varied calls of bellowing foghorn sentinels singing low, staccato songs, warning of rock and death in the tide-ripped entrance to San Francisco Bay. He understood their morbid melody.

His father cocked an ear and watched ahead, checking the compass, adjusting the wheel. His face was wet with fog, his yellow slicker thick with a tarlike oil.

On the forward deck, the two Chinese and the Filipino sat huddled, clinging to one another. Cigarettes burned close to their lips. Bare, oily feet protruded from the blanket Neil had given them.

The back deck held six more survivors: three nurses from the hospital ship, a black man in dunga-rees, and two merchant marine officers. The black man and one of the nurses were in bad condition. He and his father had found them first, clinging to the net in the center of the cork life raft, covered in bunker oil. They were vomiting, sucking breaths with screeching, high-pitched sounds. His father brought the boat to the raft. Neil took the boat hook and swung it to the stern. His father jumped into the trolling pit. The black man held the nurse up in his arms. His father bent low to the sea and pulled the oil-covered woman up and over the transom. Then the black man, his father lifting with all the strength of his upper body.

They came to the second raft outside the oil slick. Neil saw their orange life jackets first. Two more nurses and the merchant marine officers were shivering inside the ring of the oil-covered raft, like quivering fish in a net. Their lips were purple; the ocean stole language from their mouths.

The *Maria B* circled repeatedly through the floating dump of flotsam and survivors in the fog. Fishing boats, pulling survivors from the sea, appeared and disappeared in the mist. All around, unseen, behind the gray curtain, cries for help came, calling and coughing, mixing with the sounds of fishing boat engines.

Neil and his father found the last three survivors after they had already turned to run to the city. The men clung to each other in the sea. His father had to force them apart with the boat hook in order to get them out of the water. One at a time they came over the stern, and one at a time they crawled on their hands and knees, coughing and retching, to the bow, where they reassembled, clinging just as they had done when they were found in the water.

His father arranged the other survivors around the outside of the engine compartment, where the heat from the wood would help them to get warm. He placed the black man and the nurse on top of the engine compartment, covering them with the fo'c'sle sleeping bags. The survivors said little. They were like people at church, silent during a long mass.

The story of the disaster came in pieces on the radio as they ran in. A hospital ship on sea trials had been struck by a tanker. The tanker remained, but the hospital ship was gone. On his father's instructions, Neil picked up the oil-stained salmon in the deck bins and threw them overboard. One by one, their floating white bellies disappeared in the fog, like the woman in white.

The horns from rock and tower passed astern. They moved into the safety of San Francisco Bay. His father took his hands from the wheel to light a cigarette as he squinted into the darkening fog. Beads of moisture gathered on his eyebrows.

Neil thought of that morning several hours and a thousand years ago. The day before. The sea lion's

death. His difficult conversation with his father. The

shark angel. Time was backward, inside out. His mind searched for meaning, and he sensed that, somehow, it was all gathered together in the sea, but he was lost in a fog floating over it. A vision returned of the floating woman. Staring downward into the depths. What did she know, what had she seen?

Chapter Six

Neil could not see it, but he felt its presence following the raft. Real, unseen, stalking. A shark was hovering in the depths. It had always been there. Neil knew that death was swimming ever closer. Knew it, but the final clarity hurt more than he would ever have thought it could.

His whole life had been but a posture against it. The realization overwhelmed him. He was ashamed of his weakness. He would drift on. Wind and sun would weaken the fabric on which his life floated. Glue and stitch would dissolve, unraveling bit by bit in the kneading of the sea. He *would be alone, in the water. Tired. Weak. Weaker still, until he slipped away into dreams not remembered and sleep without morning. Arms spread, embracing.*

Neil pushed these thoughts and images from his mind, trying hard to think of other things, hating the cowardice of his own forced self-deception. The wind slackened further. The raft was caught in a tide rip, turning slowly despite the sea anchor. The set of the current swirled him on. Thirst returned. He finished his water. Unthinking, as if there were plenty to come. He finished the rations. Unthinking, as if there were plenty to come.

Hours passed, each minute eternal. The wind picked up. Southwest. A squall came. Once more, Neil sucked moisture from his shirt. Night was returning to the sea, and with it came fear, following below. He was floating facedown, watching its approach, eyes wide open, like the drowned woman of his childhood.

The sleeping lady of Point Reyes called again. This time, however, her voice didn't whisper with fog. This time, she sang of wind.

The Half Moon Bay boats and the rest of the fishing fleet trolled west of Point Reyes. The sky was clear, the sea increasing. Neil sat on the edge of the trolling pit, across from his father. Early that afternoon, the wind's first song came to him, humming through trolling wire and rigging. Small, isolated whitecaps broke, hissing like snakes all around the boat. East and inshore, atop the high promontory of Point Reyes, a thin mist formed, then dissipated on the lady's head and face. She was calling, warning the boats to run for safety. But Neil's father trolled on, even though the lines had been without fish for hours.

A white fishing boat passed on an opposite course, tacking uphill toward Bodega Bay. Her deck and trolling pit empty, she resembled a ghost boat rising and falling over large blue white-tipped swells beneath a cloudless sky. The *Evon, Marina, Norland,* and *Cefula* were scattered abreast, port and starboard on his father's tack. Their mastheads played hide-and-seek in the troughs of seas.

As they tacked on, swells like walls rose high behind the *Maria B,* spilling more and more water at their crests. A salmon came to the line, and his father brought it to the boat, playing the leader in his hand in a following swell that was higher than their heads. Neil saw the fish in the green transparency of water. It was a kite on a string, twisting and turning. His father gaffed the fish out of the approaching wall of water. The swell passed beneath the stern, lifting the boat high as the fish slammed to the deck in blood and death.

They trolled on. No more fish came to the lines. 127

Neil waited patiently for his father to give the word to pull the gear, but he had said little all day.

"It's picking up," Neil said finally, to break the monotony, hoping to plant the seed of escape in his father's mind.

His father looked at the following seas and nodded a yes, but then he turned away, cupping his hands to his mouth to light a cigarette. The smoke trailed off with the breeze.

More and more, his father seemed preoccupied. Was it the memory of the people they had fished from the water, or were his thoughts of home and his mother and her job at the cannery? Up and down the coast, the Italian fish buyers had cut the price of salmon. His father and other fishermen spoke about it angrily on the radio. The anger continued when his father spoke of the fish buyers with Neil's mother at home. His mother said she was "trying to make ends meet" by working at the cannery, but his father replied that the Patroni brothers were taking food from their table. Neil was caught in the middle. He imagined a fish with a hook in its mouth and a hook in its tail, pulled both ways at once. His mother put food on the table from the very men who took food off the table. The world was a confusing place.

Worst of all, his mother was changing. All of her money did not go to making ends meet. She charged new clothes and cheap jewelry, and now looked more like the magazine ladies with each passing week. One night Father Kerrigan came to the door and sat with his mother in quiet conversation. She had joined a club forbidden by the church, but after the priest left, his mother said it was her life and he could go to hell. The angelic voice from church that made old women cry sent the priest away with a curse.

Neil's grandmother cooked and cleaned at home, taking care of the baby while his mother was gone, all the time claiming her own daughter had turned her into a slave because she had married a fisherman. His mother fought back. All she had asked for was "a little help" from a mother who couldn't learn to mind her own business. At night in bed, Neil imagined the family home as a solitary vessel upon the sea, beset by storm, lost in a fog.

A boat payment was late. His mother said it was "either that or the mortgage." His father told her to "stop charging junk." His mother said it was her own money and that he wasted too much on the boat. Neil and Paul took their baby brother, Philip, outside, seeking refuge from the storm. They made him a prince in a castle of fish boxes in the weeds. Paul was a king of a rich island, with a beautiful queen; Neil was a pirate in his fish box ship. Their wooden swords struck with intensity, as Philip laughed with glee.

.   .   .

Weeks had passed since Neil had seen the floating woman, but he thought of her often. His mind conjured up the image of her again and again on the sea's surface, in the foamy edge of tide rips, afloat with discarded bait cartons, garbage, and driftwood white with barnacles. His father never mentioned her. A dark thought haunted Neil. What if she was not dead as they passed, simply too weak to move? Did she drift farther out to sea? Did she glide to the bottom? Did God find her floating soul, or did she slip down into a cold liquid nothing, to wait with all the rest?

They had been back to Half Moon Bay once since the oil tanker struck the hospital ship. Hazel's coffee shop buzzed with conversation about the newspaper account of the fishing boats saving so many. Neil felt proud.

His brother Paul asked a hundred questions. "Did the ship blow up in front of your eyes? Did you see it go down? Did it suck people under? Were there dollar bills floating in the sea? Did sharks eat off the arms and legs of floating people? Could it have really been a Commie torpedo?"

Neil measured out his answers in small portions, savoring his own importance to the rescue. It was also a sort of revenge: for Paul had told him that "nobody misses you at home" and his mother was glad that he was gone.

But soon the harbor returned to business. The

newspapers spoke of other things, and his father and his friends were once again mere fishermen.

In the coffee shop, his father and Henry discussed forming a fishermen's association to fight the dealers.

"We'd have a chance if we all stuck together," his father said.

Henry agreed but said, "It won't be easy."

Neil had been glad when the fish moved north. The boats loaded bait, ice, and groceries, and ran through the night in pursuit. Neil once again left Paul to his island home and sailed away with the roaming pirates.

"Hold on!" his father yelled, shattering his thoughts.

A crisp sound of breaking water came from behind. Neil turned as a loud slap struck the stern and an avalanche of green-white water broke toward him, filling the pit and drenching him. The chill took his breath away. The stern rose, yawing sideways. Neil was floating out of the boat into the sea! He reached out, flailing for anything solid connected to the boat, but the churning water held his arms. His feet floated above his waist as the wave took him up and out of the pit. He was going; there was nothing he could do.

Suddenly, Neil realized that something had his shirt. He lay across the front edge of the pit, his boots against a bin board. His stomach hurt. His clothes were soaked. The sneaker wave passed as quickly as it had come. Water drained from the deck, rushing through the scuppers, carrying plugs, hootchies, and leaders. It was then that he saw his father's arm and felt the strong grip of his fingers at his shirt. His father had wedged himself into the pit as the breaking wall of water fell down on them. His face came up from the pit, dripping water. A yellow plastic bucket floated at his father's knees as the pit continued to drain into the bilge. A stupid smile came to his face as he spit out his soggy cigarette and released his grip. His father was laughing.

"Whoa, honey. The *Flying Dutchman* pissed on us. Snuck up. Caught us sleeping."

Neil fought anger. He was hurt, wet, and terrified, yet his father thought it was a joke.

Neil shivered as he changed his clothes in the fo'c'sle, but it wasn't just the cold that numbed his body. He looked down at his wet boots. He had heard stories of fishermen swept into the deep, paralyzed by cold, dragged down by boots they could not remove. He thought about Henry's uncle. Was that how the sea had taken him? The sneaker came like a stalking animal, intent on snatching Neil into the ocean with its cold claws. It was sudden, unexpected. Was something after him?

Neil slipped a dry shirt over his head. The image of the woman facedown in the water came once more—

her waving hair, her outstretched arms. His chill deepened. God had not found her. Her soul was trapped in the ocean. She was searching in the waves for a friend. A premonition came, dark and bad: Someday, he would join her.

Back on deck, his father had retrieved the scattered fishing gear that lay about the stern. He was putting the lines on board, glancing over his shoulder as each following sea approached the boat. His pants, his canvas jacket, his wool sweater, all were wet, but he did not appear to be cold. The wave had changed his father's attitude, had washed away whatever was bothering him. His eyes were alert. His gaze met Neil's. His father cringed, turning slowly in mock fear of the high seas running up on the stern. He straightened, and a smile came to his face. It was a joke, a near-fatal accident a joke. Neil turned away.

The pitch of the engine changed, and they were under way. The *Maria B* slid sharply from side to side as she surfed down the swells at the stern. After setting the autopilot for the tip of the point, his father lit the stove in the cabin and warmed his hands.

"What did you mean, *Flying Dutchman*?" Neil asked, taking advantage of his father's buoyant mood.

His father looked at Neil. A subtle smile came to his lips. He turned and reached for a cigar from a box above the stove, lit it, and turned back to watch the sea ahead. The unseen hand of the autopilot turned the helm left and right, searching out their course. The stench of blue smoke came.

"Don't they teach you anything in school?" his father finally said. His voice was edged with the sarcasm Neil had come to hate. "It's a ghost ship. Sails the seas to the end of time. That's what. You see it, and the jig is up."

"The *Dutchman* almost got *me*," Neil said, feeling a private self-pity he knew his father would not understand.

"Nah, honey, *I* got you. Sometimes, the *Dutchman* comes close. Her sailors piss over the rail, down on our heads, for a little joke. A warning to keep our eyes on the game. That's all."

Neil wanted to ask how his father would have felt had he been washed out of the pit, but he was reluctant to do so. His father was the captain, Neil was crew. It wasn't his place to ask what was in his captain's heart. That was not the way it worked. A certain silence was always between them, a silence as deep as the sea itself. His father's quick, strong grasp had saved him, yet he had then turned it into a joke. Why? Was *Neil* a joke? He searched for the courage to confront his father, to be taken seriously, but he knew if he was rebuffed it would tear from him forever what little courage he had.

134   Gradually, the seas built in white anger as the *Maria*

B ran on. An hour passed, and they rounded the high, jagged tip of Point Reyes. His father set a close course along the lee side of her sheer bluffs, seeking protection from the wind, following the fifteen-fathom line down to Drake's Bay. The cliff, over two miles long, was a castle wall, and they were seeking a gate to escape a dragon called wind. To the southeast, Neil saw the Italians, the city boats, running one behind the other, as he'd seen them in the fog, hunting people in the sea. The Half Moon Bay fishermen called them the "Yukon Gang." Henry said that in the old days they loaded their boats on the decks of steamers and sailed to Alaska to net salmon. They fished in formation, ran in formation. Neil imagined them as soldiers of the sea—descendants of Caesar's legions. Now the wind was driving them from the battlefield.

At the east end of the point, they came to a sea buoy, and his father turned the boat north, past Chimney Rock and into Drake's Bay. The deep-green ocean water became milky—it was water his father called "beach water." In fog, water like this was a warning that land was near, but there was no fog, the wind owned the sky, and as they passed Chimney Rock into the open bay, the full force of the gale struck the boat, sending white spray over the bow, drenching the pilothouse. But once inside the bay, the wind was robbed of its alliance with the swells of the open sea. They beat on steadily toward the anchorage.

As each buffet of spray drained from the windows, Neil saw the Italian fish houses, tucked into the armpit of the bay atop rickety pilings. High, chalky bluffs loomed ahead, bluffs under which the boats would anchor as close as possible to the beach.

Astern, Henry, Cort, Carmelo, and Ott followed, bucking the wind chop in explosions of white that extended halfway to the tips of their masts. Twenty minutes later, the Half Moon Bay boats came to several dozen fishing boats swinging on anchor cables under the bluffs. Neil went to the wet bow and awaited his father's signal.

That night, the wind played an evil symphony. The boat swung back and forth on its anchor cable, making short tacks to port and starboard with each heavy gust. The hull was a resonance chamber as each pull on the cable sent a dull hum, then a loud twang, through the fo'c'sle when the boat came up hard on the anchor. The wind played the boat like a fish on the end of a leader. In the dark, Neil's father left his bunk several times to see if they were dragging anchor, checking the boat's position relative to the other fishing boats. But all was well, save for the constant undulating scream of wind through the rigging.

At dawn, the wind continued to howl. A big northern boat left the anchorage to check the sea, but it soon returned: The ocean was not fishable. Neil spent the day watching the bluffs as the boat swung on its anchor. The gale blew hard down onto the bay from the tops of the cliffs. In their sandstone whiteness, they looked like tombstones. Gulls gliding above the bluffs were struck by sudden gusts that twisted their wings askew, sending them plummeting until they regained their gracefulness. There was nothing to do except watch the small events of the day: the change of light on the windy bay; a distant someone walking on the beach.

A second windy dawn came at anchor. His father started the engine and pumped the bilge of melting ice. By early afternoon, Neil had read, for a second time, all of his father's reading material on the boat: *Popular Mechanics, Argosy, True,* and one old newspaper with a picture of the President on Cape Cod Bay, cruising in his sailboat with a wife who looked like a movie star. His father said little, content to sleep through the day as the wind blew on. Neil was in solitary confinement, guarded by a hibernating bear.

That night, Neil woke to the loud twang of cable. The bear snored on. Neil went up into the cabin. The anchor lights of nearby boats were as they should have been. Off the stern, the distant city lit up the sky. Millions of lights twinkled in the wind. The deck was cold and damp on his bare feet. A chill came. He was trapped on the boat, trapped on the sea—captured by fishermen, held against his will. He looked again at the distant lights, beautiful and alluring. Was he a person from another world, looking at a place he would never know?

A third windy dawn arrived. Occasionally, the bear awoke to do odd jobs in the cabin on fishing gear, or switched on the broadcast band and listened to what Neil's mother called "hillbilly music," songs that sounded nothing like her favorites on the *Hit Parade*. The boat was out of meat and bread, even Spam. His father sent Neil to the hold for a salmon. But after lunch, dinner, and breakfast the next morning, he was sick of the rich red flesh.

For a change in menu, Neil fished with a drop line from the stern, huddled low in the pit against the wind. He caught several stary flounder. His father sliced them into strips, floured them, and sizzled the white flesh in a pan for dinner. At first bite, a pungent, medicinal taste of iodine came. Their flesh was inedible. His father said the fish had been eating seaweed. They scraped their plates into the wind and the bay. After this failed meal, they returned to salmon and old cans tinged with rust, stashed under the bunks in the fo'c'sle.

A fourth day at anchor saw no letup of the gale. Time moved backward and blew away with the wind. In the afternoon, Neil sat in the cabin, on the countertop between stove and sink, watching the cliffs inshore. The wind sent waves of motion through hillsides of grass in the gullies that lay between the bluffs.

The land was treeless and without people. Neil took the rifle and went to the bow. He leaned into the wind, shooting bullets shoreward into the cliffs and the bleakness of it all. The wind blew the sound of the gun away. The bear slept on. Neil was trapped inside himself. That night, the voices in the rigging screamed louder than ever.

By noon of the fifth day, the fifty-knot gale had moderated to a stiff twenty-knot wind, but the sea was too rough to fish. His father spoke on the radio to Henry, inviting the Half Moon Bay fishermen to the *Maria B*. His father had a bag of beans left, Henry two ham hocks, Ott one onion.

The *Evon* pulled anchor and came across the choppy bay to the side of his father's boat. On board were Ott from the *Norland* and Carmelo and his son Nicki from the *Cefula*. The fishermen rafted the boats together with bow, stern, and spring lines, using tire casings to cushion the hulls. On the radio, Cort said he would join them later by skiff. He said he had no taste for Neil's father's "*Gott*-damn bean pot."

After five days of windy monotony, it was like a Christmas of voices as Ott, Carmelo, Henry, and his father crowded in the *Maria B*'s small cabin. The windows were steamed from the bubbling bean pot and boiling coffee. Because there was no room for Neil or Nicki in the top cabin, they went below into the fo'c'sle and sat on the bunks, balancing plates on

139

their laps while the men ate and talked above. The air reeked of cigarette smoke, beans, and garlic, of fish blood dried on unwashed pants, of feet too long in socks, but none of this mattered. The easy laughter of the men made Neil human again. The cold wind had less of a hold. It wasn't home, but it felt like family.

Neil and Nicki sat opposite each other and shared complaints. Nicki, like Neil, was his father's prisoner. Nicki's skin was dark, like Carmelo's, but he was several inches taller than his father. Nicki's hair was greased back into a ducktail. Neil told Nicki of his terror in the sneaker wave. Nicki told Neil of a girl-friend he was certain had forgotten him during his long summer absence with his father. Carmelo had come to Half Moon Bay years before to fish black cod in the deep canyons outside the hundred-fathom curve. The family bought a house and stayed. The *Cefula* was the only Italian boat in Half Moon Bay.

"Jesus, goddamn it to hell, Ernie, them Dago deal-ers won't go for it." Ott Bergstrom's voice boomed from the cabin above, interrupting Neil and Nicki's quiet conversation.

Neil looked up into the cabin. Ott shook his open hands in the air at some unseen adversary. His face was red. Neil went to school with his two sons, Billy, crippled by polio and in a wheelchair, and Billy's older brother, Rudy. Rudy often pushed Billy out onto the dock to watch Ott unload. Billy loved the boats and the ocean. Rudy did not.

"Every goomball cousin from the city to Monterey will get the word from the big salami himself," Ott went on. "None of them boats will join. Forget marketing association. Forget it. Jesus, they're all married to each other's sisters. It's one big fucking pot of spaghetti for those guys. Nickel a pound under the table to Uncle Sal, three cents to brother Guido. The Wops have got us by the balls."

Neil looked at Nicki, who shook his head in silent disgust. Nicki made a pistol fist and stuck the gun to his head, pulled the imaginary thumb hammer, rolled his eyes back, smiling.

They had all heard Ott's arguments before, in Hazel's coffee shop. According to Ott, the marketing association that his father and Henry were attempting to form was crazy. Fishermen would never get one fair price for their fish. The Italian fishermen would remain loyal to the Italian dealers. Fishermen Ott called "scissorbills" and "Okies," incompetents and newcomers to fishing, would help by fishing for whatever price the dealers offered, no matter how low.

"You got a big wrong idea 'bout some of these people, Ott."

The smile left Nicki's face. Carmelo was answering Ott in his broken English.

Above the fo'c'sle steps, Neil saw Carmelo's brown

woolen pants legs dangling as he sat on the sideboard next to the sink. Henry sat below him, on an overturned bucket. Nicki's father was hard to understand, but he spoke softly, slow, like fog moving across the water.

"Everybody not so stupid like you say, Ott," Carmelo went on. "Fishermen, all time, are like little fish. Here, there, all alone in the water like little anchovy. Big fish see 'em, he catch 'em easy all by himself. No matter where big fish come from—Italia, the Chicago, the New Yorka, the city, Halfa Moon Bay—they all the same. Big fish got big belly, and they eat little 'chovies or they own babies if they want. But how do all the little anchovies not get caught one at time? Easy. They go together in big school. That's how they do it. Big fish come. They see 'em, but who they gotta bite first? Big fish circle around. Anchovies ball up and look like something else. Something big. Something big fish is scared to eat. And what, Ott? You think little fish not so smart? What big fish wants is same as little fish. All the same. Everybody wantsa money. Needs money. You show little fish more money, and they swim your way all together."

"He's right, Ott," Neil's father said. Neil couldn't see him, but he knew he was sitting on a box next to Henry, his back to the port cabin door. "Forget where they come from. Forget who they married. The city and Monterey boats have to feed their families too."

At home, his father's anger about the Italian fish dealers was constant. Like Ott, he complained that the city and Monterey boats were in the dealers' pockets. Now he was coming to Carmelo's defense, and to the defense of Italian boats too. They lived together on the boat, but his father was still a mystery to Neil.

"Maybe, Ernie, but I'll be goddamned if I can understand what he's saying with a mouth full of spaghetti."

The cabin went silent at Ott's insult. Chop on the bay lapped the outer hull. The anchor cable groaned. Neil could not look at Nicki.

His father spoke, his voice at the edge of anger.

"For Christ's sake, Ott, don't be such a goddamned knucklehead. Carmelo makes more sense than you ever will. That kind of crap keeps us apart."

Ott folded his big arms across his plaid shirt.

"Forty cents a pound when the season opens," his father continued. "Cut back a nickel after the first week because they always say the market's flooded. You know they're lying. They stack the fish in freezers like money in the bank. Dump it anytime they want when the market is as high as gold. You bitch and moan about Dagos, but they take it in the shorts just like us, no matter who they know, no matter how they talk."

Thinking, Ott moved his jaw back and forth below his closed mouth. "Maybe they do, Ernie, but none of those goomba bastards is gonna roll over for this all-for-one bullshit. I can hear what the city boats are talking about on the radio. In American, no less. They're not talking to each other. They're talking for the big salami. You hear what they say? The big salami's got big attorneys. And the big salami's got the government on their side. The dealers are talking about antitrust suits against us if we get together on the price, 'cause every one of us is a little business. Monopoly. That's what they say. The government can swallow us all up. In one big mouthful."

"Bullshit, Ott," his father came back. "You think you're eating on Rockefeller's yacht here? The government didn't make those laws to get the little guy."

"They get whoever the politicians tell 'em to get, Ernie. Whoever arrives first with the long green. This ain't no football game, Ernie, with rules and referees. They play by rules you didn't learn in college."

Neil's heart beat faster. Ott was baiting his father. His father rarely, if ever, spoke of his past. But Neil's mother had given him and Paul little bits of information. His father had gone to college as a football player. Once, Neil and Paul snuck into their father's gun closet and found an old scrapbook full of news clippings and pictures of a young man in a football uniform. On his father's dresser, a dusty, partially deflated football rested on a tarnished metal pedestal. Faded writing on the ball read "Sugar Bowl. Rice 0, Santa Clara 6." Their mother told them their father had been captain of the team and was given the game ball. Neil had no idea how a football player had come to be on the sea. Was Ott saying his father was stupid because he had been to college? That he was a fool to become a fisherman? But his father and Ott had fished crabs together for many winters. If they hadn't killed each other before, they wouldn't do so now. They liked to argue—it wasn't the first time Neil had heard them. It was who they were. They spoke exactly what they thought and felt.

"Ott, I don't know much about this government stuff, but I see the way things have gone with the fish." Henry spoke, filling the silence that had over-taken the conversation. His words came quietly, like Carmelo's.

Neil sat forward, craning his neck to see Henry as he spoke. He saw Henry's hand with the missing fin-ger gesturing gently in the air.

"You know, Ott, we got to do something soon," Henry continued. "Something. Else we'll end up like the purse-seine fishermen with the sardines. When's the last time you saw a sardine in a salmon's belly? They caught 'em all. Wiped out because fishermen couldn't get together for a price and the canneries knew it. The boats fished nonstop, from sundown to sunup, for years, just to break even. In the end, the fish were all gone. Monterey, Moss Landing, they became parking lots for derelict boats nobody could sell. Ott, I've told you this before: When Cort and me started out, you could walk on those fish at night. All the way from Half Moon to the islands. The salmon are no different.

"My father had friends. His *simpatias,* he called them. They farmed the valley over by Merced. He'd take us there every year in the fall to trade for sacks of fava beans and cook the salt water and the fog out of his joints and bones. His *simpatias* lived near the San Joaquin River. The salmon went up the Tuolomne, the Stanislaus and Chowchilla, rivers off the San Joaquin. The farmers took wagons to the water's edge and pitchforked the spawned-out carcasses into the wagons to feed their pigs. Wagonful after wagonful. The roads to the river stank for weeks. Now those rivers are all dammed up so that the big-time farmers can have lots of water to grow things the government pays them money to later plow under. The few fish that still make it to the San Joaquin search for spawning gravel that's already been scooped up and hauled away to make highways. They die before they spawn in dirty pools of silt. We either do something now—catch less for more money, start saving some fish—or it's too late. We got to have a say. If not, the government will step in, and it will all be over. Not a fishing boat on the ocean."

Once more, the cabin grew silent. The wind increased through the rigging. Neil looked at Nicki, whose dark eyes betrayed the same fear Neil had in *his* heart. To be stuck on the boat was no fun, but who would their fathers be without fish? Neil tried to imagine the sea without salmon boats. A sea empty of men, alone with its own dark cruelty.

The conversation turned, without resolution. It was the way they did it.

The fishermen spoke of other things. The coming full moon and minus tides, a time when the fish went off the bite. They spoke of the wind, and the cold water it would bring, cold water the salmon loved. If Neil's father and his friends worried about the future, it was quickly put away. Their life was now. The sea, wind, fog, and the fish made it that way. If they got angry with each other, they put it aside until it was time to be angry once more. He knew that to save one another, they would risk their lives and boats. And if they failed to do so, they would be nothing ever again to other fishermen.

His father told the story of the sea lion tearing the salmon from his hands and how he subsequently tricked it to its death. Ott recalled a story from his youth. Pissed off, working on his uncle's halibut schooner in southeast Alaska, he had waited for the boat to anchor up, then jumped ship, rowing ashore into a remote region. Ott had been chased by bears on a rocky beach and had escaped to an abandoned lighthouse, which days later he set on fire for rescue. There were no books on his father's boat. The fishermen were Neil's library.

Carmelo spoke of his first job in the new country, working on a drag boat out of the city, the *Achilli Jocomella*—a boat without radio or Fathometer. This boat, Carmelo said, "had two small compartments at the side of the wheelhouse, and two doors."

"What for?" his father asked.

Carmelo paused. "Well, you know, Ernie, with the net on the bottom and two cables tight to the boat, it maka you helpless target in the fog when the steamers come. So you open one little door. You got a little kneel-down rail, like the churcha. On bulkhead over rail, a nice statue of Blessed Virgin, tied down with net twine. You geta scared, you talka to God's mama."

"And what was behind the other door? A barrel of wine?" Ott interrupted.

"No, Ott. They gotta the toilet that never stops flushing off the engine pump. Lika your mouth."

Neil looked at Nicki, whose hand was to his mouth, smothering laughter.

"See how they are," Ott shot back after Henry and

his father stopped laughing. "They ship 'em like boatloads of monkeys from Italy. Stick 'em on leaky company boats for a loaf of bread and a bottle of Dago red. If the whole shitworks goes down, there's plenty more walking down the gangplank."

Once more, the cabin above grew silent.

"No, that's not like you say, Ott. I no come from the Italia."

Nicki's face again had turned to anger, but Carmelo's soft voice had a calming effect.

"I come from the Sicily, Ott, a kid, but it's no Italia boat that brings me to America."

"Okay, so you shipped over on a Black Hand boat with a fresh load of Pistol Petes."

"No. I come here on a shipa from the Stockholm, SS *Gottland*. It gotta square-head captain with straw hair. Nice smile and thin lips like eel. This shipa comes to Palermo for olive oil to take to the New Yorka. Me, Guido Piozza, Tucchi Aloimia, Dominic Bosco—we all fisherman sons from Cefalú."

"Yah, what kind of fish they got there?" Ott interrupted again, less forcefully this time, his steam dissipated by Carmelo's patience.

"Our fathers go for the tuna every year in the Tyrrhenian Sea. Big fish. All the fishermen go together, with the big hempa net owned by Dom Viedo. They make the churcha of death with the net with all the boats around. When we big enough, we go too. Sometimes they let us dance on the net. Climb down onto the big mesh next to boat. Holda on with one hand, and with the other set the long gaff hook into the gills of fish for the men to pull into the boats."

"So if fishing was so good there, why did you come here?" Ott wouldn't let up.

" 'Causa the currents go bad for two years. Dom Viedo wants the bigger share of what few tuna we catch. Bad times come to Cefalú. We want to go to new country, so *Gottland* captain tell us if we worka on his ship, he take us to America. He hides us in hold to clear the customs. But when ship leaves Palermo, he doesn't let us out. He keep us there inside the belly of the ship like rats. Instead of straight to the New Yorka, he takes us someplace else. They leave hatch plank open high above for little light. They give bucket on rope with water jug. Bread, cheese, sometime can of sardines. Same bucket comes down for shit and piss. Two weeks later, we hear the fall of chain like thunder through the hull. Hatch opens above. The air is hot and thick. For days we take bunches of bananas from cargo net and stack in hold. The captain he take us to the South America. Shipa goes on. Then we loada cases of canned meat from someplace else.

"Shipa goes on again for long, long time. The cold comes. We sing our fathers' fisherman's songs from Cefalú to stay warm. The shipa rolls heavy in bad weather. Tucchi gets sick. He shakes like a fish on the deck. He cries for his mother, his father, his sister. After a while, he thinka he's back in Cefalú. He's dancing on the net. He sees the white eyes of the tuna as it rolls in the water red with blood. We take the turns holding him in our arms. Lika baby.

"When Tucchi die, they make us put him in the empty oil barrel. They haul him up with ropes. Me, Guido, and Dominic maka the knife out of sardine can and swear to cut captain's throat. But when shipa finally comes to America, the captain cuts our hatred up into little pieces. Dominic is brought up and left in one port. I thinka the Charleston. Guido someplace else. When they take me out, I come into the street of the New Yorka City. Snow is falling down."

The men above were still. Water slapped between the rafted hulls. Neil looked at Nicki. Nicki looked away.

But the men were talking again. First quietly, then with vigor. About weather, and fish, sailing away with words from Carmelo's story.

Nicki and Neil talked, below the voices of the men. Neil told Nicki of the loneliness he felt fishing with his father. Nicki talked about not wanting to be a fisherman. He wanted to be like Joe DiMaggio—make it big someplace, maybe open a restaurant on Fisherman's Wharf. But as Nicki spoke of his dreams away from the sea, a thump came to the stern, resounding through the hull. Footsteps came across the deck. The cabin door slid open.

"Huntsmen, what is this? A bunch of old hens cackling on the eggs?"

Cort Heinkel stepped into the crowded pilothouse.

"*Mein Gott,* Ernie," Cort continued. "I won't eat your slop beans, but I'd paddle across this windy shithole anytime with my board to take all of your money."

Up and past Ott Bergstrom's legs, Neil saw Cort's florid, smiling face. A glowing blunt cigar rested between two fingers of one hand. In his other hand, he carried his cribbage board, a polished piece of mahogany inset with little holes rimmed in ivory. Brass anchors decorated the board at each end. Cort wore a flat cap, like Ott Bergstrom. Unlike Ott, his face was not serious. The ocean, the worst of everything, seemed like one big joke to Cort.

"So what will it be? Cutthroat? Partners? Ott, you never catch a salmon, but I take your marker. Carmelo, my *pisano,* you got money 'cause you catchee more fishee than sailors catch clap. Henry, *mein* huntsman, I bet your backyard is still full of buried coffee cans from the old days. Remember the morning they made you piss in your pants on the road over the hill? By *Gott,* I'm on the right boat now. This black wind has got me crazy, but now I'll make back all the fish I haven't caught, peg you all out for the last nickel in your dirty pockets."

Neil's father retrieved two more empty bait buckets from the back deck and offered Cort a seat on one of them. He placed the plywood cutting board from the sink on the other and made a low table. The men were knee-to-knee in the cabin, but the cramped space did not matter. Within minutes they were absorbed in a sometimes boisterous, sometimes quiet game in the middle of the choppy, cold bay.

Neil lay down on his father's bunk. His father's hair and body scent, mingling with cigarette and cigar smoke, descended into the fo'c'sle with heat from the galley stove. Nicki stretched out on the opposite bunk and clenched his fists together as if handcuffed, gesturing toward the men in the cabin. They were prisoners, chained to the conversation above. But Neil was content and drowsy from the heavy meal, and the voices of the fishermen were his book and radio.

Nicki fell asleep. His arm, dangling over the edge of the bunk, moved back and forth with the swells of the bay. Neil imagined himself a gull in the wind outside the boat, saw himself flying, blowing across the ocean swells and back toward Half Moon Bay. He thought of home and of his mother. Above him, the men were laughing again, harassing Ott, who was slow to play his cards. Neil closed his eyes. The laughter became the laughter of women, the laughter of his mother and her friends in another world.

His mother was in a "secret pal" club. Each month she sent and received a present, each recipient not knowing who the sender was. After several months, the women had a party to reveal themselves to one another. Most of the women were fishermen's wives— his mother's friends from the cannery. They opened their gifts with glee, gifts they never received from their husbands, gone on the sea. They exchanged things that made them look and smell better, knick-knacks, cheap copies of things movie stars and rich magazine women had in their homes: plastic fruit bowls made to look like crystal; plaster-of-paris ballerinas, made in Japan, that danced on top of music boxes like expensive French porcelains. Sometimes these same women dressed up for Tupperware parties and get-togethers where salesmen who looked nothing like fishermen sold pots and pans. The women spoke of better homes they would someday get to live in, homes without stacks of crab pots in the yard. Neil knew his mother wanted more out of life than a full bin of silver fish, or a four-day nap in the wind. The sea had made his father a solitary seabird. His mother, on the land, was a social swallow, flying this way and that in pursuit of her dream. She was now a full-fledged member of the Rebecca's Lodge, the club Father Kerrigan came to warn her about, a club that was Protestant to the point of mortal sin.

On Friday nights, she would go to the Rebecca's meeting upstairs at the Odd Fellows Hall on Main Street in town, while he and Paul went to the movies. One night they came back from the show early, waiting in a kitchen with long tables for her meeting to finish. The entrance to the meeting room was blocked by a big door, which had a peephole in it, covered by a swinging oval of wood. The door was guarded by a huge woman in an apron, who worked in the kitchen. When the woman wasn't looking, he and Paul stole a peek through the peephole.

What they saw was a wonder, an astonishment: On a platform in the center of the room, a line of women sat like a court of stately queens and obedient princesses. Their mother, dressed in a pink satin gown with a floral corsage pinned to her waist, paraded before the platform, along with other women wearing satin gowns and broad sashes of silk. Their mother looked like a movie star in a musical. Neil and Paul could see Bernice Bergstrom—she was one of the ladies on a throne. At the cannery, Ott's wife was just another woman standing on the fish line, digging her fingers into cooked fish. Here, she was a queen, ruling a court of housewives, cannery workers, and fishermen's wives. The women were like magic caterpillars changing themselves into butterflies and back again anytime they chose. They lived in a world of secret dreams. They wanted more than the cold, constant world of the fishermen. Neil's mother tolerated the here and now, and dreamed of a beautiful tomorrow. His father and his friends lived only in a cold, windy today.

"Ach der lieber, Ott," Cort's voice shouted, bringing Neil back from his mother to the sounds of the men as they dealt their cards and moved matchsticks around the cribbage board. "You and Ernie here are on the front porch of home, and Henry and me are only halfway down Second Street. Jesus, Henry, watch their greedy fingers on the wood. Someone is hauling lumber on us."

The conversation moved from the card game to the wind. Cort said this blow was nothing. He had anchored at the point when the wind tore winches from the bows of boats.

Henry agreed. As Neil listened, Henry told of a time when he and Cort were young—eighteen, nineteen years old, fishing crab with ring nets off the *Elizabeth.* A southeaster suddenly blew up, pushing them off the crab grounds northwest of Half Moon. There was nowhere to go except with the wind, straight up to the point, where they sought protection anchored close under the cliff near the coast guard boat station. The southeaster blew for days—at times, eighty, ninety miles an hour. The seas were green mountains. Nothing but a kerosene lantern and their own body heat kept them from freezing. They huddled together with one blanket in the low forepeak of the Monterey, on a bed of wet rope.

"*Ja,* and all night long, Henry keeps giving me a big hug, crying out, 'Annie, Annie, Annie.' Jesus-to-Jimmy Christ, I think I'm gonna have to jump in and swim to save myself."

The cards shuffled again. The game went on. The women lived for the future. The men lived in the past. Neil drifted between two worlds. The game grew quiet.

Henry spoke again, this time of his father. Tony Cabral had been a man full of advice, who became quiet and moody only when the fog came between the first strong northwesters of March and April. This was when he grieved the loss of his brother.

"*Gott* damn old Tony," Cort broke in, dominating the conversation. "That old bastard. He sure showed me the ropes when I was a young huntsman fresh off the beach. And fresh off the beach is no joke. Isn't that right, Henry?"

Neil saw Henry smile, a single eyebrow rise.

"But you know, Hen, it pissed him off bad when we started with those bootleggers. Not that he gave a shit about the law or didn't take a shot of grappa when his bones hurt. What did he call those guys? They weren't fishermen, and he didn't trust a man who lived only for an easy buck. Nothing like my old man. Jesus, what a *sheiskopf! Mein Gott,* I won't forget that day. How old was I? *Ja,* fifteen, sixteen? A pup hardly off the tit. My father comes home from the customhouse, late, his breath full of beer and peppermint schnapps. 'The *Krieg bald kommen!'* he yells, the old fart's voice bouncing off the walls like a cannonball. There's going to be a war, and he's happy as hell. The Kaiser is going to kick ass. He gets his sword down from the mantel, waves it around, shooting off his mouth about riding with Moltke into Paris when he was a young huntsman. Tells me it's the cavalry for my butt too. He's going to give me the *Gott* damn sword soon as I join up. *Mein Gott,* my mother and sisters, they are scared to death. I hate horses. I wanted to live and have a new machine, full of good-looking women. So I tell him. *Mein Gott,* he knocks the holy shit out of me. Then he goes next door to Muester's house. Later that night, he's climbed up to the roof of the house, waving the sword like a crazy man, and my mother is yelling for him to come down before the *Polizei* come.''

"Krauts are all nuts."

Cort took no notice of Ott's interruption. Neil

liked the way Cort talked, the way his words came in quick bursts. Again, Neil was sailing into the past of a man who had once been as young as *he* now was. A man with a difficult father.

"*Ja,* so the next morning, before my old man gets over his hangover, I'm down on the Hamburg docks, looking for a boat to the New World, where the only war they got is with the Indians, and the Indians are all dead. I got no papers, but they sneak me on board a *Gott* damn sailing ship, the *Mecklenburg,* one of the last—a rusty, plate-steel three-master. Jesus, that night we're down the Elbe, lashed to a tug, and I'm thinking, What the hell have I done? The tug lets us go in the North Sea and *das ist das.* I'm no sailor, but those huntsmen make me one quick.

"We load coal in Cardiff after I puke out my guts running down the English Channel. We missed getting caught by the English by four days, because right after we load and put our stern to Land's End, the Kaiser tried to ram his sword up the English ass, and every German ship in an English port is confiscated. But by then it's off we sail to San Francisco.

"The captain, he's a cheap old huntsman, and crafty too. He goes right down the coast of South America, passing the brand-new Panama Canal and any English ship that might be waiting there. He plans to take the coal to San Francisco for running expenses, then load up with food—wheat, beans, dried apples, canned salmon. Sail back to Europe after changing registry and make a killing on the war.

"Loaded with coal, the ship sails like a turd in the sea. All the time, I'm thinking about passing into the lower forties and getting drowned off Cape Horn, instead of shot off a horse by a Frenchman. My huntsmen tell me that down there the wind can blow the hair off your balls and the seas rise up higher than the sails.

"We get east-southeast of the Falklands, and she blows so bad you have to keep your mouth shut to save your teeth. But Jesus Christ, we go down further into that ice wind from the South Pole, and it backs around, moderating all the time until we get near the Cape, and the ocean is like glass, smooth as a baby's ass. A big, long lump from the southwest, that's it. That and a sea of fog. The captain runs all the sail out to catch what breeze he can, but it takes two weeks to round the Horn, and I never see it, to boot. I'm happy as a clam. But the old huntsmen in the crew don't like it. They say what the ocean gives she takes away later, and no wind at the Horn is an expensive debt. A very expensive debt.

"The southeast trades are limp. It takes a half month to move up the west coast of Chile. The ocean turns to a desert. The seawater is piss warm when it should have been cold from the Humboldt Current.

Outside Lima, we come on a fish boat, an anchovy seiner. These poor huntsmen come alongside, nets piled high on their stern bleached in the sun. *Mein Gott,* what skeletons! No boots, rag shirts and pants. They beg fresh water and food, anything we got. In the rigging they got salted flying fish, twisting in the hot breeze, and three stinking terrapin shells on top of the cabin. They touch their stomachs and point down into the clear blue water. '*El Niño, El Niño,*' they say. Our cook was in Spain. He said he knew what they meant: *El Niño,* the little baby Christ child. Christ child, shit! A present from the devil on Christ's birth-day—the rich, cold water that comes each December, to make the plankton grow, comes no more. The rivers of life in the sea go someplace else. For bread and a few tins of fish, the captain traded for the terrapin shells to sell to Chinamen in San Francisco. When those poor huntsmen fell off our stern, I felt sorry for them. But pretty soon I had my own trouble.

"Jesus, finally we cross over into Central American water and a big *chabasco* picks us up, and we start flying up the coast of Mexico. Six mornings later, we tack inshore. I see the sun come up over Point Concepción, and then America, for the first time. By *Gott,* almost the last time too, 'cause next thing I know, we run into a wall of fog. And wind! It blows northwest, pretty damn good. The captain's got men on the bow and in the mast twenty-four hours, watching ahead for steamers. The current runs uphill into the wind, and the captain keeps the ship offshore, but the next night he makes his move. So from Hamburg, past England, round Cape Horn, halfway around the world I come, and in a few hours more I'll be a new huntsman in San Francisco. The captain has it all figured out: tack inshore south of the Gate, wait till the man in the bow with the lead line strikes twenty fathoms, then tack uphill on the twenty-fathom curve, which puts us right outside the lightship on an incoming tide. Perfect.

"But what the old huntsmen on board said was true. The most dangerous part of any journey is coming home.

"On the back deck, I see the first mate is not so happy with the captain's plan. He wants to take down sail. Drop the hook when we hit twenty fathoms, wait for the fog to clear off. But the captain drives on, and the lineman walks the dog down the railing, calling out the depth with every heave of the cord. The big war money can't wait. We hit the twenty-fathom line. The wax head in the lead shows sand. The captain figures he's coming in good, somewhere below the San Francisco bar. The crew is on deck, everyone with their ears out, listening for the bell on the lightship. Jesus, we're still making a good eight knots on that black wind.

"The lookouts hear the bell. We listen. There it is,

ringing through the fog. Ding-dong, clear as music. *'Lichtschiff,'* says the captain, laughing at the first mate. The ship turns in toward the bell. But then we hear it no more. We run on. Soon the mate is waving his arms, pleading with the captain to come about, to put the bow back to sea.

"First I think it's another sailing ship. I see something. A big white sail. Schooner, I think. But Jesus to *Gott,* this big sail has got no schooner under it! It's got white water all around. Our ship goes past like in a dream. It's a big white rock covered with bird shit! Christ, then the whole works goes. We hit so hard the ship turns round ass backward. The deck pitches up. We slide down to the rail. Oh boy, that plate hull full of coal rips and fills so fast she leaves the deck and rigging behind. Mast and sail come down like falling trees. Nobody makes a peep. When you fall in that water, you shut up right now, like a mouse caught by a cat. I see two huntsmen in the sea close by. The forestaysail comes down on them like a mother putting a blanket on a baby. I can see bumps under the wet canvas where their heads are. That was that."

Cort paused to reflect. The wind reached a higher pitch through the rigging. The ropes between the boats creaked with strain. Henry shuffled the cards.

"So what was that bell?" Neil's father said, breaking the silence.

"*Ja*, Ernie, for a long time I think about that too. Because that bell brings me all the way round the world to Half Moon Bay.

"When the deck split, one part came ashore north of Pillar Point, with me, the cook, and two other huntsmen. The rest of the shitworks comes ashore way up by Fleishacker's beach, with nobody else. I figure, if I come that far, if the ocean stops me twenty-five miles short, that's where she wants me to be.

"Henry's old man and some of his huntsmen pick us off the beach in a horse wagon. I get a job on the dock and soon work on a boat. Two years later, Henry and me are down at Patroni's wharf, weaving ring nets for his old man. Foggy morning, but windy, just like that morning the *Mecklenburg* cracked up. By *Gott*, I hear that *Gott* damn bell again! I almost shit my pants. *Was ist das?* I'm so nervous I start with the German, which was not good because by then America was in the war too. My huntsman here, Henry, tells me not to get excited. It's only the bell from the schoolhouse in Moss Beach. It carries through the wet air on foggy mornings."

The light in the fo'c'sle grew dim. Up and out through the skylight, the sky was turning dark. Nicki slumbered. The men resumed their stories, their laughter, and the war of cards.

Neil knew that bell—it was the one in his grammar school. Sometimes, Mrs. Scott made him bell monitor. He pulled on the rope that led up through a hole in the ceiling to a stucco tower. He rang recess, lunch, and school's end. A child rang the men of long ago to their doom.

Neil closed his eyes. Again, he saw the woman in the water, felt the sea's cold hand that tried to snatch him from the trolling pit. Foreboding washed over him as the men played on, moving their matchsticks on the cribbage board. The wind sighed through the mast stays. The fishing boats creaked together. The anchor cable hummed its low underwater lament. He thought of Carmelo's boyhood friend dying in his arms, Cort's quiet sailors put to sleep in the water, and the *Flying Dutchman* in search of souls. He thought of the night his father first took him to sea. His first sight of Half Moon Bay from the ocean the afternoon of their return. The white houses. The tall church where the beautiful young queen brought her crown of silver each spring, to pay for deliverance from the sea. But where was the crown hidden the rest of the year? He tried hard to remember. Beneath his closed eyes, a white building appeared, a white stucco building on the far end of town, where the Chamarita parade began. The building had stairs leading up to doors beneath an arching facade. On top of the facade, the symbol of a crown rested above tall capital letters— IDES. Inside the building, the silver crown of the young queen rested on an altar surrounded by flowers.   165

Neil had always wondered about the strange letters. What did they mean? One day he asked Henry, who was working alone, weaving crab traps in Neil's father's backyard. Henry raised an eyebrow and said, *"Irmão Deus Espírito Santo*—Brotherhood of the Holy Ghost." There was no further explanation. Henry quietly went back to weaving the crab-trap wire.

Neil opened his eyes. Stars appeared through the fo'c'sle skylight. The fishermen played on. He was on a ghost boat. His father and the fishermen were spirits of the sea. The crown was theirs. Time did not matter. He had been captured by a brotherhood of spirits, sailing forever in and out of a fog.

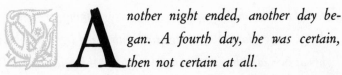

Chapter Seven

A nother night ended, another day began. A fourth day, he was certain,
then not certain at all.

The southerly seas decreased as the wind let up, and there
was no more rain. The storm was passing. Neil was thirsty
again and hungry. He drifted into another rip, curving outward toward the lowering sun. He was moving farther from
the coast, farther from shore, well beyond the shipping lanes.

Before dark, a seagull came and alighted on top of the
canopy. He saw its shadow through the fabric, the indenta-
tions of its webbed feet. Thinking it was alone on the sea,

the bird squawked to itself, ugly and loud. Neil was starving. He imagined seizing it, his hand darting out of the canopy's opening to snatch it, twisting its neck to kill it. But it was only a story he told to himself. The gull flew away as quickly as it came, stealing ending.

The sun descended, and night came to the sea. He fell into a hungry sleep without dreams. When he awoke, the stars shone above: Cassiopeia, the Big Dipper, the North Star. He had a bearing. The swells had grown larger while he slept, and they had also swung around to the northwest. The raft rose and fell. Rose again. Fell. He peered into the night, imagining the mothership coming toward him once more.

The wait was over. It came dead ahead, dark form in the night—he could hear its engine resonating low across the water. He saw the phosphorescent wake coming on like a wide, glowing mouth. Paul signaled with a red light. A blue light answered, the prearranged signals that Taylor and Smith had given them. The ship slowed further.

"Payday," Paul said.

Neil saw Paul's face washed in binnacle light in the dark cabin. Paul returned his look. For a moment, they were boys again, listening to Henry Cabral in the backyard by their father's crab pots. Now they chased the night fish. Besides, what had they said? "Everyone's doing it. You'd be surprised to know." It was a bad excuse for a choice.

With the coming of fall, Neil's first summer at sea was over. He was back in school, but his thoughts floated upon the sea and the work of the fishermen. Sometimes at night, the floating woman came to him, but all that remained of the salmon season were memories and a framed coast guard commendation hanging over his father's dresser. The fishermen now cast their steel traps into the sea for crab. His father joined Ott Bergstrom on the *Norland*. Cort Heinkel paired up with Henry Cabral on the *Evon*. Carmelo Denari, shunning the crabs, went to deep water with baskets of long-line gear, setting gangions of hooks in the dark depths for black cod. The fishermen had formed their marketing association, but after the first two abundant weeks of the crab season, the dealers had cut the market price. In the meantime, Neil and Paul turned to minor crimes amidst tide pools. On low tides, after school or on the weekends, they poached abalones out of season and sold them to the cook at the back door of Nerli's restaurant.

Neil and Paul had spent the early, minus-tide morning searching for abalone, and they were returning from the beach, climbing a steep slope, with their illegal bounty.

"This sack is killing me, Neil. We took too many. We should've stuck to the trail like I said."

Paul had been complaining ever since they left the beach with the wet sacks on their backs, moving up through a shale gully through tick brush and yellow lupine. Neil looked back at his brother, bent with his load. His abalone iron was stuck through his belt like a short sword. His face was red with strain.

"This way, the game warden won't see us," Neil called back. "We gotta go this way."

But even without sacks, the climb would have been hard. Seawater and abalone slime saturated his shirt and chilled his back.

"This way. This way. It's always your way, the hard way," Paul mimicked behind him, between gasps. Paul was getting older, less sneaky, more openly rebellious to Neil's lead. The idea of poaching abalones out of season was as much Paul's as it was his. At home, money was scarce, arguments about it plentiful. The lack of cash brought their mother to a rage or reduced her to tears. Their father said he was doing all that he could, but it was never enough. Neil was sympathetic to his father—he had seen how hard he worked. Paul was sympathetic to his mother—he was there when others were gone. The little altar boy had become a priest in his mother's confessional of grief and complaint.

Saving his breath, Neil forwent argument and kept climbing. Eventually, he came to a protruding rock, rested his sack upon it, and looked out to sea. Welcoming the chance to rest, Paul collapsed into the slope below him, sucking air.

"Whadda you see?" Paul asked, following Neil's gaze, when his breath returned.

"Nothing."

Offshore, outside the point, the white mass of Sail Rock rose from the sea. Its triangular shape did look like a sail, but Neil didn't want to take the time to explain it to his brother. The fishermen's stories were his, not Paul's.

Neil tried to imagine Sail Rock as Cort Heinkel first saw it from the sea when he was a young man, with the sound of the ringing bell coming through the fog before disaster struck. Below, the incoming tide was covering the rocks and tide pools of Whalemen's Cove with a blanket of white—the cove where he and Paul had spent the morning prying abalones from beneath rocks, bent over in freezing waist-deep water. They had felt under rocks, reaching into dark crevices for the succulent mollusks that hid in red shells resembling large ears. But Cort Heinkel's story was with him constantly as his freezing fingertips felt their way. The beach at Whalemen's Cove was the one on which Henry's father found the shipwrecked Cort. As Neil's hands felt for abalones through seaweed and the touch of anemone tentacles, he feared not only the nip of eel or spider crab but also the barnacle-encrusted skull of a long-drowned sailor.

171

Later, with pounding hearts, Neil and Paul finally came to the crest of the cliff. The climb took the sea's chill from their bodies. Once over the cliff's edge, they dropped their sacks and collapsed on a soft mass of wild strawberry plants.

When his breathing returned to normal, Neil sat up and looked at Half Moon Bay, open before him. The sky was cloudless and blue. The anchored fishing boats looked like toys bobbing on lines of swells that moved relentlessly in from the sea. The fish docks, cutting through the surf-washed beach, were tiny bridges to nowhere. Miles to the southeast, the spire of Our Lady of the Pillar Church and the town of Half Moon Bay rested like a miniature village beneath a Christmas tree.

Below, at the Princeton end of the curving bay, the old dock next to Hazel's coffee shop pointed out to sea. This was the pier Henry and Cort spoke of when they told stories about the old days. Across the road from Hazel's sat Nerli's restaurant, their immediate economic destination, where Louie Campini, the cook, promised them fifty cents a shell. Up the street from Nerli's, the old Patroni House stood alone, tall and mysterious. Along the beach in the harbor below, the cannery, sprawling like a dark castle, spewed steam and smoke. At its foot lay Patroni's wharf, where he had first gone out with the fishermen. Neil's eyes moved across a sandy beach, washed with waves—the very beach where fire had consumed his father's first boat and where the drowned rag-doll fisherman was taken from the angry surf. Neil's life was here, in this place along the sea—he felt it with every beat of his heart.

"The boats are moving," Paul said, bringing him back from his thoughts.

Down on the bay, beyond Patroni's wharf, puffs of smoke came from two fishing boats. Neil could make out the *Norland* leaving its mooring. Nearby, the *Evon,* trailing a skiff, followed.

"What are they doing, Neil?"

"I don't know. It's too late in the day to go out and pull pots if the strike is over. Let's go. We've got money to make."

Neil and his brother walked down toward Patroni's dock. Gulls sat like sentinels on the roof of the gray fish house at the end of the wharf. Here and there, at the edge of the long pier, other solitary seabirds rested, waiting for the pump from the cannery to discharge its pink waste into the sea. It was a Saturday, but the cannery was working overtime to process the summer fish. Behind the cannery, near the entrance to the wharf, women in black boots, fish aprons, and white kerchiefs sat on stacked pallets, eating their lunches from paper bags.

"Damn, lookit there," Paul said as they trudged along the beach.

The green car of the state game warden drove

slowly out onto the wharf. Instinctively, Neil and Paul ran toward a low hill of sand and Bermuda grass on the upper beach. Concealed, they peered over the sand, through the grass. The car stopped at the fish house, and a man got out.

"Did he see us?" Paul asked nervously.

"I don't know. Shut up," Neil answered.

"Mom will kill us if we get caught," Paul whispered.

"Kill me, you mean." Neil pressed a firm finger to Paul's lips, hushing him.

They knew the man. The game warden wore a gold badge on a tan shirt that covered a belly overhanging his belt. Binoculars were slung around his neck. He sometimes checked the boats for short salmon and crabs when they unloaded at the docks, but he also drank coffee, joked, and played cribbage with the fishermen at Hazel's. Even so, the game warden was the law. Frush was the man who came to remind everyone to play by the rules. Neil and Paul weren't playing by the rules with two sacks of undersized, out-of-season abalones and no licenses.

"What's he looking at?" Paul whispered, as if the game warden were ten feet away instead of three hundred.

"I don't know. Not us. He's looking toward the bay. He's watching the boats."

"Why?"

"How should I know? Looks like they're picking up live boxes. Maybe the strike is over. Look, let's walk to the cannery, see what's happening. Leave the abalone here. We can wait until he leaves, then come back and get them."

It was a good plan. They pushed the wet sacks under a patch of beach grass, carefully bending the stalks to shield the abalone from the sun. That done, they rose and walked toward the dock, innocent boys on a lark. The game warden turned, looked their way, even spied them with his glasses. But then he turned back to the boats on the bay.

Neil and Paul approached the women at the rear of the cannery. Annie Cabral and Bethel Heinkel sat with Neil's mother, all of them watching the bay as they ate. Because she worked in the office, his mother now wore slacks and a flower-print blouse—no more black apron, boots, and white hat for her. Nearby, Bernice Bergstrom, with another group of cannery women, munched on a sandwich. The beautiful, satin butterflies of the Rebecca's Lodge had all returned to earth. The women weren't talking much. They were watching the boats on the bay. Something was up. It felt like trouble.

Out on the water, the *Norland* was turning. Ott was at the wheel, at the back of the pilothouse. Neil's father was on the stern with a boat hook, pulling in a string of live boxes.

175

Their mother saw Neil and Paul approach. A smile came to her face.

"What are you guys doing here?" she asked.

Her smile disappeared as she looked closer.

"Your clothes—what happened to your clothes? You're all wet. What's going on?"

"Nothing," Neil answered. "Horsing around on the beach, that's all." Poaching was something his mother did not want to hear about, especially if it also involved his brother. Thankfully, his mother's attention returned to the boats.

"They're gonna try something, Emily," Bethel said to his mother. Bethel seemed pleased. Not his mother. Whatever was happening, she didn't like it.

"Honey," Bethel went on, "they've got to do something. Those crabs have been in the water two days since they cut the price. Another day, and they'll stink to high heaven."

"Bethel, believe me, I know all about it," his mother said.

Neil knew about it too. The night before, his father's anger with the fish dealers had broken like a wave, washing across the dinner table toward his mother. His father denounced Joe Patroni, as well as Patroni's brother, Tony, who ran the dock. His mother defended herself, telling his father she had nothing to do with the company's business decisions. She was only the bookkeeper. His father said the Patronis had always been crooks. His mother said that old man Patroni might have been crooked, but his sons were not, and if it hadn't been for her checks from the cannery the previous winter, his father would have lost the boat. Neil wanted his father and mother to stop, but his grandmother joined in, telling his father that if he didn't stop yelling, she was going to call the sheriff and have him hauled off to jail. His mother screamed at his grandmother, demanding that she stop butting into family business. His grandmother burst into tears. Wasn't she part of the family? Neil fled from the table. The whole family seemed like scattered boats lost in a fog, running full speed without a compass, shrieking their horns without listening.

The fishing boats started slowly for the dock.

Several cars and pickups pulled into the parking lot next to the cannery. Fishermen got out, fishermen from other ports who had brought their boats and gear to Half Moon Bay for the crab season. These men also had waiting crates of live crabs in the water that they had refused to sell at a reduced price. The gulls along the dock glided away as the men walked casually out onto the pier. Neil and Paul exchanged a glance and started after the men.

"Wait a minute. Where do you think you're taking your brother?"

Neil turned back to his mother. He pointed to the dock.

"No," she said. "I don't want you out there right now."

He opened his mouth to protest.

"Emily, they'll be okay," Bethel said. "Nothing's gonna happen." Neil had always liked Cort's wife. He wished he knew the hush-hush story at which his grandmother hinted. All he did know was that when Bethel was young, Henry and Cort had called her "Dance"; that was about it.

His mother started to say something else, but Mr. Patroni appeared at the cannery door. He wore loose brown trousers and a brown vest over a white shirt. No tie. A Toscani cigar rested in his mouth below a black mustache. He wasn't like the fishermen—he was a businessman. He commanded the conveyor belts to move and changed the silver fish into money.

Mr. Patroni looked to the bay, took the Toscani out of his mouth, and called the women back to work.

The women went back into the cannery. When their mother was out of sight, Neil and Paul followed the men onto the dock and into the fish house at the end of the wharf.

Several fishermen, in black jeans and plaid shirts, stood watching the slow approach of the *Norland,* the game warden among them. Neil and his brother moved around the men to get a better view. The *Norland* was towing five crates the size of bathtubs, roped in tandem, at its stern. The boat and crates moved up and down on the swells, and thousands of wiggling crab legs protruded through the slits, making the crates look like floating porcupines.

Tony Patroni stood near his scales. Tony was smaller than his brother, clean shaven, a quiet man. Neil liked him. When Neil was younger, he had often come to the dock with his mother and brother to wait for his father to come in with his catch. Sometimes, Tony took them all upstairs, treating Neil and his brother to slices of focaccia or creamy Italian pastries in the fish house kitchen. Today, however, Tony was nervous as he looked down at Ott and Neil's father on the *Norland*. The boat came to the dock, reversing its engine. His father grabbed the dangling tie-up lines.

"Ernie, what's going on?" Tony called down. His voice was matter-of-fact. Deliberate, but friendly.

His father stood on the back deck of the *Norland* in black boots, yellow bib oilskins, and woolen watch cap. He looked up at Tony. A smile came to his face. Ott Bergstrom stood implacable, silent near the wheelhouse.

"Business, Tony, that's all. We're gonna pull our crabs out of the water."

"Good. That's fine, Ernie. I was hoping you boys would come around. But you know the price hasn't changed."

His father shrugged his shoulders. Nearby, Henry and Cort stood on the flying bridge of the *Evon*. They also towed a string of crab crates, coming close and abeam of the *Norland*. Henry took his boat out of gear. The men on the boats and the men on the dock focused on his father's and Tony's words.

"We're not selling these crabs to you," his father called back. "They're going someplace else. A new buyer. Someplace where they'll pay a man what they're worth."

Tony ran his hand across his head. "Jesus, Ernie, the market's flooded. We can't *give* them away. You know that." Tony's face was pained.

His father's eyes narrowed, as the smile left his face. It was the face of the man who had hunted a sea lion. "Tony, stand aside and let us get on with our business. A few hours more, and these crabs won't be good to nobody—"

"Flooded. That's bullshit, Tony," Ott Bergstrom interrupted. He was raging with anger. "It ain't flooded in the city, where your Dago pals are selling them ten cents under the table and fifteen cents under the association's asking price. Don't give us that crap. It's dealer bullshit. What kind of fools do you think we are?"

His father motioned for Ott to shut up. The fishermen on the dock moved closer to the edge of the wharf. Their faces were implacable, like the faces of men on a jury. Ignoring Ott's insult, Tony shook his head from side to side.

"Tony, look." His father spoke again. "You won't buy the crabs for fifty cents, and we're not taking twenty-five. Hell, we can't pay for bait and gear loss at that price. We bring you all our salmon. All we're asking for is a little slack here, Tony. A little help. A little fairness. If you don't want them at a fair price, fine. We'll unload them ourselves, take them someplace else. We can't wait any longer. We got families to feed."

Tony spread his arms out in a gesture of helplessness. "Ernie, my hands are tied. If you don't want to unload for twenty-five cents, what can I do?"

"Let us use the winch. Get out of our way," his father answered. His stare was unwavering.

"Ernie, you know I can't do that. We got responsibilities. We got a business here, Ernie. Expenses, upkeep on the dock. You use the winch to take to someone else, and we're cutting our own throats—"

"Weigh the goddamn crabs. We'll pay a penny a pound to unload. That'll take care of your expenses," his father interrupted.

Tony fell silent. His teeth moved across his upper lip. The *Norland*'s engine idled on. The fishermen on the dock spoke low among themselves. Neil couldn't hear what they said.

Tony spoke again. "Ernie, you got to understand. I can't do it. This is a business. We can't take pennies while someone else takes dollars."

"Let 'em use the winch," a fisherman on the dock called out. Tony turned from his father to the men.

"C'mon, we'll make it right in salmon season. Bring you all the fish you want," a second fisherman added.

"Boys, you heard what I'm trying to tell Ernie here. I can't do it—"

"Forget it, huntsmen." Cort Heinkel's voice came loud across the water. His hands were cupped to his mouth. "We're not beggars here. We're *gott* damn Americans. Ernie, we stop begging now. Take our business someplace else. And we go damn quick about it."

Ott Bergstrom went to the bow, untied the line, and threw it into the pilings with force. Neil's father let loose the stern line from its cleat. A puff of smoke came from the *Norland*'s exhaust stack. Water boiled at its stern. Neil watched the boat crawl away from the dock, crates in tow. Henry Cabral and Cort Heinkel followed on the *Evon*.

Neil and Paul followed the men from the fish house. Where were the boats going? They moved slowly around the tip of the dock and made for the beach near the cannery's parking lot. Minutes later, they turned parallel to the beach outside the breaker line. The *Norland* dropped anchor, and the *Evon* rafted alongside. Soon two men appeared in a skiff, rowing away from the *Evon*. Neil saw his father in the skiff's stern and Cort at the oars. His father was paying out line from the skiff. The line floated back to the *Norland*'s stern, where Henry and Ott were creating one continuous rope by attaching crab line after crab line. The skiff rowed straight for the white surf.

"They're taking them through the surf," a fisherman yelled. Neil and Paul caught the men's excitement as they hurried to the beach to watch.

The waves were low—nothing like the storm seas he had once seen buffeting the stranded *Norland*. Nor were they the roaring peaks of destruction that demolished the family boat when he was a young child. Nevertheless, the moderate swells rose to several feet as the skiff, men, and rope rowed toward the breaker line.

Eventually, the skiff reached the breaking waves. Cort reversed oar blades, holding it in place, waiting for the right wave as several swells passed beneath. Neil understood: The trick was to hitch a ride on a swell, pick up speed, and shoot in on top of its breaking turbulence, rather than be struck and swamped by a wave overrunning the tiny boat.

A sudden shout came from the skiff.

"Oh boy!" Paul called.

Cort dug the oars hard into the water, rowing fast, trying to catch the crest of the oncoming swell before it passed. Neil's father pushed on the oars to make the skiff go faster. The skiff hung on the top of a 183 crest, tipped forward, and plunged down into white turbulence. Quickly, Cort swung an oar from its lock, passing it to Neil's father, who held the oar to the stern like a long tail. The skiff shot forward toward the beach, riding a white wall of water.

"Whoa, look at that!" Paul shouted in triumph.

The skiff came to an abrupt halt in a shallow wash of foam. The men jumped out. Cort took the painter from the bow and pulled the skiff farther up the beach. Neil's father followed, taking the rope that paid back through the surf to the fishing boats.

Neil hurried from the wharf. Paul followed. "What are they doing?" Paul asked.

"I think they're going to take the live boxes through the surf. Unload them on the beach."

"Unload to what?"

It was a good question, but Neil knew the fishermen would not be doing what they were doing unless they had a plan.

The boys cleared the wharf and ran across the beach. Their father smiled as they approached. There were beads of water on his forehead. His shirt was soaked with spray from the ride down the breaker.

"Holy Christ, help is here, Ernie." Cort grinned.

"Just in time, boys," their father said. "Take this line. Run up the beach to hard ground. By the parking lot. Coil it up when you see us pulling it in."

He walked toward the parking lot near the cannery. Neil and Paul took the rope as ordered. The crab line was wet, the hemp fibers were prickly, but the boys were part of it now.

The fishermen from the dock came to help. Neil's father backed Ott's pickup to the edge of the parking lot. He got out, opened the tailgate, took three lengths of pipe from the pickup bed, hoisted them to his shoulder, and came back down onto the beach.

Cort, Neil's father, and the men who had come to help walked knee deep out into the surf, taking positions along the rope.

"When we start pulling, take it up the beach, boys, like I said," their father called back.

Cort waved his arm, signaling to the men on the anchored boats. The men in the surf heaved together on the rope. Neil and Paul started up the beach with the rope's end. Neil looked back. A single live box attached to the rope came away from the stern of the *Norland* toward the breaker line.

Neil and Paul reached the edge of the parking lot. They stopped and began coiling crab line into a wet pile. The live box came to the breaker line, rising up on a swell. Cort waved to the men on the boat, who put strain on the line, preventing the wave from smashing the box in the fall of surf. The swell passed. The men on the beach pulled once more. Another wave came. Cort signaled. The fishermen on the boat held the live box back again. The wave passed. The men on the beach pulled once more. Laboriously, the men repeated their actions, over and over, until they successfully eased the first live box through the breaking water into the shallows. The men untied the live box. They took the pipes and placed them through the highest gap between the boards of the crate. Three on a side, the men lifted. The live box came from the water, across the wet sand, up and onto the beach, dripping water. Sharp-pointed crab legs and blunt pincers moved menacingly through the narrow spaces between the live-box boards. The men moved with shuffling steps, keeping the sides of the box at a safe distance. Neil thought of Egyptians moving stone for a cruel king. The men reached the parking lot. With one final effort, they heaved the live box into the back of the truck.

The men hurried back to the beach to bring another crate through the surf. Despite the weight of the crates, the fishermen's work was like a game. They laughed and made fun of each other's struggles. After an hour, five live boxes, dripping seawater, were weighing down the back of Ott's truck. The men covered the crates with sacks wetted with buckets of seawater. They spread a canvas tarp over the load and roped it down. Neil's father went for a second truck.

Once more, the slow process of easing the live boxes through the surf began. The wet, sandy pile of spent rope rose waist high as Neil and Paul coiled on.

As they watched another live box float toward the waves, smoke wafted by. Turning, they saw Joe Patroni, cigar in his mouth, come across the parking lot, together with his brother Tony and the game warden.

"Hey, you boys. What are you doing, making that big pile of spaghetti there?" Mr. Patroni's voice was not hostile, but neither was his joke genuine.

They said nothing.

"So how about one of you run down and get your old man," Mr. Patroni commanded.

To stall, Neil thought of asking why, but before he did so Paul dropped the rope and was off toward the men on the beach. Neil could not blame him—these men meant business.

Behind the cannery, women came to the open dock door, first one or two, then more, until a crowd was watching. Neil saw his mother among them.

Paul trailed his father as he approached Mr. Patroni.

"Joe," his father said simply. Down in the surf, Cort and the other fishermen began easing another box through the waves, but they were glancing back nervously at his father. Laughter had left the beach.

"Ernie, I'm sorry to see this," Joe Patroni said.

His voice was calm, slow. "Maybe something could have been worked out. I don't like to see a man do all this work for nothing."

"Nothing? Does it look like we're doing nothing here, Joe? We got a Jap in Moss Landing who'll buy our crabs. Market order price. You better tell Tony here, Joe, that the business is changing. Independent buyers are coming in. The old days are over. The city can't run the whole show anymore."

His father's face was set and determined. Neil felt proud.

"That's fine, Ernie. That's good. But this is one business here. The dock, the cannery, this parking lot right here where you're loading your truck. To me, this is a little thing, but my brother is upset. He tries to do the best for his boats, but right now everything is mixed up with the crab price. Too much product on the market."

"Joe, get to the point." Neil sensed his father already knew the point. Down the beach, Cort and the other fishermen strained at the pipe ends as they brought the next crate from the surf.

"The point? I think you understand the point, Ernie. The point is that you're doing your business on top of my business. This is the cannery's parking lot here. It's cannery property. You boys are fishermen. You buy a fishing license and catch fish. We're dealers. We buy a seller's license and sell fish. You got a fishing license, we got a dealer's license. That's the way it is."

Neil looked at the game warden, who stood silent. Several women from the cannery walked toward the parking lot.

"*Mein* huntsman. What happens?" Cort called, as he and the men struggled closer with the crate.

"Bullshit," Neil's father called back, his reply intense. He looked straight at the game warden, then once more at Mr. Patroni.

"We don't need a goddamn license to sell crab to feed our families."

"Family? What are you talking about, family?" Mr. Patroni was no longer calm. His words came quickly. "What do you think my business is all about? I got family. My brother's got a family. You think we can take from us to feed yours?"

"You can take your ass the hell out of my way. I'm wet, I'm tired, and I'm in a hurry to get these crabs to market."

Neil was awash with fear. Was his father going to strike Mr. Patroni? Would he fight the game warden too? Would the game warden bring the sheriff to stop the fishermen? Was his father going to prison? His father and Joe Patroni were two circling sharks with nothing to eat but each other. The women from the cannery reached the trucks. Bethel Heinkel, Annie Cabral, Bernice Bergstrom, and others. They said nothing, but they heard everything. Neil saw his mother approach. She looked worried.

"That's no way to talk," Mr. Patroni answered. He took the cigar from his mouth and pointed it at Neil's father. He was angry. "Those goddamned crabs don't cross my property."

Mr. Patroni looked at the game warden. "Al," he said, "I got a business here."

Frush looked uncomfortable. He held up his hands, attempting to stop an imaginary something. "Joe, I'm a game warden. I got nothing to do with private property. Maybe you better call—"

"And we're in business too, Al," Neil's father interrupted. "What the hell do you think we do? We ain't got big money, but if this is still a free country, the little man's got as much right as the big. All we're doing is going about our work, unloading to sell where we want. If somebody thinks they can stop us, well . . ."

Joe Patroni stuck his cigar back in his mouth and sucked hard. He didn't move. Neil's father stepped toward the Patroni brothers.

"Ernie, stop it! You've got to stop this." Neil heard his mother's voice. She stepped in front of Bethel Heinkel and Annie Cabral.

190   "Stop what?" his father said.

"What you're doing. This isn't worth it."

His father fell silent. Neil stared direcly at his mother. What was she doing? His father was not a child. For a moment, his father looked down at the sand by his boots, thinking. He looked up again.

"Emily, it's worth everything." The anger had drained from his voice.

"Everything? Getting arrested? Making a spectacle of yourself?"

Neil wanted to run away. He could not believe what was happening between his parents. But he could not run. Everyone was watching.

"Emily, what I'm doing is right. We've broken our backs for these crabs. What are we supposed to do? Jesus Christ, whose side are you on?" His father looked at his mother with a face Neil had never seen before. A face that betrayed helplessness.

Neil wanted to run into the surf, drown in a sea of shame. What was his mother doing? Was she defending the Patroni brothers? Was she trying to save his father from trouble? A sneaker wave was taking him, cold and terrible, washing him from his mother.

"*Gott* damn it!" Cort's call was filled with loud disgust.

Neil looked to the beach. Crabs were spilling from the bottom of a live box, crawling over the fishermen's boots, pinching at their legs. The bottom boards of the crate had burst. The men on one side let go of their pipes. The crate fell on its side, spilling more crabs to the sand. They were getting away, dancing sideways down the beach to the water.

"Ernie, quick! Hammer, nails. This shitbox hit hard coming in. Quick, or we lose the whole works," Cort called from the beach.

His father ran to the pickup, pulled a hammer and a coffee can of nails from the passenger compartment.

"Buckets, boxes," Bethel Heinkel called back to the cannery workers watching from the loading dock. "Bring buckets."

Bethel started toward the beach, Annie Cabral and Bernice Bergstrom following.

"Bethel, what are you doing? Get back on the line," Joe Patroni commanded as Bethel and the other women passed.

"Crab break, Joe. Take it out of my wages. Your old man already took it out of my butt," Bethel replied. The other women laughed. "Go get those buckets, boys," Bethel said, tapping Neil and Paul on the head as she passed.

"Neil, Paul," Neil heard his mother call, as they started for the loading dock. "Stay right here."

They stopped. Neil turned toward his mother. Her face was angry.

Carrying hammer and nails, his father hurried toward the beach, passing his mother without a word.

Neil looked at Paul, frozen in place, then briefly back

at his mother, before reeling and running on to the loading dock. Several women ran past him, carrying buckets toward the beach. Mr. Patroni shouted at the running women. But they, too, did not turn back.

Neil reached the loading dock. Hands reached down, loaded with buckets with wire handles. He took as many as he could carry and ran back to the beach. Avoiding his mother. Avoiding his brother.

Determined to reach the sea, the escaping crabs fanned out, chased by fishermen and cannery women. The pursuers flipped the crabs onto their backs with the toes of their boots, then picked them up by their back legs as carefully as cooks removing food from a hot griddle. The crabs snapped back. The women pulled their fish aprons up into sacks, filling them.

"Not a moment too soon. These babies were about to start nursing," Bethel exclaimed as Neil handed her a bucket, into which she promptly poured her chestful of crabs.

Red-faced, Neil took the bucket and went to the broken live box with the crabs. Pincers opened and closed. Spit formed on their ugly faces.

His father nailed the broken bottom. Neil dumped the crabs back in and ran quickly down the beach for another load.

The beach had turned into a carnival. Cannery workers and fishermen raced crabs across the wet sand. Laughter and screams of pursuit rose above the sound of surf. The live box refilled. Joe Patroni walked back to his cannery, shooing the more timid workers back to the line.

For several minutes, his mother stood alone with Paul near the trucks, watching. Briefly, his father looked her way. Neil saw their eyes meet across an invisible line. Then, his mother walked away. Paul looked toward Neil, turned, and followed her.

By midafternoon, the fishermen had brought the remaining live boxes to the pickups. The trucks drove away, dripping seawater, as the fishermen and several women waved them on.

With the game warden still near, Neil and Paul decided to wait until morning to take the abalones to the restaurant. That evening, after their mother left the cannery, they took a rope and returned to the hiding place in the beach grass. They carried their sacks to the wharf, and when they were certain no one was watching, they walked out beyond the breaker line to lower the sacks into the sea. They were in a dark mood. Neil called Paul a "mama's boy." Paul told him he was "going to hell" for not respecting his mother. But their criminal proceedings at hand proved more important than their anger. They placed their differences inside the abalone sacks and lowered them beneath the cold water of the bay. They would return in the morning when the coast was clear.

That night, their father did not return home. Their

mother was quiet. She went to bed early, shutting the bedroom door behind her.

The following morning, Neil, Paul, their young brother, Philip, and their grandmother drove with their mother to mass. Neil knew he should have confessed the sinful bitterness he had felt toward his mother on the beach, but he did not do so. As she stood singing by Mrs. Riley, playing the organ, his mother's voice reverberated off the walls, hung with the stations of the cross. The statue of the Blessed Mother, clothed in a blue mantle, opened her arms in love near the altar. But Neil's thoughts were not on the mass. Nor were they on Paul as he rang the bell in his altar boy habit when Father Kerigan raised the Eucharist and goblet above the heads of the kneeling people, invoking them to partake in the flesh of God.

His thoughts were on his father and the fishermen who came to mass only for funerals. He closed his eyes. He imagined the sea pouring in through the stained-glass windows, inundating all, washing him from the church until he surfaced alone, far, far at sea, with no people, no sullen and angry parents, and no land in sight.

After mass, Neil and Paul slipped away from the house, walking and running straight for the dock in Princeton.

"What if the game warden found the rope? What if   195

he's waiting for us?'' Paul asked as they took a short-cut through an artichoke field.

Neil didn't answer. His thoughts now were on his mother and father.

The cannery parking lot was empty, save for the car that belonged to the watchman who kept the cannery's boilers running when the women were not there. The wharf, too, was deserted. On the bay, the boats swung on their moorings. No one was watching. Neil and Paul went out on the dock and pulled their illegal treasure from the sea.

Once more, they trudged along the beach with the wet sacks on their backs, heading for Nerli's restaurant.

"What's that?"

Paul saw the fishermen first. Ahead, where the sand of the beach met a low clay bank near the mouth of Princeton Creek, his father's and Ott's pickups were backed to the top edge of the low cliff. The men worked at the rear of the truck beds. He saw his father, Henry, Ott, and Cort sliding and lifting a live box from the bed of a truck.

"Looks like they're bringing the empty crates back to the beach," Neil said.

"Why?" Paul asked.

"To take back out through the surf. Start all over again. I think they're finished using the parking lot by the cannery."

Neil quickened his pace. Paul followed.

But as they hurried down the beach, a closer vision of the men's labor came to them. Neil slowed. Stopped. An invisible thing struck his heart. He did not want to believe what he saw.

At the edge of the bank, the men turned a crate on its side. An avalanche of crabs fell toward the sand. The men brought another crate. The crabs fell again. As they slid downward, their legs and claws moved. But as the pile of crabs grew on the sand, they moved no more. The edge of the pile did not crawl back to the sea. The crabs were dead.

Neil and Paul climbed up the bank and came to the fishermen as they dumped the final crate. The men pushed the crate back in the truck. His father sat on a tailgate with Cort. Henry and Ott lingered at the bank's edge, looking down at the tall mound of shells. His father lit a cigarette.

"What happened?" Neil asked his father.

His father's head turned. A forced smile came to his face. He looked at the wet sacks by Neil and Paul's feet. His eyes were weary. He shook his head, sucked on his cigarette, and turned away.

"Somebody made a phone call."

Neil did not understand. His father was tired. He didn't want to press him further.

"*Ja,* that sure the hell is right," Cort added. "Somebody made a phone call, and the Jap closed the doors in our face. Poor little *Japanisch* had to save his ass. Somebody made a phone call. If he bought from us, they were gonna flood his customers with cheap fish till he had to go back to picking strawberries. That was that."

Ott cursed the Italians. Henry pulled his felt hat low on his forehead, telling Ott to calm down.

Before the fishermen left, his father walked to the bank's edge. Looking down, he stood for a minute, hands in pockets. Then he turned and walked back to the cab of the pickup. His step seemed uneven, hesitant, as if he were walking across the deck of a boat in a big sea. Had the fishermen been drinking? Neil smelled no alcohol. He wanted to say something to his father, to comfort him, but nothing came. Comfort was buried beneath the hill of death on the beach.

As the men drove off, Neil and Paul picked up their sacks. They made their way along the bank above the beach, descending on a trail down through the willows and wild blackberry vines of Princeton Creek, once more emerging onto the beach. They hurried along the sand's edge until they came to the rocks near Hazel's. Climbing the rocks, they stayed low as they came to the highway across from Nerli's restaurant. His father's and Ott's trucks were parked down the street in front of the coffee shop. He and Paul dashed across the road as fast as their sacks would allow and went to the rear of the restaurant.

Louie the cook came to the back door, his hands and arms covered with flour. He looked around, signaled them inside. He took the sacks and dumped them one at a time into a deep sink. Louie took a fork, testing the black flesh at the edge of the abalone shells for signs of life. The black flesh moved. He counted the shells out loud in Italian, whistled, and exclaimed, *"Gusto!"*

The cook counted single dollar bills into a small pile on a table strewn with uncooked ravioli. Neil picked up the money, blowing the white dust off the bills into Paul's beaming face.

"We're rich," Paul said, with his eyes closed tight.

Neil and Paul left the back of the restaurant with their empty sacks. Neil could feel the money in his pocket.

"Let's split it now," Paul insisted.

Neil took the folded bills from his pocket, but as he looked around, his heart missed a beat.

Across and down the street, in front of Hazel's, sat the game warden's car. In their haste to get to the restaurant, they had missed it. Frush stood at the side of his car, binoculars hanging on his chest. His arms were folded. He was looking straight at them.

"Jeez," Paul murmured through his teeth.

They were caught. His mother would never forgive Neil for leading his brother into crime. The trouble at home would multiply. He thought of escaping into a nearby field, but the game warden knew where they lived.

Nothing happened, though. The game warden turned, got into his green car, and drove away.

"I almost pissed my pants," Paul said, excited and relieved all at once. "What luck!"

But Neil knew it was not luck. It was pity—one man's gift to the sons of another man, whose luck had run bad.

Their triumph diminished, Neil and Paul crossed down to the beach once more. They came to the mountain of shell and claw. An army of gulls stood near the base of the pile, spreading their wings, screeching, pecking, and jousting for position as they gorged on the fishermen's dead catch. Their yellow beaks broke repeatedly through the backs of the dead crabs. The heads of the gulls tilted to the sky, gulping torn organs and tissue.

Neil's mouth was dry. He closed his eyes to the carnage, but the stench would not go away. He thought of the priest at mass, raising his chalice high in the mystery of sacred ceremony and goodness. Secretly, Neil prayed for meaning and justice, but when he opened his eyes again, nothing came. The birds were eating his father's flesh.

Chapter Eight

The circumpolar stars were turning, brothers and sisters of the Big Dipper and Cassiopeia—Draco, Lynx, Cepheus—familiar constellations, companions of fishermen on clear night seas. The swells continued from the northwest, but a subsurface current, the storm's dissipating power trapped in the sea, pushed the raft on from the south. With menacing sword forever drawn, Orion the hunter rose high in the east. Neil thought of distant stars, distant oceans, distant fishermen, a distant fisherman drifting on, gazing heavenward. What storm, what accident, what scheme, took him to that place? What did he see in his distant night?

The mothership came, smelling of rust, barnacles, and bunker oil. They maneuvered to its lee side as a single line fell forward to the bow of the Redeemer. The mothership ran slow ahead into the easy night seas. Neil spun the Redeemer's wheel hard to starboard and left the engine in gear. He felt the hull stick hard to the collapsible fuel tank inflated with air, which served as a fender at the ship's waterline.

Paul stood by the hold. The hatch cover was pulled back. Taylor was looking down from the rail of the mothership. Smith appeared and scrambled down the ship's hull on a rope ladder, but before he came to the deck, he called back for the load.

That's when Neil saw the first crewman. A yellowfish. Then another, and hurried looks over the side as the cargo net swung out. This was not the deal. The Redeemer was supposed to be the last pickup boat. The yellowfish, smuggled immigrant Asians, should have been gone already, offloaded on other boats. But there was no time to ask. The Redeemer settled in the stern as the net came to rest. Paul jumped down as Smith tossed the bundles taped in plastic into the hold. Neil hurried to help.

"What about those guys?" Neil shouted to Smith, taking a bundle, pointing up to the ship.

Smith tossed the bundle down to Paul, then another. Paul stashed them in empty fish bins.

"Change of plans. They're getting off at the next stop," Smith said.

They unloaded the net as fast as they could. A fortune was being secured in the hold.

Lost in task, Neil didn't see Taylor descend, did not see him loosen the line from the bow, didn't understand until the first yellowfish called. Asian sounds. Unintelligible, angry, desperate. Taylor had cast the Redeemer free from the ship.

The boat was in gear. Neil ran for the wheelhouse, but already the Redeemer was steering away from the mothership. A man was screaming. Neil looked back through the open door at the rear of the cabin. He saw a yellowfish standing on the fender, beseeching. Two more came down the rope ladder. The man on the fender dropped to his knees. He was begging. The men above, clamoring at the mothership's rail, were waving him back. Cursing. This was not the deal.

Stars disappeared and reappeared as Neil continued to watch the heavens through the opening in the raft's canopy. Saturn was descending in the west to join him in the sea. The flotation chamber had grown soft again, and he pumped for a long time. But it was the second time that night: Slowly, bit by bit, somewhere at a seam, maybe through a fastening, air was escaping. He was still afloat, but at some point the equation would shift. The expelling air would increase. He would not be able to keep up. He was thirsty. Hungry.

He stopped pumping and looked heavenward at the clustered Pleiades, seven daughters of Atlas cast into the sky. He would not be remembered as a star. Nor would his father and the fishermen. When memory ceased, they would all vanish, falling away into the sea, dissipating in the currents, scattering in the waves. What had Henry Cabral said when he and Paul had been boys? A story Henry's father told?

A sound of breaking water came from outside the raft. Something had swirled on the black surface of the water. He looked toward the sound. Silence, there was nothing but silence on the surface of the sea, save for the rustle of the raft's fabric moving on the swells. A fish? A shark? A shark would stay, wait, come again. What, then? Something deeper. Cuttlefish? Or unknown things hiding in the depths by day, ascending toward the stars at night?

The raft drifted on beneath the Milky Way. He was crippled by the cold. He brought his knees to his chest, held his legs, shivered hard. He remembered prayers from his youth, recited them. Prayed for rescue. "Hail Mary, full of grace . . . Forgive me, Father, for I have sinned . . ."

But the prayers went away. Small, whispered lies on the dark sea all around him.

Later, he heard engines on the sea. Fishing boats. His father was coming. Henry Cabral, Cort Heinkel, Carmelo Denari, Ott Bergstrom. They were searching. They would find him. He would be saved.

It was winter, the most beautiful time of the year in Half Moon Bay. The sun was shining, the fog was gone from the ocean and the coast, and first rains had turned the coastal hills to springlike green. It was also a deceptive time for the sea, a time when a calm day could change rapidly as southeast storms raced down from the Gulf of Alaska.

Neil, Paul, Nicki, Bobby, Rudy, and the Raisin. They were all in it together.

"The hell with your old man, Rudy. I say if the Raisin wants to go, we take him. It's my boat," Bobby said, grasping the handles on Billy Bergstrom's wheelchair, pushing it toward the dangling hooks at the end of the winch cable.

Nicki stood by the ladder.

Rudy Bergstrom did not want to lower his crippled brother into the sea, to the waiting boat below. Not because he feared for his brother's safety, but because he feared for himself if Ott found out.

"You're chickenshit if you don't let him go," Paul teased, clanging the hooks at the ends of their short chains in Rudy's direction. Paul was changing, overflowing with bravado as he drew even closer to his mother. But only with their friends. It was a side of Paul his mother never saw.

"How about it, Billy? You sure about this?" Rudy asked again, his voice begging no.

"Damn right. Let's do it. The boats won't be in for hours. We'll be back in plenty of time. The old man will never know the difference."

He looked down from the dock at the lapstrake lifeboat tied against the pilings, twenty feet below. It was a long way down for a kid in a wheelchair. They were on the old dock that ran out from Hazel's.

Bobby pushed Billy to the edge of the wharf. Billy looked down, smiling, fearless. Bobby Azevedo was a tough kid too. Muscular, with greasy hair combed back under a close-cropped crown. Neil had met him in school, where they dreamed of cars and girls together. His father wasn't a fisherman—he was a mechanic.

In contrast, Billy Bergstrom looked like a ventriloquist's dummy. Pencil-thin paralyzed legs in black jeans dangled from the seat of his metal chair. He wore a checkered flannel shirt. His upper body was normal, except for a withered left arm, which fell to his lap, ending in a hand with clawlike fingers. At school, they called Billy "Raisin." If it bothered him, he never said so. His outer deformities hid an inner strength.

Billy had pleaded to go trolling halibut with the gang. Ott was out pulling pots with Neil's father on the *Norland*. Now that they had given in, his strong, tall brother, Rudy, was chickening out. Ott Bergstrom had marked Rudy to follow him to the boat, to become a fisherman. Rudy wanted no part of it. It was a mystery. The strong brother hated the sea. The Raisin loved it.

Bobby wheeled the Raisin to the edge of the wharf, and Paul snapped the hooks to the chair's metal frame, one on each side of the seat. Rudy stood petrified in place.

Nicki climbed down the ladder, while Neil went to the winch controls, inside the fish house. Everybody except Bobby and the Raisin scrambled down the ladder, leaping dexterously into the open boat, one by one, when it rose on a swell.

"Ready," Bobby called.

"Wait a minute, wait a minute," the Raisin said. "Rope me in."

"What for? You can't swim," Bobby said, laughing. He rocked the Raisin's wheelchair for effect.

"That's why I don't want to fall out." For emphasis, the Raisin hit Bobby on his arm with his good hand.

Bobby tied him in with crab line. Inside the fish house, Neil switched on the motor, letting it whine up before putting the cable drum in gear. The slack in the cable came taut. The Raisin rose in the air.

"Whooo," the Raisin sang out, a big smile on his face. The Raisin had guts.

Nicki pushed the boom away from the dock. The Raisin swung out, back and forth above boat and bay.

"We ought to leave your skinny butt hanging right there," Bobby taunted.

"Try it, snot head. I'll cut myself loose and drop through your boat like a cannonball."

Slowly, carefully, Neil lowered the Raisin to the boat. Paul caught his chair on an upswell, guiding him in the bow facing aft, to a round of cheers. The Raisin was speechless, as Nicki lashed his chair tight to the forepeak. The Raisin's face beamed as his body felt the pitch of the sea for the very first time.

Neil switched off the winch, descended the ladder to the old lifeboat, and sat in the stern on the floor slats. Paul sat across from him. Nicki and Rudy took the boat's single plank seat, amidships. Bobby pulled on the outboard motor, which was rigged over the lifeboat's pointed stern on a metal frame. The motor sputtered to life. The dock lines were loosed, and the boat moved from the wharf. A slap of spray splashed over the gunnel, striking the Raisin's head. His tongue came to the edge of his mouth. Tasting. The sleeve of his good arm wiped the water from his face, but a smile remained.

At full throttle, the motor made conversation a shout. Bobby kept a steady course toward the breakers outside Miramar Beach. It was the time of year when halibut came close to shore to spawn. They lay on the bottom, half buried in rifting sand. Henry and Cort had shown them how to rig bare treble hooks weighted with folded sheet lead. The hooks were trolled along the sand in hopes of snagging the tough, scaleless skin of the large flat fish.

"Snag 'em in the eye sockets. That's the best," Cort had told them.

An easy breeze blew from the northwest. The sky was free of cloud. The bay was milky green, the swells were moderate. The ocean without his father gave Neil a different sense of the sea. Released from his father's decision and rule, he was free, even if that freedom hid a nervous current at the edge of self-reliance.

A year had gone by since his father and mother confronted each other in the parking lot behind the cannery. That summer, Neil continued to chase salmon with his father. From Monterey Bay to Cape Mendocino, the hunt continued. Much had happened, but little too. The fishermen had lost their crab strike, but the association had held together in the ensuing salmon season, enabling some negotiations with the dealers. Neil's mother and father had now completely withdrawn to their separate worlds—she to the cannery's front office, he to his boat and the sea. His mother made more money now, and his father was having his second bad crab season in a row. Two weeks before, a bad southeaster had struck. A river of sand was pushed by the storm's current along the bottom of the sea. Many of his father's and Ott's crab traps were buried forever. The sway in his father's walk increased, coming on suddenly, disappearing just as quickly. His father went to see the doctor, but nothing was found. Maybe it was an old football injury.

On the other hand, there was new quickness to his mother's step. She was elected grand marshal at the Rebecca's Lodge. Some said she ran the cannery when Joe Patroni was out of town. Neil, Paul, and Philip went better dressed on her charge accounts. Since the strike, his parents seldom talked about the fishing business. A silent line had been drawn between them. When his father was away, his mother still warned Neil against fishing as a way of life. She wanted him to go to college, to get an education. Though he listened without argument, he felt resentment. Who would pay for college? His mother was ambitious but hardly realistic. She wanted him to grow into one of the men she saw in magazines. He knew only the men on the boats. He was drifting into the future.

Half Moon Bay was changing too. Different people were coming, spilling over the hills from the suburbs, people who didn't grow artichokes or own a fishing boat. People who got into cars in the morning and returned at night, headlights on, to the foggy coast, people you did not know and who did not want to know you. There was talk of a breakwater, a wall of rocks to protect the bay from the sea. Ott Bergstrom cursed the idea, claiming protection would turn the bay into a refuge for seagoing fools, recreational yachtsmen, and dumb Okies.

The world beyond Half Moon Bay was changing too, but Neil wondered whether it was worth going there. The President was shot. The handsome man tacking windward in his sailboat on Cape Cod was dead. The nation grieved. At mass, the priest preached acceptance while the women wept; however, the fishermen went on, weaving wire to trap, splicing rope, painting buoys. The sea was their country. There were assassins enough in wind and fog. Beyond Half Moon Bay, the country was changing, but Neil was a fisherman's son. Everything else was far away.

"Smoke?" Bobby called above the noise of the outboard motor, taking his hand from the tiller. He pulled a pack of Lucky Strikes from his shirt pocket, extracted a cigarette, cupped it to his mouth. Blue smoke trailed from his head. Bobby extended the pack. Neil shook his head.

It had been Bobby's idea to bring the Raisin along. It was always Bobby's idea when it came to trouble. Neil's grandmother said that if he kept hanging out with Bobby, he'd "end up in San Quentin." At school, Bobby was a troublemaker. He stole a car from his father's shop and drove it down onto the beach to spin hookers in the sand. The car got stuck, and when the tide came in, waves and sand took it. All that remained was a shiny top at low tide. Bobby thought it was funny, even after his father beat him senseless.

Bobby called his father "old man," a name Neil would never call *his* father. Bobby's father was a drinker and a bar fighter. His car shop was next to the Feed and Fuel in town, but he spent his afternoons up the street at the Half Moon Bay Inn, drinking, waiting like a spider to sucker-punch drunken farmhands and truck drivers. The fishermen shunned him.

Bobby said he was going to become a fisherman. He pestered Neil's father about boats, gear, engines. Sometimes, Neil resented it when his father answered Bobby at length. Bobby was stealing some of his father away from him. But Bobby was also his friend, a wild brother who often spoke bluntly of his inner secrets and desires. Bobby claimed he had been south of town to Terrible T's, a bar where Mexican and Filipino sprout pickers drank, a place that, Bobby said, had a gypsy whore.

The sound of the outboard slowed, and conversation again became possible. The lifeboat rolled slowly in the moderate swell. Neil looked shoreward. They were outside Miramar Beach, fifty yards beyond the breaker line but still well inside the south reef. In a storm, this water between the south reef and the beach could be dangerous. The fishermen avoided it. The seas could break on the reef and sweep to the beach. But now it was safe.

"How's this?" Bobby called out.

"Close enough," Nicki answered. "Turn it downhill."

Bobby turned the boat parallel to the shoreline and tacked south. The swells grew as the bottom shallowed.

Shoreward, spray blew back from waves beating upon the beach.

"Pole, Rudy." The Raisin's exuberant voice came from the bow. "Give it to me. I'm gonna snag a big one. Show you squid heads how to fish."

"You'll never be a fisherman, Captain Two-Wheel," Bobby mocked, as Rudy handed the Raisin a pole.

"Yeah?" the Raisin shot back. Rudy stuck the butt end of the pole under his bad arm, and the Raisin swung the pole over the side, releasing the brake on the fishing reel with his good hand.

"You're dreaming," Bobby continued. "Who ever heard of a fisherman in a wheelchair?"

"Knock it off, Bobby," Nicki broke in.

"No. He can say whatever," the Raisin said. "I've thought about it. A lot. I'm gonna fish. Have my own boat. Got it figured. Special cabin, special controls, elevator down to the engine room."

"You're nuts." Bobby laughed.

"No I'm not," the Raisin replied, flipping Bobby the bird with his good hand.

"You ain't normal." The smile left Bobby's face. The Raisin was wearing him down.

The Raisin continued: "You don't have to be normal to go to sea. Fact is, normal people avoid it. I've sat in this seat watching the ocean for a long time. I've listened. I've heard some things. Read all the books I can. At night, I dream of it. Just the sea. Nothing else."

"Figures."

"Yah, figures," the Raisin replied, nodding to Bobby's implied meaning. "I may not be the freak you think I am, Bobby. I know why I want to be here."

"Why's that?" Feigning boredom, Bobby flicked his butt into the water.

" 'Cause there's no pity out here. None. Not a single drop. Not a teaspoon of sympathy. I like it."

The open boat rose and fell on a swell. Bobby was thinking about it but had nothing further to say.

"C'mon, let's fish," Nicki said, breaking the silence.

Nicki and Paul let drop lines out on opposite sides of the boat. Rudy took a second pole and lowered his weighted treble hook beneath the green water.

Without a line, Neil sat back and looked shoreward, watching the beach move slowly by, as Bobby steered the boat south. He imagined the hooked sinkers moving along the bottom, kicking up sand in deadly formation. He imagined the flat backs of unsuspecting halibut, their big eyes peering up into underwater light, as death bounced their way.

The sun burned Neil's neck. Bobby's hand moved back and forth, adjusting the motor's tiller to the movement of the sea. The noise of the outboard made Neil sleepy. The Raisin watched the vibrating tip of his pole as his hooks plowed the sandy bottom. Nicki and Paul held their drops lines over the gunnels, intent on the feel of cord disappearing into the depths. Their bodies swayed with each swell that passed. Close by, two black cormorants flew low to the water.

"Hey, Neil." Bobby's voice took him from his thoughts.

"What?"

"I saw your old man coming out of the workshop last week. He looked like he was drunk. Almost fell over. What's the matter with him?"

"Don't worry about it. It's none of your business," Neil said, as if not talking about it could make it go away.

Neil turned aside, watching the offshore swells. He knew what Bobby was talking about. When it happened, it looked like his father was walking across a rolling deck at sea. Because his father said nothing about it, Neil said nothing, either. His father was working too hard. That was all.

The outboard ran on. Nothing came to the lines, save bits of seaweed snagged on hooks.

"It's a desert here," the Raisin called. "Three Rocks. We got to pull our lines and run down past Three Rocks. My father never sets the halibut nets above Three Rocks. Does he, Rudy?"

"Too far," Rudy answered, swatting a kelp fly that attacked his ear.

"Too far? It's my boat," Bobby interrupted. "I say what's too far."

"The gas can says what's too far," Nicki broke in.

"We got plenty of gas. At least half of the five-gallon can the motor's been sucking on, and a whole extra tank under the seat between the oars," Bobby replied.

Neil looked forward at the can under the seat, then at Nicki. Their eyes met for a moment.

"Bit of a stretch if the wind comes up," Nick said, looking to the horizon.

"What wind?" Bobby answered.

"Let's run down the line," the Raisin insisted. "Martin's Beach. That's where the smelt run. That's what the halibut eat. Come on."

They went.

As they ran south again, the low sandstone bluffs above the beach grew gradually higher. A half hour later, they came to three flat rocks along the shore-line, set in breaking white water. A flock of murrelets lifted from the sea, taking flight off the lifeboat's bow.

The open boat passed into blue water filled with moon jellies. The surface of the sea looked like cobblestones. Tentacles with purple veins of poison stretched downward into the depths, as the gelatinous monsters drifted with the tide, trolling for tiny victims. Bobby shouted delight as the propeller tore through them and the stern wake churned with chopped brown Jell-O.

They came to brown water.

"Holy cow, what's that?" Paul called, rising to his feet and pointing ahead.

Nicki stood bracing himself, one hand on Rudy's

shoulder. The Raisin turned in his wheelchair, straining to see.

In the trough of a swell, Neil saw nothing but open ocean. But when the boat rose again, there it was: a fin, a dark fin protruding high out of the water.

"Oh, God!" Rudy yelled. "Look at that! Look at that fin! Look at that tail! Let's get out of here! Turn away, turn away!"

Bobby slowed the motor, turning away, circling to starboard. Neil stood holding tight to the gunnel, watching the swimming creature. Several feet behind the fin, the upper half of a crescent tail swept back and forth, slow across the surface. As they approached, a dark outline showed beneath the water. It was huge, larger than their small boat. Bobby straightened course. They came abeam of the submerged monster. A broad head moved forward beneath the water. An eye looked up through the sea. Gill slits opened and closed.

"C'mon, let's go," Rudy called again.

"Take it easy, Rudy," Nicki replied. "Unless you're afraid of getting gummed to death. Basking shark—toothless old bastard. Nothing to worry about. I see them all the time in Monterey Bay with my father when we fish for black cod. They eat plankton, not people."

Everyone—except Rudy—laughed. Bobby circled the
218   creature as it moved on through the sea. The basking

shark was indifferent to their presence. It was a creature in another world, a million miles away.

Bobby circled again, passing closer to the shark. There was menace in his heart, but striking the fin with an oar was quickly vetoed by all, and the lifeboat ran on, leaving the creature behind.

They returned to milky green beach water, and Bobby slowed, turning the boat in as Nicki cautioned him again to be alert to shifting shoals of sand out beyond the beach. Neil saw the sandstone pinnacles that marked the north end of Martin's Beach, landmarks he had seen many times from his father's boat. He knew Nicki had too. Once more, the boat slowed, and the fishing lines went back into the water.

Subtly, the swells grew taller, broader. Neil sensed wind in the distance. He wondered if Nicki did, but a smooth surface and a clear horizon meant it was hours away—they would be home before it arrived. Perhaps they had gone too far, but the farther he ventured without his father, the more capable he felt. A vision of the basking shark came, alone, swimming relentlessly forward. His resentment toward his mother softened. Maybe his father was like the shark, tied to his place in the sea, oblivious to change. Maybe he *should* do something about his education. He'd try harder to please her. But summers with his father and the fishermen took him to a place that tempted his heart.

"Got something!" the Raisin screeched with excitement, the tip of his pole bent hard to the sea.

"Jesus, big one," the Raisin called again.

"Me too," Paul said. His drop line was taut against the hull.

"Cut your line, Paul," Nicki commanded. "Cut it. You're hung up with the Raisin under the boat."

Paul fumbled for a pocket knife and cut his line. Immediately, the Raisin's line whizzed along the surface, stretching sideways from the boat.

"It's pulling the boat, it's pulling the boat!" the Raisin said with delight.

"Turn toward the line," Nicki said.

Bobby turned the motor toward the pull of the fish. With his pole tight to the gunnel and the butt tucked beneath his bad arm, the Raisin reeled hard in the bow.

"Who needs a motor?" the Raisin shouted. "Leave me alone," he called, chastising his brother, who wanted to help.

The Raisin struggled, reeling hard, resting as the fish took the boat, reeling again as it slowed. Everybody shouted instructions and encouragement. Slowly, the angle of line rose toward the surface. The fish stopped pulling. A white tail slapped water off the bow. A flash of white underbelly came as it twisted, attempting to dive. The Raisin pulled up on his pole. The fish slapped water once more.

Minutes later, the exhausted halibut was next to the boat. The treble hook was embedded in its head.

"Watch the tail," Nicki called, striking the fish with a gaff hook. He missed, and blood appeared in the water. He struck again, sinking the hook in solid flesh.

Neil moved to Nicki's aid, adding his hands to the bat end of the gaff. Straining, they brought the broad, convulsing halibut head-up against the hull. Rudy, Bobby, and Paul cheered. The Raisin was too excited to say anything. Everyone leaned to the opposite side of the boat to counterbalance their pull. The fish came from the sea, over the side, tail slapping wildly, and fell to the bottom of the boat, thrashing, sending sea-water, slime, and blood everywhere. Nicki beat on its head until the thrashing stopped.

The cheers subsided. The halibut quivered in final submission. All turned to the Raisin and cheered again. The Raisin's eyes were big, his smile was wide. A drop of blood dribbled down his forehead. Rudy's hand moved to wipe it away from his brother's face, but as he did so his hand froze and his face drained of color. He pointed seaward, his mouth open. Rudy shouted one word, quick and urgent.

"Comber."

Neil saw it too. A massive swell, humped wall of dark water growing higher, moving on relentlessly toward the broadside of the boat. Neil was paralyzed with fear. The top of the wall was translucent with sunlight. A jellyfish and a floating strand of kelp revealed themselves like paintings on the comber's vertical mass. It was at once horrible and beautiful. In the excitement of landing the fish, they had run up over a shoal.

"We're dead!" Rudy's voice came as a scream.

"Turn the bow. Turn it, Bobby. Gas! Bobby, give it gas!" Nicki's words were quick, decisive.

Neil understood. It was their only chance. They had to get the bow around, or else the cresting wall was sure to roll them under.

Bobby put the motor in gear, swung the outboard hard over. The bow began to swing.

"Hold on, get down," Neil shouted to Paul.

"No good. Faster. Get around. More gas," Nicki yelled.

"It's wide open," Bobby screamed, twisting the throttle.

The bow swung further, but the first sound of falling water came above the whine of the motor. The wall was turning white all along its crest.

"Son of a bitch. Come on," Bobby called to the boat. His face was wild with fear.

The boat lurched forward, gaining speed. Nicki crouched low, wedging himself under the plank seat. Rudy did the same. Neil's heart raced.

"Hold on," he yelled to Paul, pushing him to the bottom of the boat.

The wall closed, rising higher. It was falling over on itself. There was no escape. An exhilaration came, numbing but clear. Neil saw the simple equation of finality. The momentum of the boat had to clear the mass of wave, or they were dead. Nothing else mattered. The bow pointed. Bobby raced the motor for all it was worth. They were running at the wall of water as fast as it was racing toward them.

The boat dipped down into the hollow of water being sucked up into the wall. Shadow and a stillness of air on faces. The bow shot up, as the boat turned skyward. A falling oar struck Neil in the shoulder. A red gas tank whizzed past his face. The halibut slid by Paul and into the sea. Cans, rope, fishing poles. A bucket fell, but still the boat climbed. Neil's fingers were locked into the stringer at the gunnel edge of the boat. His legs slid away. Rudy and Nicki held on to the seat above him, like boys dangling from monkey bars. They were mountain climbers suspended on a thread. The boat was vertical on the wall of the wave. The equation was falling apart. The comber roared deep and final as it broke. The sky was gone. The boat was pitching over. They would be crushed and drowned in one final blow. Weightlessness came. The last thing he saw was the Raisin above him, lashed to his chair. His good arm and his withered arm spread wide, as cold white ocean thundered down.

Looking up at the stars once more, he realized that he wasn't as cold as before. He saw the Raisin's arms again, arms of his youth. Again, he thought of other oceans in the stars. How different could they be? Would you float in the air? Would the sea be your sky? Fearing delusion, he willed the thought away.

Neil switched on the flashlight. Its bulb was dim. He removed his last flare from the survival pouch and held it precious in his hands. The air was clear for miles around. Perhaps someone would see. Should he fire it now or wait for the light of ship or plane? Fearing failure, he willed the decision away and made a plan for the morning. He would take hook and line from the pouch, rip fabric from his shirt to make a lure, catch fish to eat, catch fish to suck moisture from their flesh.

The stars moved, time wore on, but the black night remained. A moment came when he felt that he was not alone on the raft. Paul, Bobby, Nicki, Rudy, the Raisin, they sat with him under the canopy. They said nothing, but he heard them breathing, shivering. He reached out to touch them, but they were gone. Frightened, he aimed the last flare through the opening in the canopy and fired. It rose as a meteor, incandescent red, assaulting the stars, filling him *with hope. But his comet diminished, falling to the black ocean. For a long time he waited, but nobody came.*

Maybe we can make a signal fire," Bobby said, between recurrent spasms of chattering teeth. Neil sat shivering in the dark, wrapped in his own arms, slumped forward to avoid the wind.

"With what?" Nicki answered. "What can we light? We're lucky this tub is floating. That crappy frame you made cost us the motor when we bucked over the comber. The gas cans went overboard with your ass. We lost the oars because you didn't tie 'em down. No flashlight. You don't even have an anchor. Nothing."

Neil, Bobby, and Nicki had kept up their argument since the current took them from the shoal. Through his wet clothes, Neil could feel his brother shivering next to him. Forward, the Raisin sat in his chair, Rudy's jacket covering his shoulders and head. Each time the boat rose, he became a dark form against a background of night and stars. It was a miracle he and his wheelchair had not torn loose when the boat shot over the breaker. Rudy lay at the Raisin's feet, knees to chest, clutching his legs for a little warmth. The cold wind was stealing their lives away, sucking it from their wet bodies, scattering it over the night sea.

Neil closed his eyes. The wall of water came again, its snarling crest, the bow of the lifeboat pointing skyward, the Raisin's arms wide. He saw Bobby in the water, fingers gripping the stern where once the motor had been. He saw the second hump of sea approach. The boat, sluggish with water, climbing its dark mass. He felt once more the downward plunge as the second comber raced by, exploding behind them.

Current and current alone took them clear of the breaking sandbar. Bobby vomited seawater as they pulled him in. They bailed with cupped hands and a single can found wedged beneath the stern seat. Motor, oars, gas tanks, poles—everything had fallen into the sea. The wave left behind only their lives.

Above, the stars oscillated with the roll of the boat. Orion rose to the east. Polaris stood fixed above the bay, miles to the north. A strange sensation came. Neil felt he had been here before, some other time, drifting through stars.

He had no idea how far the land breeze had taken them from shore. It had come before dusk, scented with grass, warm and strong from the beach, rippling across the water in whirling gusts like passing ghosts, pushing their helpless boat out to sea and into the descending darkness. When the warm ghosts had left, the ever-chill spirits from the northwest came in the night with their mocking whitecaps. The wind took them south, farther and farther from Half Moon Bay.

"Keeps up like this, we'll be in Monterey for breakfast," the Raisin said.

"How would you know?" Bobby shivered with anger.

"I pay attention. I got charts in my bedroom. I'd bet right now we're in about thirty fathoms between Pescadero and San Gregorio Creek. Making two, maybe two and a half knots in this wind."

"Jesus, Captain Two-Wheel," Bobby replied.

"You got us here," the Raisin said, his voice trailing off into the wind.

They drifted on, pushed by wind.

"Pigeon. I think I see Pigeon Point," Nicki said after a while.

Neil looked ahead and realized the Raisin's guess at their position was right. The eye of the lighthouse turned inshore in the distance.

"They're coming," Neil said. He was certain.

"Coming? How can you be sure? Nobody saw us when we went." Bobby's voice was edged with despair. "How can they find us in this goddamn ocean?"

All were silent. The wind rose and fell in gusts. The whitecaps hissed in the night. After a time, Rudy spoke in hushed sobbing tones to his brother in the bow. Neil thought of Carmelo Denari, Nicki's father, of the story he had told about young men imprisoned at sea. They, too, were prisoners, prisoners of their own stupidity. If they had watched the game, they would have seen the shoal ahead, a change in the height of the swells, a change in the sea's color. Neil said a silent Act of Contrition. But the prayer felt empty as they drifted on through the night. They were in a place without forgiveness.

The turning arc of the Pigeon Point light grew closer. The northwester was pushing the open boat back toward the land. Land was safety, but safety would be guarded by rolling surf and rocks.

"Do you think they'll really come?" Paul whispered in the dark.

"They're fishermen," was all Neil could answer.

"Because our father loves us? He never says it. Mom does. She says it, but he doesn't. Sometimes, I think he doesn't."

"You can love without saying it." Again, it was all Neil could answer.

"The ocean wants to kill us," his brother went on.

"Don't think about it. It'll be okay," he answered. But his brother was right. At the top of an oncoming swell a whitecap washed by, hissing. It would kill them if it could—effortlessly, accidentally, without intent, spilling and filling up the boat. They had nothing but their hopes, and the waves were laughing.

The boat dropped into a trough between seas. They were in a black valley surrounded by walls of water. Flickers of light went off beneath the surface. A galaxy of glowing bait was revealed upon a watery screen.

Smelt, anchovies, squid? Underwater phantoms pursued the bait, meteors outlined in phosphorescence. Were they salmon, diving birds, or something else? The ocean of their death was filled with life.

Time changed to the rise and fall of swells. The cold hurt. Far out to sea, a ship passed, heading north. All watched its passage without a word. Slowly, they drifted past the Pigeon Point light. Neil thought of the trouble between his parents. His anger at his mother. He prayed again for forgiveness, but forgiveness no longer mattered. The God of his childhood was going away, he knew not where.

"I think I see the beach," the Raisin called from the bow.

Nicki rose to his knees, peering east into the dark. They all saw it: a thin glow of surf beneath the hills of the coast, outlined in stars.

"Now what?" Bobby asked.

"Pray for sand," was all that Nicki could answer.

Driven by the wind, they drifted on. Sometime later, Neil felt the swells heighten as the boat drifted closer to shore.

"There's a house or something. I see a house," the Raisin called again.

"Damn," Nicki answered. "It's got to be Año Nuevo Island. The abandoned lifeboat station, where the elephant seals haul out and screw all winter. There's nothing but rocks for miles."

They strained their eyes toward shore. Dawn's first faint light shone above the hills. Each swell, each gust of wind, pushed them closer. Neil saw the house. They were helpless, broadside to the waves. The wind and current were taking them to destruction. The pounding surf would roll them over in the rocks far from shore. Some might make it. But the Raisin? His brother? He saw them settling down through the night sea beneath the boiling surf, passing downward in a final cold sleep, through the twinkling lights of bell jellies. Even those strong enough to swim in the numbing cold would be beaten against stone and hammered into crevices of seaweed.

Neil pulled his shivering brother closer. The swells grew higher and higher. The sound of breaking waves came. He watched the abandoned coast guard house as the pale shape became distinct. Roof, walls, windows, a door. It was the empty house where death lived, the house to which they all were going.

Beneath the wind, Rudy sobbed quietly in the bow.

"A boat. Is that a boat?" Paul said, pushing himself away, pointing to the northwest.

Outside the lighthouse well above them, a mast light appeared, then a second. Searching beams swept the sea.

"They're too far. We're too close. They'll never see us in here," Nicki said. "If this pisspot had an anchor, we could hold on till daylight."

The seas grew higher, the pounding surf louder, closer. Neil saw three mast lights now. The fishing boats were fanned out in a search pattern, running down the coast. His father was coming, Henry Cabral, Cort Heinkel, Ott Bergstrom, Carmelo Denari. He saw the red and green running lights on the boats, eyes in the night, heading their way.

But they were too far. Even if they had a flashlight, they were still too far. They were caught. Time grew shorter with each pushing swell, with each gust of wind.

"Get me out of this goddamn chair now," the Raisin commanded from the bow. "C'mon, get me out."

"Yah, get him out. Tie his legs around my neck. I can use him as a life jacket," Bobby said.

"I got an idea. Get me out," the Raisin shot back. "Lookit. Use my chair for an anchor. It's heavy. The crab line for an anchor line."

For a moment, there was no reply.

"C'mon," Nicki said, breaking the silence.

Neil and Nicki climbed over the seat, past Rudy, slumped in despair. Nicki untied one end of the rope at the Raisin's waist, and Neil untied the other end from the post at the bow.

"Unravel the line to make it long enough," the Raisin said. "There's rocks on the beach. There's a good chance there's rocks under us. The frame, the wheels—they'll snag something."

The Raisin put his good and his bad arm around Neil's neck as he lifted him from the chair. His thin, useless legs flopped against Neil's body. Neil took the Raisin to the stern and placed him next to Paul, while Nicki hurriedly unraveled the rope that held the chair. The height of the swells increased; the sounds of breaking waves grew louder. Neil scrambled back to the bow. They worked quickly at the rope, twisting off the first and second strands.

"Not much better than string. But it's a shot," Nicki said, tying the strands together.

Nicki secured one end of the rope to the bowring. Neil tied the other end of the line to the Raisin's chair. Together, they lifted the wheels to the gunnel.

"Now," Nicki said, heaving it into the wind. The wheelchair sank into darkness, trailing phosphorescence.

Minutes later—forever later—the bow slowly came round, pointing into wind and sea. The boat was fast, snagged on the bottom, hanging on a thread. Cheers and laughter came from the dark sea.

At first light, the fishing boats saw them. The *Norland* came first, with his father and Ott, then the *Evon,* with Henry and Cort. The *Cefula* too, which had run in from the black cod grounds to join the search. Neil saw the faces of the fishermen as the boats approached, felt the power of their arms as he was pulled up and onto the deck. There were no recriminations, only smiles. His father and the fishermen turned their near deaths into jokes, vowed with laughter to replace their forged anchors with wheelchairs. They wrapped wet bodies in blankets and stripped the clothes from the Raisin's frail body. They rubbed his blue flesh pink again. They had beaten the sea with a cripple's brain.

Chapter Nine

He knew the stars signaled the passing of the storm. Scattered clouds, pink with the coming dawn, were sailing away. There would be no more squalls, which meant no more fresh water. How long could he go?

He was drifting toward death. He tried to imagine its position, its exact line of latitude, its precise degree of longitude—the last intersection point on his wayward course of life. If he had chart, dividers, compass rose, plotter, direction, speed of drift, he could plot it. How many knots did he drift in an hour? In a day? Years? Looking back, the *way points were clear, but where was that final point of position to which he was drifting?*

The separation between the mothership and the Redeemer increased. He should have seen what Smith and Taylor were up to; maybe he chose not to see. He put the mothership on the stern and pegged the engine. It would be easier without the yellowfish. Neil was sure about that.

Paul secured the hold. Smith came to the cabin, buoyant, optimistic, and false.

"We shouldn't leave them," Neil was saying to Smith, as Taylor stepped into the cabin.

"We already did," Taylor answered. "They're not worth the risk."

Smith was nervous, but he smiled weakly.

Neil stared ahead into the night. He held the helm in his hands, glanced at the course in the binnacle light, but hesitated to engage the pilot. It was not right. They were sailors. Men like him. Worse, it was stupid. Having crossed the Pacific, the ship would run out of fuel, water, provisions, and be found. The crew were living evidence. The abandoned sailors would name his boat. They would tell everything. But he kept the helm on course. They were already two hundred yards from the mothership. Three hundred. Something about the situation did not add up. How could Smith and Taylor not see it?

He sensed that they were one step ahead of him. In an instant, he understood, and his heart was cut from his chest.

"What about . . . ," he started to say.

The sound came from beneath the sea. Neil felt it in the soles of his boots. Resonating. A quick, horrible explosion telegraphed through the ocean. That was the plan.

"No!" he said.

"Yes," Smith said, with exaggerated jubilance. Taylor was laughing.

Smith and Taylor congratulated themselves on the details: Twenty pounds of explosives planted in the shaft alley. The radio sabotaged. The next stop for the mothership was the bottom of the sea.

In his shock and confusion, Neil knew one thing: He had to come about. He measured the consequences, calculating how far his false companions would go. He wondered if they had sabotaged the lifeboats too. He was certain they had.

He had to turn around. He thought of his father, Henry Cabral, Carmelo Denari, Ott Bergstrom, Cort Heinkel. They were all fishermen. He, too, was a fisherman. A fisherman's son.

He sank back in the raft. Watched the stars once more, turning, disappearing one by one with the coming dawn.

237

A time came when he was no longer a boy.

The bow of the *Maria B* pointed to the sun descending into an oily red sea. The ocean's surface was as flat as a tabletop. On this oncoming night, the sea wore a mask of serenity—it was asleep and dreaming. On this night, Neil Kruger began the last trip with his father.

Years had passed, yet the sea was constant in its changing moods. His father's loss of balance worsened, but he went on fishing. His mother's life improved as she made more money at the cannery. Her dreams became more real, and a silent truce reigned in the no-man's-land between them. A distant war began and soon spread like a raging storm across the land, but the fishermen took little notice as arrogant fools fought for the helm of a foundering ship.

From the wheelhouse door, Neil watched a drag boat on the starboard beam, lumbering northward, pulling its net across the ocean's bottom inside the southeast Farallon. Two deckhands in bloodied slickers stood like guards on the back deck. Smoke from the vessel's engine rose straight up into a windless sky, mingling with trailing gulls. In the diminishing light, the drag boat was more apparition than fishing boat.

Neil's father had set the course an hour earlier, before descending into the fo'c'sle to get some sleep.

Between the mechanical oscillations of the autopilot and above the drone of the engine, Neil heard his snore. At midnight, they would change places, outward bound 290 degrees on a course that would take them well outside the Cordell banks toward the trackless depths of the Bodega canyon. The racing *Maria B,* low in the water with a deckload of fuel in fifty-gallon drums and a ton of chip ice in her hold, was chasing yesterday's rumor of albacore—long-fin tuna—the fastest fish in the sea. For weeks, the salmon had been off the bite. The northwest winds had been still, the fog had not come, and the sea along the coast had turned warm. In consequence, the salmon had vanished into the deepest secrets of their travels: deep, cold, hidden places that even the fishermen could not discover.

Up ahead, Cort Heinkel, alone on the *Marina,* led the way toward the afterglow of the drowned sun. Henry Cabral followed on the *Evon,* Carmelo Denari and Nicki on the *Cefula* followed Henry. Ott Bergstrom ran behind the *Cefula* on the *Norland,* and Neil and his father brought up the rear. They were a chain of tiny boats bound into darkness, into the open emptiness beyond.

Neil took the glasses from the console and watched the drag boat. Its deck lights came on, and the deckhands came to life as the cable drums behind the wheelhouse turned. After some time, the deckhands secured rusty net doors to each side of the stern. Seagulls soared in agitation as the net came to the surface, heeling the drag boat to starboard. The deckhands moved the net to the boom and lifted it into the air. Water drained from the sack end of the net, gorged with bottom fish. Once they had swung the net inboard above the deck, a deckhand pulled the pucker line and jumped back. The fish exploded to the deck. The pucker was retied and the net once more swung into the sea. Black smoke came from the boat's exhaust as the skipper put the vessel in gear. The deckhands released the metal doors, and the net fell away, into the depths, dragging the bottom, the net's wide mouth devouring all.

Neil took the glasses away from his eyes, checked compass and course, and placed the glasses back in their case. The drag boat fell away to the northeast. The deckhands were sorting the catch, shoveling the junk fish back into the sea. Gulls dove upon their dead and dying bodies, plucking at eyes and bellies. Neil hated the drag boats, hated the waste, hated their net's wide mouth, taking all.

The sea embraced the night as stars appeared between the mast lights ahead. To the southwest, a sliver of moon lowered in the sky, reflecting a thin path of light upon the sea. Neil switched on the binnacle light and then made a pot of coffee. Over the glowing stern wake, the revolving eye of the Farallon light grew smaller, disappearing into the distance.

As darkness deepened, Neil Kruger recalled the moment he had changed from a child to a man. He saw the open boat of his youth once again—the open boat in the cold night sea in which the Raisin saved their lives.

Several fishing seasons later, the letter from the government took Bobby first. Then it was Neil's turn. The wide-mouth net descended, taking the sons of fishermen, of mechanics, of farmers, far across the sea. Rudy and Nicki were spared the net's tight weave. Paul escaped by the luck of the draw. Before the net took Neil away, he went to Our Lady of the Pillar Church with his mother. The church was empty and cold. He and his mother knelt at the candle rail beneath the Blessed Virgin. Two small candles flickered without warmth before them. His mother touched his hand.

A band played on the dock in San Francisco as the troopship left. Its decks and holds were filled with sons. Outward bound, they saw the Golden Gate disappear on the stern. The ship passed south of the main Farallon, sailing through the kingdom of Neil's youth. To the southeast, he saw the faint pulse of

Pigeon Point light. The smell of vomit on metal companionways came as boy comrades without sea legs left their country behind.

And then they found themselves in the sack end of the net.

Neil saw the sharp geysers of bullets in the paddy, the boys fall, blood in the brown, fecal water; he inhaled the sulfur smell of entrails, the pungent sweetness of burning flesh. He saw the rain, endless rain, washing all away—screams, tears, laughter, boredom, fear, blood—away to earth, away to ditch, away to stream, away to river, away to sea. For a time, his heart was cut from his body, held beating and helpless in some great hand. The child was gone. Bobby was dead. Not at sea, not as the fisherman he had dreamed of being, but simply as a mistake: a pilot's error, the plane flown into a mountain. His country gone, Neil returned to the men of his youth in search of his heart.

Half Moon Bay had changed too. The government had built a breakwater. The bay was now walled with rocks against the fierce southeast storms. Just as Ott had once warned, the breakwater brought Okies in junk boats, yachtsmen with fantasies they played out on the land while their expensive craft lay moored and protected in the bay. The beach by Patroni's wharf would never again know the towering fury of the sea's anger, in that place where his mother had once shed tears while his father burned a dream.

His young brother Philip was now a boy of eleven. Paul had become an abalone diver, with his own small boat. His grandmother was gone, dead and in the cemetery on a weedy hill above Half Moon Bay. Neil went alone to her grave. From the hill where she was at rest, he saw the sea beyond the town, and he felt sorrow for the first time since escaping the net, sorrow for an old lady who tried to protect him from the sea, the sea in which he now sought escape.

While Neil was gone, a profound change had come over his father. His condition was much worse—his walk was now very unsteady. Something in the depths of his heart had changed too. He had grown pensive. His mother was also different. She was filled with energy, and she now ran the cannery when Joe Patroni was absent. The angry flood of arguments between his mother and his father had ebbed to a placid, exposed mudflat of silence. Paul was his mother's confidant. They talked long into the night over coffee at the kitchen table, while his father toiled in his workshop or fell asleep on the couch. Neil knew that his father silently resented their intimacy, for he heaped sarcasm on Paul's budding ambitions, ridiculing his calling beneath the sea. Paul retreated further into the depths. In his diving suit, he searched the rocks of the bay's outer reef, seeking abalone and a father's approval that never would come.

Had his mother's withdrawal produced his father's unsteady gait? Was he a victim of his own self-pity, or was there a true worm of disease boring through the hull of his being? Neil saw his father again in a childhood vision, swimming strong for the towline in the crashing surf, pulling survivors from an oily sea. Did this man pity himself? He was a man from a place without pity. He had cut beating hearts from fish and shot sea lions in the head. He had abandoned the dead to save the living.

A fisherman's life was empty of pity. Was his father's body out of balance because his mind was? Was it that simple? Or was it something else? Could it be that all men were fishermen, sailors on a pitiless sea, carried this way and that by tide and current, lost in fog, lashed by endless waves of uncertainty? Was life itself without balance? Did his father mirror it in the unseen depths of his heart?

Neil looked out on the night sea as the boat ran on. He imagined the dark void below the thin hull, pictured great whales, giant squid, the unknown things of the depths swimming, floating there. The thinnest of membranes—a half inch of wood, nails, and caulking—separated him and his father from the clutch of eternity, in which the unknown swam in eternal silence.

They were racing over the night sea on a naked skin of nothingness.

His father was a fisherman, a man skilled at lures and traps, a man who covered the sharp truth of a pointed hook with succulent bait. Deception was his skill. If there was self-pity, was it also deception? But who was deceived? When he was young on his father's boat, he saw him with certainty. Now he seemed fleeting, the brief sum of a series of moments. He wasn't the great basking shark, moving inexorably forward. He was a flickering silver school of fish, each one a thought or a feeling. His father was many fish, and no fish at all.

"Huntsmen, awake! Am I the only man here whose eyes are open? Talk to me, huntsmen."

Cort Heinkel's words broke the static silence of the radio, the drone of the engine, and Neil's drifting thoughts.

Henry Cabral came back, as did Ott Bergstrom and Nicki, speaking for Carmelo, who was asleep in his bunk. Neil keyed the mike, answering in turn. Ott had called him "soldier boy" since his return. Neil hated it and loved it. It acknowledged his sudden harsh transition to manhood, but it signaled his return to where he could begin to forget.

Cort announced that he had overheard a good report ten degrees below their present course. The voices on the radio agreed to change direction. Without waking his father, Neil followed suit. For a while, Cort talked to Henry about the old days, before iron mikes, long runs and no sleep, steering by hand until they could run no more, then shutting down, drifting to sleep on deck boards above the warmth of the engine, until the engines cooled and they awoke in the cold to run some more. Then the two of them stopped talking. Straight off the bow, the thin moon was setting. The silhouette of a steamer crossed its narrow reflection. Moving on to the north.

To escape the drone of the engine, Neil left the wheelhouse for the deck. He checked the lashings on the fuel drums and watched the glowing sea rush past the hull. The calm sea made him uneasy. He could have set a glass of water on the hatch cover and not spilled a drop. Without wind, without swell, the sea wasn't itself. It was hiding something, luring the boats on with its peaceful mask. He made out the reflected pattern of the Big Dipper and the North Star on the ocean's surface. The sea and the heavens were one. All was well, but he was filled with a loneliness. A sense of vertigo came. The Milky Way, reflected in the sea, was hypnotic. The stars whispered from the wash of the wake. Without reason, he imagined himself leaping from the deck into the night sea, imagined the boat running on without him. For no reason at all, he was suddenly terrified, feeling out of balance. He moved away from the rail. Carefully, he made his way across the deck, back toward the cabin, using the ropes his father had rigged to keep from falling into the ocean. The sea and the stars were whispering, but he feared their call.

At dawn, they set the gear as the sun rose from the sea. The coastline had vanished in the night.

Neil was first to the pit. The air was without chill, the sea flat, but his father swayed like a toddler as he went from rope to rope strategically secured along the boom. After lowering himself into the pit, his father unraveled a cord that was attached to a thermometer set on wood, weighted at one end with lead. He cast it into the sea. A minute later, he pulled the thermometer from the water, studying the glass tube in the glare of a rising sun.

"Sixty degrees," his father said, like a chef testing a roast.

Neil had never fished tuna before. The small Half Moon Bay boats seldom did. The offshore risks were too great, and it was worth it only if the fish ran close and the weather remained fair.

Neil watched as his father set the gear. Unlike the slow walking troll for salmon, the boat was flying through the water at three-quarter speed. To port and starboard, the Half Moon Bay boats fanned out in a line of attack.

"First the long lines with a jap head," his father instructed, knowing he was new to this game. "Let 'em ride the wake."

His father uncoiled three lines of thin cotton cord and cast out the tip lines attached to the ends of the outrigger poles. To each line's end his father attached a chrome bullet, its weighted head set with red glass eyes that trailed white feathers over twin barbless hooks. Then came the two and three lines hanging from springs farther down the poles, each line a few fathoms shorter than the next. These lines were retrieved by haul lines tied to the gunnels on each side of the stern. Close to the hull came the chain lines, fishing lines weighted by lead one fathom beneath the surface. As the boat moved, the chains made foam on top of the water, a foam his father told him albacore would mistake for a school of small fish escaping toward the surface.

Neil studied line and lure once they were set. The feathered jigs skipped in a V-formation in the white wake of the boat. Unlike salmon, where fish were taken from the unseen depths, albacore swam and struck near the surface.

The black water of night changed to deep transparent blue as the sun rose higher. They were sailing across the clear lens of a gigantic eye. Neil looked deep into it. There were no jellyfish, no plankton. The sea was without scent. It was not the rich green or brown water teeming with life that washed the edge of the continent. This was the sterile water of a lonely place. He and his father had arrived at the edge of a great desert.

Nothing came to the lines. His father took the temperature of the sea at ten-minute intervals. He was looking for an edge, an invisible thermal line at the limits of a current, where the albacore would feed on squid rising up from the depths.

Once more, they settled into their routine of minimal speech. After a while, his father pulled himself from the pit and moved across the deck to the cabin. He talked to Henry Cabral on the radio. Neil heard controlled excitement from other fishermen crackling from the deck speaker. Somewhere, other boats were fishing, killing.

The loop of the direction finder turned on top of the cabin. His father was hunting the excited voices. They turned to the northwest. Cort, Henry, Carmelo, and Ott soon did the same.

By late morning, the heat was oppressive. Neil was down to his T-shirt. He ran the deck hose over his head, tasting salt at his lips. There were no gulls in the sky, no kelp flies on the deck. The ocean was lifeless, save for a sunfish floating on the surface, passing close to port. Its silver-gray head had a single small fin protruding from the sea, making slow, languid motions in the air. A solitary eye stared into the empty blue sky.

Near midday, they spotted the fleet: white dots on the northwest horizon. His father stayed out of the sun, in the cabin.

Eventually, they came to the edge of the fleet. On the starboard bow, a pod of pilot whales blew, their black backs glistening like polished ebony. Moments later, the tip lines pulled back as the first fish struck.

"Pull those skippers!" His father said as his head protruded from the cabin door, a smile on his face.

Far behind the boat, two fish were bouncing along the top of the sea. His father returned to the pit, took the boat off the pilot, and put it in a circle.

"Put these on," his father said, handing him a pair of cotton gloves with the fingertips cut out.

The fish sounded as the boat started around. The pull on the line was hard. Neil used his back, turning from side to side, yarding hard on the line. He felt the albacore's struggle, the cord in his hand fluttering with vibration. A blue blur came from the sea, passing close to his head when his father pulled his first fish from the water, swinging it to the deck, where it hit with a slam and an eruption of slapping tail. Neil followed suit, yanking his fish straight up, throwing it over his shoulder like a man flinging a shovel of dirt. The fish struggled on the deck, vomiting bits of tentacles. A strange smell came: the smell of blood, urine, and salt—a smell he knew but could not place. His father took a thin knife and with a surgeon's skill made a cut at a spot behind the gill of each fish. Dark blood spurted onto the deck as the albacores' last frantic heartbeats drained their bodies of life.

Neil looked at his father with a nod, implying question.

"Blood makes them spoil," his father answered, tossing his line back into the sea.

They caught two more fish in the turn, but eventually his father steered the boat into the fleet, hoping for bigger numbers.

Neil looked at the creatures lying in their own blood on the deck. They were fish with skin instead of scales: blue black on their backs, gray white on their bellies. Long, swordlike fins extended in scimitar curves from the sides of their torpedo bodies. They were fish with wings, wings for gliding through the depths, propelled by a large, thin crescent tail. Neil ran his finger along a groove set in the side of the dead fish's body, a groove where the fin tucked in. It was a creature built for maximum speed—a jet plane of the sea.

The large fleet was circling, running and turning in

a hundred directions. This was not the slow, ordered pace of salmon fishing. This was a dangerous free-for-all.

Within minutes, every line on both outriggers came up.

"Watch the game," his father said as the boat circled. But it was difficult to watch ahead while pulling fish to the stern, hand over hand. They had reached a large school of albacore, and the fish were in a feeding frenzy. The trick was to avoid intersecting the orbit of another vessel. Neil imagined the scene from above: an ocean filled with whirling comets feeding upon their own tails.

Neil could not tell how long they rode their merry-go-round of death before they came out of the first circle. Minutes? Hours? The deck was covered with fish, the stern wake pink with blood. How many fish had he pulled and flung over the stern? Fifty? A hundred? A hundred and fifty? He lost track in the killing. His father had pulled even more. If a fish was too large to fling over the transom, his father drove a gaff hook into its head. They worked their hands together on the bat, pulling in unison to bring the struggling creature from the water. Neil was wet with seawater, sweat, and blood. Despite his gloves, his hands were blistered. His arms and back were beset with pain.

As the afternoon progressed, fewer and fewer boats circled. A broad, low sea came up. There was still no sign of wind in the blue sky. The fleet spread out, running in scattered courses.

His father called Cort, attempting to locate the scattered Half Moon Bay boats. They passed a big bait boat idling in place, carrying a large tank on its stern. At the sides of the boat, metal racks hung down into the sea. These racks held men wielding stout bamboo poles. Under a canvas sun awning, a deckhand sat atop the tank, flicking netfuls of live bait into the sea. When the fishing fell off for the jig boats, a bait boat could hold the fish near the surface with tempting morsels. The bait boat wallowed in the slight sea. The men in the racks were up to their knees in water. Neil saw one of them kicking at the head of a blue shark that had risen from the water in pursuit of a fish landed short in the rack.

The afternoon wore on. Neil descended into the hold and stacked fish his father threw down to him, then he covered them with a layer of ice. Despite the stooped work under the deck, Neil was happy to be out of the hot sun. As he worked, he thought of the trackless miles back to land. How far had they come? One hundred miles? Two hundred? The engine and fuel meant everything now, as did the wind. He dismissed the thought of wind from his mind, as if thinking about it might tempt it forward.

In the late evening, the fish came up from the depths again and bit hard. The *Maria B* circled. As the sun went red into the sea, the fish kept coming to the lures, one after the other. His father turned the stern lights on. He was breathing hard, the strain of the day showing on his weathered face—yet his eyes were wide and alert above a streak of splattered blood washing down a cheek.

"Good night, sweetheart," he called, as he slammed a fish to the deck. His father was happy.

The fish did not sound until the first stars came out. Neil and his father pulled the lines onto the boat. The fleet spread out for sea room to drift in the night. His father slowed the engine, took it out of gear; with nowhere to go, they drifted in place. When his father shut down the engine, the boat fell silent for the first time in two days. Save for the lap of the sea at the hull, the gentle slosh of bilgewater, and their own voices, he and his father were alone in the silence of the sea. The quiet ocean felt strange. Without the sound of wind or wave, the sea was whispering secrets. Secrets he could not hear. Neil looked across the dark, still water. He did not trust the silent sea.

Neil climbed from the hold and secured the hatch cover. After he'd iced the last of the evening bite, it was midnight. He took off his slicker pants. His muscles ached, his hands burned, and his stomach was hollow with hunger. He yearned for rescuing sleep. His father had long since finished his chores in the engine room, draining fuel from the deck drums into the main fuel tanks. Across the water, Neil saw scattered mast lights beneath an overturned bowl of stars. He heard the sound of music from a distant deck speaker and the steady pop of reefer engines on the larger boats. He and his father were part of a drifting city, deep in the middle of nowhere.

Neil went to the cabin. It was filled with the mingled scents of coffee and of albacore fillets sizzling in olive oil on the galley stove. A single lightbulb burned overhead. His father stood by the stove, his body swaying to its own inner sea. A smile came to his face as he handed Neil a cup of coffee.

"Coffee, fish, and bread. That's the menu tonight, pal," his father said.

"Where are we?" Neil asked, as he looked at the fish in the pan. To a man who had killed albacore all day, the prospect of eating fish was not good, but the smell was sweet and tempting.

"About one hundred and five miles west-southwest of Point Reyes. Took a reading before we shut down. We got four hundred gallons in the main tanks. About one hundred and fifty left on deck. Enough for three days' fishing and one day to run back, with eighty gallons left over, just in case."

"In case of what?"

"In case of just in case of." His father smiled. Two tons of fish in the hold had buoyed his spirits.

"What do you mean?" After an arduous day of 255

work, sun, and engine, Neil wanted the talking to continue.

"I mean it's *all* in case of, isn't it? In case of fire, in case of rain, in case of pain. You've got to look to the worried side of things if you want to stay happy."

The sun had addled his father's brain. "That's kind of grim," Neil replied.

His father turned back to the galley stove and flipped the fillets onto heavy white plates, chipped at their edges. What was he implying?

His father handed Neil his dinner. Still holding the pancake flipper, his father looked out to the night sea and drifting mast lights. After a moment, he turned back.

"I've spent some time out here," he said. "A long time looking into that ocean."

Neil felt uneasy. His father seldom spoke this way.

"It's like a mirror, isn't it?" his father continued. It was as if he had said something Neil himself had thought. The captain never shared his thoughts. Neil knew him only by his actions, by what he said to others. His father was now looking directly at Neil.

"You know what I mean? You've come home, but I'll never really know where you've been. That's the way it is between people. We guess at it. Nobody ever knows for sure, do they? We're boats in a fog. A passing wake comes to us. There's someone there, but
we never really see them."

Neil was stunned. His father clinked the edge of his plate with the pancake flipper and looked back toward the dark ocean.

Neil took a bite of the albacore. A dim perception came. His father's inner thoughts were not for children. He was a fisherman for fishermen. He was not a man for children. Never had been. At last, Neil understood.

"Yep. A mirror," his father repeated.

They finished their bread and fish with scant talk, save functional words of engine, fuel, and the high points of the day's fishing. Under starlight on the back deck, Neil did the dishes in a bucket of seawater, in which trapped glowing organisms of light swam in circles. By the time he climbed down into the fo'c'sle, his father was fast asleep. He listened to his father's breathing before falling away to his own sleep. As he closed his eyes, he saw albacore being pulled from the sea and comets swirling in his father's mind.

Neil reached back to hold on to his dream. But he was fully awake, and it was gone. He had slept through the alarm clock's ring. His father's bunk was empty. He heard him moving in the cabin above the fo'c'sle ladder. Above the skylight, stars moved back and forth. Night was yet upon the sea. The clock read 4:30 A.M., but more than time had changed in his three hours of sleep. Once more, the sea was moving. Bilgewater sloshed in the bowels of the boat. The fo'c'sle lifted and lowered. The sea had awakened while they slept.

Neil forced his stiff body from the bunk. The engine awoke, filling the fo'c'sle with a low, vibrant hum. As he dressed, his father called to him to bring up from the forepeak a canvas bag containing the staysail.

"Why?" Neil asked.

"No reason," his father replied. "Just a little something to keep the flies off the deck."

But Neil was not so sure, as he pulled the staysail from its locker and lugged it up into the cabin. There were no flies one hundred miles from shore.

"You think it's something?" Neil asked, watching a breeze wrinkle the sea's surface, scattering the reflected stars. There *was* something, though neither Neil nor his father used its name.

A half hour later, an orange glow appeared on the eastern edge of the sea. They put the boat in gear and the lines in the water. Neil noted that his father's first tack was into the emerging light. They were running to greet the sun.

At dawn, the breeze increased. The following seas approaching the stern had a scalelike, reptilian appearance. As the swells increased, the boat rode the back of an undulating serpent, but the hiss of its power did not yet make itself known. There *was* something, but it was far away, hidden. Neil watched the lines and put it out of his mind.

The dirty canvas staysail, set above the stern boom, snapped gently in the morning breeze. Within minutes of the fiery tip of the sun's rising, several albacore came to the lines. Soon Neil was breathing hard from the strain of the pull. He flung the fish to the deck. They vomited, bled, and died as a new day began.

His father joined him in the stern and put the boat in a circle. Several more fish came. Then nothing. Again, his father turned the bow east. By now, they were two miles inside the main fleet. The *Evon, Norland,* and the *Cefula* were on a similar course on the port beam. The *Marina* was nowhere in sight.

The breeze held steady at ten knots until midday, then it slackened, although the groundswell grew larger as each hour went by. A high, gray overcast came from the west, covering the blue sky. Nearby, fishing boats disappeared in the troughs of the high swells.

Continuing east, they came to the cold water edge, hooking several bonita—silver-striped clowns of the tuna family.

Neil's father saw it first, looking to the northwest behind the stern, holding on to his stern safety rope, tied to the boom's end. Neil looked in the direction of his father's stare. It came dark, and alone, low across the water, gliding up, then down, over the backs of the swells. Soon the sooty albatross, its double-jointed wings set in eternal glide, came east, rising on the updraft off the back of a large swell. As it lifted above the swell, it turned its dark head and long beak toward the *Maria B.* For an instant, Neil saw the bird's cold eye looking down upon their small boat as if in judgment. Then it turned away, gliding on effortlessly, dismissive of what it had seen.

After it had passed, Neil noticed his father gazing after the bird, following it to its disappearance.

"What's the matter?" Neil asked.

"Wind bird." For the first time that day, the unspoken word had been said.

His father pulled himself from the pit and made his way to the cabin. Soon Henry Cabral came back on the deck speaker.

"Yah, I think so, Ernie, we keep going this way."

"We keepa run to the inside too, Ernie," Carmelo Denari said, breaking in with an edge of urgency.

Before long, the radio was filled with the growing chatter of fishermen. None of it was about fishing, but all of it was calm and matter-of-fact—*too* matter-of-fact. The fleet was moving back toward land, away from an unspoken fear of an invisible enemy, amassed and marching down upon them from the distance. The men of plank and steel, of oil and engine, were surrendering the sea to a solitary bird.

Cort's voice came from the deck speaker. *"Ja,* Ernie, that's right. I'm on my way too. I think a night current takes me outside. *Schnell, mein* huntsmen, the old woman is coming."

His father leaned out the cabin door and signaled to put the lines on board. All the Half Moon Bay boats were accounted for, and they were on their way home.

With the lines on board, his father ordered them removed, stowed into buckets, and secured with lids inside the trolling pit. His father increased the engine's speed, but he did not order the stabilizers on deck.

Neil iced the morning fish in the hold, bracing himself between the ice bins to the roll of the boat. When he emerged from the hold, his father was on deck with a can of nails and a hammer. The wind was stiffening, humming a low, broken song in the rigging.

"Better safe than sunk," his father said.

Neil held the can as his father nailed the hold's hatch cover in place. Next came the engine room door, then the hatch on the lazaret, and finally the hatch cover on the trolling pit. Neil had never before see his father take such precautions.

By midafternoon, the breeze had freshened and the increasing seas were showing teeth at their crests. Something was upon them. The enemy had struck. 261

They were surrounded by its presence, though far from overwhelmed.

The wind reached twenty-five, then thirty knots, pushing hard on the staysail set over the boom on the rear deck. The sea danced with whitecaps, occasionally making the boat their partner as they slapped on board over the rails.

With the following sea pushing them on, each minute, each hour, took them closer to safety. Running in the quarter was not easy. Even with the staysail, the boat yawed sharply from side to side. His father had to steady himself in the cabin. Dishes slid in the sink, but in twenty-nine hours the boat would be home. The ride was tolerable, if not comfortable.

His father took several shots with the direction finder. He computed the loran readings, checked the course, and marched off the distance to land with dividers. They were inside and above the Taney Seamounts, running 98 degrees dead on Half Moon Bay, between the Pioneer and Guide Seamounts, underwater mountains whose peaks lay sixteen hundred fathoms under the sea. By midafternoon of the following day, the safety of the continental mass would rise on the eastern horizon. As the sun sank on their stern, his father cooked a pot of beans on the stove. They had grown used to the ride. Perhaps the nails were unnecessary.

But the real wind came in the night.

Minute by minute, hour by hour, the wind increased in intensity. Time slowed. Language stopped. Neil's mouth grew dry. In the dark pilothouse, he braced himself on one side of the cabin, while his father, with his back against the sink, did the same on the other side. It was impossible to sit. His father cut the speed of the engine to reduce yaw as they slid down the backs of large following seas. The electric motor on the autopilot whined, straining to hold the rudder on course. The night sea was covered with glowing white-caps. The ones that broke alongside the boat hissed with an intensity that covered the noise of the engine and the crackle of voices on the radio, alive with fish-ermen desperate to reach land.

By midnight, the Half Moon Bay boats were re-grouped in a loose cluster of running and mast lights that disappeared and reappeared as they rose and fell in the broad high seas. Cort Heinkel lagged behind, but they knew where he was.

The wind increased. His father slowed further, and Carmelo, Henry, Ott, and Cort agreed to change course, pointing the wallowing boats farther to the south in order to keep the growing swells and wind directly on the stern. No longer quartered into the troughs, the boats rode better, but they had traded distance for comfort and safety. The wind was forcing them to run diagonally toward the coast—a maneuver that added time and fuel consumption to the problem of survival.

The illuminated dial on the clock near the binnacle pointed to 3:00 A.M. The wind came on stronger—his father estimated fifty knots. The boats slowed to trolling speed. His father took the wheel and turned off the pilot. Whitecaps punched the stern with violence. Neil felt them through the soles of his boots as they swept the decks with carpets of white. Seawater squirted through the edges of the cabin door. The line between boat and sea was disappearing by degrees. Neil thought of the depths over which they floated, imagining wooded havens of pastoral peace atop seamounts far below. But a slap to the stern by another wave brought him back to the knowledge that there was no escape from the wind and the reality at hand. At the helm, his father struggled to keep the boat on course. One false turn could put them broadside to the full power of the breaking seas. The binnacle light cast an ashen glow on his father's face.

As the night wore on, distant calls of distress, muffled in static, filled the cabin. One vessel had lost a pole, which then fouled its rudder. Another's engine had died, making it a helpless target of the vicious seas that swept its decks, breaking cabin windows, ending the call of its terrified skipper. Neil and his father were too far away. They could only listen to the strategies of nearby boats moving to rescue. If Neil had one prayer, it was for dawn. But prayer blew away in the power of the wind. He sensed the sea and the nature of things for what they were: immensity without remorse.

"Huntsmen!" There was something wrong with the sound of Cort Heinkel's voice.

Neil's father took the mike, keeping one hand on the wheel.

"*Ja*, Ernie. I'm good and screwed here. She rolls bad. Took a comber in the cabin. I hear a lot of wood cracking."

His father motioned for Neil to take the wheel as he moved to the direction finder, trying for a shot before Cort stopped talking. Neil felt the power of the following seas in the helm as they pushed on the rudder. His father steadied himself in the roller-coaster cabin, still holding the radio mike, turning the dial on the overhead loop, searching for a compass bearing on Cort's unsettled voice.

"I got him two-ninety, Ernie," Henry Cabral shot back.

His father had a fix too. "Three-oh-five here," he called back to Henry. "Behind and above. I'm turning around."

There was no hesitation. They were going back— back around into the sea already won from the wind. Neil looked at his father.

His father returned to the helm and slowed the engine, awaiting his chance. Neil looked at him watching astern, judging the swell and the cresting white water in the dark. Coming full about would be dangerous: too slow, they could be hit broadside; too fast, they could broach. And if the stern was pushed around, the boat would roll over. The wind and sea had changed the formerly simple act of putting the boat about into a defining moment of existence.

The instant came. The boat rose to the top of a sea as his father swung the wheel. They fell down the back side of the swell, turning. There was only one thing they could do: His father had to point the bow around by the bottom of the trough in time to get it up into the next mountain of water.

Neil felt the boat drop as the wind slackened in the dark valley of water. They were abeam of disaster, vulnerable to the next sea looming broken and white. The wooden cabin, their tiny home upon the sea, was nothing to the power that approached them. Neil envisioned the cabin being swept from the deck, tumbling down into the depths—speechless, drowning men in a sinking enclosure.

His father pushed the throttle to full power. Bracing himself, he swung the wheel as far as it would go. The engine strained. The bow came about. It was not enough. The fishing boat began to lift into the oncoming white. They heeled hard to port. The starboard

266

stabilizer flew from the water like a shooting star, trailing a fiery tail of phosphorescence. But his father's decision to increase power at the last moment kicked the stern around, allowing them to quarter the white violence that shook the boat. The breaking crest and swell passed as they plunged down its back side. They had made it.

His father struggled to keep the boat on course toward Cort's distress. They met the next wall—up and over, down and up, and on. Each wall of water was a new eternity, each wave at its crest a death. The hull resonated with every impact to the bow. The sound was chilling. Neil imagined planks separating, caulking spewing out, the sea coming in. Deep down in a coward's place, he wanted his father to turn back. They would never make it. Worse, they would destroy themselves trying. White water came over the bow and struck the cabin hard. He was certain the plate on the windows would go. The bow dipped down; it rose again. On they went. Each swell was an ordeal in an eternity of water. Struggling to keep his balance, his father swung the wheel, cutting back on the throttle as they came to the tops of waves, pouring it on as they raced down their back sides again. The engine and the hull were part of his father's body.

"Hold me," his father yelled. "Catch me if I start to go."

Neil understood. In the pitching, dropping, and ris- 267

ing cabin, his father's equilibrium was beginning to fail. His powerful legs fought the roll of the boat, but his head betrayed him. Neil moved behind his father, put his hands on his shoulders, gathered his shirt in his fingers, and held on.

They were not alone. All the Half Moon Bay boats made it around, even the tiny *Cefula*. At the tops of waves, Neil looked back to their red and green running lights, driving hard toward a friend's voice in the night.

But the wind took its toll as the boats ran on.

"*Ja,* come back, Henry. I think—I think I'm pretty good screwed here, boys. Locked in tight." Cort's voice was filled with fatigue, resignation, and truth.

Cort was trapped. The comber had cracked the cabin hard. With each new wave, water came in through its splintered side. Two windows were gone, but worse, the doorjamb was crushed. Cort could not escape to the deck.

"Chop the door out," his father commanded on the microphone. For a long minute, the radio was silent.

"Good idea, Ernie. But no deal, huntsman. It rolled over me like a steamroller. A black cat couldn't squeeze out. And jimmy Jesus, where could I go? Pumps can't hold it. Stern is down. I got a swimming pool for a deck—"

A thud came through the speaker. A half word more, and Cort went silent. Another wave had struck.

Henry called. His father called. Ott called. Carmelo. Reassuring they were on their way.

Cort's voice did not come back. The bow pitched up. Another wave punched the hull. White came to the windows. Neil felt the cabin shudder. He held tight to his father. Down they went. Down and on.

But Cort was not gone. A half hour later, a hundred years later, they saw a lone mast light ahead at the top of a sea. His father took the mike and called Cort to come back, commanding him to flash his mast light three times if his transmitter was gone.

The light up ahead went off and on three times.

"Keepa your pants dry, Cort. We almosta there," Carmelo sang out with encouragement.

"*Ja,* I see you boys." The signal was weak, but they had him in sight.

Carmelo came back again. He said Nicki was ready. He had an ax and a crowbar, and a line attached to himself, secured to the inside of the cabin. If Carmelo could maneuver close enough, Nicki would chance a jump to the *Marina.*

"*Nein, nein,* Carmelo. Too much sea. Too much wind. Too much water over the decks. Don't risk your son to catch my fat ass."

"Hold on there, Cort," Henry's voice came. Cort's weak signal came back in turn.

"Henry . . . ," Cort replied, but his signal cut out once more.

They came to the *Marina,* foundering in sea and wind. His father maneuvered as close as he dared. The back deck was under, washed with white water. Only the bow and the top of the cabin, crushed in on its starboard side, remained afloat. The running lights and mast light were on, which meant Cort still had batteries. The stricken fishing boat lay below them, then rose high above as each sea passed. It was impossible to get a man to the deck. The wind smelled of oil and blood from the vessel's flooding hold. The *Evon* came and heaved to, as did the *Cefula* and the *Norland.* On the radio, the fishermen searched for a plan, a response if Cort could still hear. Neil saw the *Marina*'s radio antenna above its mast light as the fishing boats rose and fell all around the helpless vessel.

The blink of a flashlight came from the cabin's port window.

"Huntsmen, you're here." Cort's voice came again. "I see your lights." Static came to the radio. A long pause, then Cort's voice returned. "Huntsmen, home. We'll sail again. . . ."

The transmission broke up, then came back again.

"Give my Bethel goodbye. Home, boys, home. . . . I see your lights. *Vergissmeinnicht.* The old man is calling. . . ."

The *Marina* rose up to meet the teeth at the top of a sea. The wave washed over. The sea fell away. The *Marina* was gone. Only its mast remained.

"Ahhhhh!" his father called out, his very voice a defiant curse in the wind.

The mast and its light slid away, disappearing by feet. The antenna was going. A word came. Feeble yet clear. In the cabin, under the sea, in a pocket of air, Cort Heinkel was alive.

"Huntsmen."

Another sea came, dark and tall. They fell into the trough. Neil looked into the sea above. The mast light was there, underwater, dimmer and dimmer. Sailing down. Sailing on.

Chapter Ten

The halyard to the sea anchor, attached to the raft, hung straight down in the sea. Hand over hand, Neil pulled it in. The current had stopped pushing the raft. He was no longer moving. He was at a fixed point on the sea, and it filled him with fear. Through the canopy opening, he stretched his hands toward the dawn, beseeching it to come. When he fell back into the raft, he put his forehead to its chamber and heard someone crying, far away, deep in the depths.

·   ·   ·

There were other hands on the Redeemer's helm as it raced away from the mothership. He felt them. One hand for each spoke on the wheel. His father's hands. Cort's hands. Henry's. Ott's. Carmelo's. It's what they would have done. Without question. They were fishermen. He, too, was a fisherman.

He put the helm about. Taylor and Smith didn't notice until the boat was halfway through the turn. They had gone to the back deck to secure the hold cover and gloat over their treasure.

Neil called Paul to the cabin. It was on Paul's face too, leaving the men. He told Paul to shut the cabin door. Take the sea lion gun. Paul understood immediately. They were not going to be rich, but Neil could not betray the men who had showed him the way.

Smith and Taylor had no weapons. They beat on the door, calling them fools.

Paul fired a round of double aught through the porthole window on the door.

"Good," Neil called, with ringing ears.

Paul jacked home another round. Taylor and Smith retreated behind the cabin.

The mothership was settling fast in the stern. The yellowfish had switched on the deck lights. When they saw the Redeemer returning, they began waving at the rail, exuberant. The fender came level with the deck. They climbed over the rail and waited as the boat approached. Smith went to the pit and pulled away the hatch.

He tried to steer the boat away with the small metal wheel in the stern, but the wheel in the cabin was larger—more leveraged. Neil held the Redeemer *on course straight for the mothership—full throttle, with everything he had.*

Neil reversed hard to the fender. The yellowfish leaped on board. Screaming with joy, screaming with hate.

Consequences were swift. With knives and hands, the yellowfish moved quickly. Taylor was cut down next to the hold. Smith made it as far as the flying bridge, yelling for Neil and Paul to do something. They heard the scuffle on the cabin roof as Neil turned the boat away from the sinking mothership.

The yellowfish threw Smith's body down to the deck and dragged it to the stern, placing it with Taylor's. As the deck lights of the mothership went under, they rolled the limp bodies into the sea.

Then they came to the cabin door. Paul readied the shotgun. Neil put the wheel on pilot and took a knife from the galley. He and Paul stepped carefully out on the deck. But the heads of the yellowfish were lowered with gratitude. One man knelt on the deck, his knees in blood. Carefully, delicately, the yellowfish took Neil's hand and pressed it to his forehead.

The sun was coming—a new day was coming. Neil's fear was gone. He was hungry and thirsty, but he was hopeful,   275 *more so than he could remember being since he joined with the raft. They would see him. The sky was clear.*

The rim of the red disk rose from the sea. He saw a flock of seabirds silhouetted against it. Murre, cormorant, brant? Too far to tell. Winging south. They flew on, but he was certain they saw him too.

The sun rose fully from the sea, warming Neil's cold body. He looked away, thinking. His thoughts came slower, but it was not an unpleasant feeling. Once more, he brought to mind Cort's death years before. And for the first time in years, he thought about his father's death as well. His father did not die at sea, but when he went under, he, too, drifted alone.

For weeks after Cort's death, the men spoke little of him as they prepared their crab pots for the coming winter season. Cort's skiff remained tied to its mooring out in the bay, lifting and falling in the swells, pointing into the shifting wind. Nobody retrieved it, as if all were awaiting its owner's return. As the weeks went by, it was painted white with seagull droppings. Seaweed grew at its waterline. With the first rain, it filled half full, and Henry Cabral and Neil's father brought it to the wharf, lifted it from the sea, and trucked it to his father's backyard. The following spring it floated alone on a sea of grass amidst wild mustard plants, solitary monument to a fisherman's end.

Neil's father's condition grew worse. That crab season, he fell into the sea while reaching for a crab buoy. He saved himself with one of his own boots, filling it with air, holding it under his chin, floating long enough for Ott Bergstrom to get a line around him and use the crab block to haul him back to the deck.

The doctors didn't know what was wrong. They examined his inner ear and an old injured knee. When salmon season arrived, it became harder and harder for his father to walk. The land had become an ocean. He reached to steady himself wherever he walked. They X-rayed his skull and his spine. A day came when he could no longer walk out on the wharf in the dark, or climb down the ladder to his skiff. His friends sailed away. He went back to the doctors. The bills piled up.

Once again, Neil drove his father back from the hospital.

"They say I got a chance," his father said, as they drove down the coast highway. He looked out the window toward the ocean. "All I want is a chance."

The doctors had a theory: A vertebra had grown thick inside with calcium, pressing on his spinal cord. They wanted to go fishing inside his body, scrape away the deposit. His father agreed.

"Barnacles on the spine," his father said, making a joke. Neil did not think it was funny, but it was a chance.

The first operation would go through the front of his neck, the second through the back. His father would have six months in between to recover.

After the first operation, his father came home from the hospital in a wheelchair. Neil built a ramp up the back porch stairs. The bills increased. His father made a decision: He would sell his boat. Neil's mother said nothing. Their mutual dreams had parted company years before. She had a career of her own, separate, apart from his father's dealings on the ocean.

The day the boat was sold, Neil drove his father to the customhouse, where papers were signed to transfer ownership of the boat. The buyer was an Okie, a fool who said he loved the sea. His father got up out of his wheelchair to sign the papers. He introduced the fool to the customs man, the customs man to the fool. His father's tone was formal and serious as he attempted to add dignity to an ignoble twist of fate. The bureaucrat and the Okie did not understand. The boat was sold. The Okie sailed away. His father stayed home. Neil felt hurt on his father's behalf and resentful of his mother's indifference.

But his father thought differently. He had a plan. The second operation was the key. Well and upright once again, he would buy a new boat with what money was left. A smaller boat, yes, but it would be a new start.

Neil drove his father to the hospital for the second operation. His father was hopeful that in six more months he'd be back at sea. He waved and smiled at Neil as the nurses pushed him away, just as he did on the ocean to a passing fisherman.

But things went wrong. The doctors proclaimed the operation a success, but it went on too long. The anesthetic poisoned his father's liver. His skin became yellow with jaundice.

Neil entered his father's hospital room, he was moaning in a metal bed. Neil thought of a crab caught in a trap. His father's arms were strapped down, but his fingers were clawing. His eyes were open. His mother came too. His father beseeched her to go. Neil looked into his father's eyes. They were the eyes of a fish on a leader, open and wide, a fish on the stern pulled to the gaff.

"I know," his father said. "I know."

By morning, he was adrift in a coma, moored to his bed. There were tubes in his arms, his mouth, and his nose. It went on for days. Neil stood by his father's bed, watching his chest rise and fall like swells on the sea. The storm was inside, beneath the surface. What did his father know?

On the second night of Neil's vigil, two memories

came. He remembered the winter of the crab strike, the winter his father and his friends dumped their dead crabs on the beach. Rather than fish for a reduced price, the fishermen pulled their crab pots and brought them back to their yards. His father was forced to take a job on the land, going to work in the shipyards in the city as a welder. Each day, he would leave on a Greyhound in the early morning and return late at night. One such night, Neil met his father at the bus stop and walked home with him. His father carried a lunch box and handed Neil his aluminum helmet to carry. His father was tired, his pace unsteady; Neil had never seen him this tired before. He was a repairer of ships that then went back to his sea. He worked for the sake of his family, not for himself.

The second memory came from the following summer, when the fishermen once more went in chase of salmon. Neil rejoined his father after school was out. They pursued the schools of silver, north along the coast, above the point and above Bodega Bay, past Salt Point and Fish Rock to Point Arena. The schools of fish were concentrated, and the fishing was good.

In the morning, the wind came up. Cort, Henry, Ott, Carmelo, and Neil's father brought their boats to a rickety old dock in the Point Arena cove, open to the sea. They rafted the boats to the wharf with header and spring lines. In the late morning, his father went to the icehouse for two cases of bait, bait ordered by the Half Moon Bay boats and sent the night before up the coast on a fish truck.

As his father carried two cases from the freezer, he was met in the icehouse by an Okie boat puller trying to impress his skipper. The Okie demanded half of the bait. The man was tall and thin, and much younger than his father. His father put the bait down and told the Okie to whom it belonged. The Okie was insulting. He struck his father with his fist. His father stepped back, raised his fists like a boxer, and hit the Okie hard in the face. The Okie struck back, wild and strong. Other fishermen came. The Okie dove into his father, scratching at his eyes, digging his fingers into his neck.

"Fight fair," his father cried out.

The Okie was choking his father. Neil had to do something. He grabbed an ice hook from on top of a box and ran at the Okie, raising the hook to strike him in the back. But just as he was about to strike, he felt himself rise in the air, grabbed by his wrist.

"No you don't, boy." A voice came at his back, as Ott Bergstrom held him tight.

His father broke free from the Okie's clutch, gasping for air. He pushed the Okie away, hitting hard with his fists. The Okie too was out of breath. For a long time, they stood face-to-face, with heaving chests. The fight was finished.

Ott carried the bait back to the boats, hoisted on

his shoulders. Neil accompanied his father from the icehouse. Neil was trembling. His father touched Neil's shoulder, patting it gently.

"That's okay, honey," was all his father said. There was no further explanation. His father had fought for the sake of his friends, not for himself.

On the fourth day of his father's coma, his breathing became labored. Neil spoke to him, but there was no real response: Garbled words came and went from his mouth. His father was elsewhere. On an ocean, by himself. Drifting on.

Neil was driving to the hospital two days later when his father died. Afterward, he went to a promontory overlooking the sea. A hard northwester blew waves to the beach. Whitecaps marched in from the horizon. There were no fishing boats in sight.

Wearing suits, the fishermen carried his father's coffin from the mortuary. On the ride to the crematorium, his mother complained of the expense of it all. Paul consoled her like the good son he was. Neil was angry and despised them both.

Three days later, Neil, Paul, and Philip took their father's ashes in a concrete urn to the wharf. Henry Cabral brought the *Evon* to the pier. They all sat on the bow and went out to sea, past the breakwater, past the reef, past the moan of the sea buoy on a southwest course. There was no wind. The sea was still, but a low fog bank loomed. They sailed into the fog, which obscured the morning sun. They ran through openings of light, clouds of mist, opening light once more.

Standing alone on the flying bridge, Henry Cabral slowed the boat. He took it out of gear, and the *Evon* slowed to a drift. Neil looked down at the final, dark water and cast his father's urn into the sea. It fell from sight vanishing in the deep. There was nothing to say.

They sat drifting for a time before Henry put the boat in gear. As they started to go, a sound came from port. Then another. The blow of whales, a gray whale cow and a gray whale calf moving north. Neil saw the dark hump of the mother, her barnacled skin, the slender calf at her side. He heard the inhale of breath. The animals dove, and came up no more. It was nothing, it meant nothing—neither symbol nor sign. The creatures swam on, oblivious to his grief.

H*e knew too. He sucked the final drop from the last water sachet. The sun was descending to the other side of the horizon. The sky was clear, but nobody had seen him. No ships had passed.*

In the late afternoon, a lone airliner etched contrails in the blue far overhead. He became excited. He signaled with

his mirror. Imagined people comfortable inside. Eating off
trays. Sipping cool drinks. "Look down," he said quietly.
"Look down on a fisherman lost on the sea."

    The plane flew on. He was alone.

The sun fell away. Stars rose in the east. He slumped in the
raft. The chambers were soft. A thought of surrender came.
He imagined the raft without air, a tattered shroud entan-
gling his body as he sank to the depths. He took the pump
and pumped some more.

In time, Neil became a fisherman too. He bought
the *Redeemer,* forty-two feet of old yet reliable wood.
Detroit diesel in the engine room, knuckle stern,
sharp entry in the bow, flying bridge atop its cabin, a
deep hold for the fish he would catch.

    The seasons went on. His mother married again
and moved to the city, away from the sea. Her new
husband was a good man, an ordinary man, who measured his dreams in paychecks and fulfilled his life in
pension. Neil and Paul raised Philip as best they
could. Soon Philip was a fisherman too.

    As the years drifted by, Carmelo Denari and Nicki
were lost at sea, disappearing on an uneventful day.

    Three years later, on a windy night, the *Norland*
broke free of its mooring and crashed on the breakwa-

ter. Ott Bergstrom was crushed between the *Norland* and the rocks, trying to save his boat.

After Henry Cabral's wife, Annie, died, Henry seldom went home. He was an old man living on his boat. In his fo'c'sle, he fastened her picture to a bulkhead. Below it, wired to a shelf, he kept a small lantern fired by cooking oil.

Long before he suffocated in his sleep, the Raisin became a fisherman too. He bought a cruiser and hired a Samoan to take him to and from his boat. The Raisin sat in his wheelchair, strapped to the deck, steering the boat, issuing commands to his Samoan deckhand. Neil passed the Raisin one day off Bodega Head, bucking into the wind. Spray rained down on his body and chair. His face was beaming. His good arm waved. He was the happiest man Neil had ever seen.

Over time, everything changed. Fishermen changed, cabins bristled with electronics. The fish couldn't hide. New boats were made of steel. The new men were made of deals and debt. They went longer and farther, for less and less. Competition increased. The fish declined. The government came in, and all was lost.

Somebody was laughing in the night. Neil got up on his knees, looked around at the sea and sky. Each star was a   285 *knot in a net. He was trapped. He had to get out. He picked up a plastic paddle. Dug hard at the water. Dug hard and paddled on. Round and round and round.*

When he came to a stop, he heard someone crying. He was thirsty, but there was nothing to drink. He tasted a tear with the tip of his tongue. A taste of betrayal. A taste of the sea. He tried to spit on his hand, but nothing came. He lay down in the raft, his ear to the sea.

Sounds came from below, strange sounds, the sounds of yellowfish beseeching, killing. The yellowfish were swimming his way, telling him something. Paul was with them. They were all swimming, calling to him, trying to tell him something.

Henry Cabral saw them as Neil and Paul slipped out on the *Redeemer*. Old Henry sitting on his back deck, fast to his mooring, weaving wire on a salmon scoop. Henry waved, but his wrinkled face watched without smiling. He knew. They told no one they were leaving, where they were going. If anything happened, nobody would know, nobody but Henry, but whom would he tell?

With the death of the dealers, the deal wasn't a deal. Paul and the yellowfish cast the bales one after the other into the sea, ripping them open, sending them back to the mothership that had brought them. The yellowfish didn't care. They were sailor immigrants, bound for a promised new port.

They ran hard for the coast. At daylight, Neil and Paul hid the men in the hold and gave them cans of Coke, bread, and a jug of water. The sea was warm, flat, and greasy, but at midday high clouds pressed in. A lump from the south arose. Past noon, the higher mountains of the coast came in sight. Neil slowed the boat, to approach in the dark. On the flying bridge, Paul scanned the horizon for cutters, while Neil watched the radar for converging blips. Their plan was simple. Run for home in the dark. Go on the mooring and row each man ashore, one at a time.

But as darkness came, the clouds lowered and the wind came on. Then rain and wind. Thirty knots, forty knots, gusting faster. A southeaster had struck.

Twelve miles from the coast, a blip appeared on the screen, northwest and coming their way. Drag boat? Fishing boat running for cover? Coast Guard cutter? In the night, there was no way to know.

They bucked east-southeast for the beach, their running lights off. In five fathoms of water outside and below the town of Half Moon Bay, they turned north toward home, hugging the cliffs, hugging the coast on a course only a fisherman would know, losing themselves in the coastal clutter of anyone's radar screen. The blip passed away, running south, well off the coast.

But in shallow water, the seas rose and the waves toppled over. Paul secured the hatches and went to the bridge to spot the way. They'd take the chance. They'd squeeze inside the south reef and the beach. A treacherous spot in a storm, but they knew it well. They'd taken some chances. One more wouldn't hurt.

Neil felt the boat drop before the comber hit. It was sudden, like an elevator falling. The strike of a hammer, and then he was thrown onto the wall of the cabin, sliding down to the ceiling. The windows burst, exploding with water. Something cracked in the bowels of the boat. Above him, the muffled screams of trapped men came from behind a bulkhead. He was floating, swimming in blackness, feeling his way. The bottom of the door was the top of the door. He pushed through.

He came to the surface. Pain exploded in his chest. How long had he been under? He gasped for air. The raft rose to the surface, inflating nearby, blowing away in the wind. He swam to the raft and pulled himself inside.

He rose on a sea. The overturned hull of the *Redeemer* was awash nearby, its propeller still turning. Wind and current were pushing him away. He saw a form on the upturned hull. He called for his brother. The wind howled back. He called again. The wind howled back. A comber came, and all was gone.

Neil awoke with his ear still pressed to the fabric, listening to the sea. But no more memories came and no sound save the lap of water at the edge of the raft. He felt better, refreshed. Things would be fine. He would be saved. He had come this far.

He crawled to the edge of the raft. The stars had turned but not gone away. Orion was high overhead. He watched the stars' reflection on the sea mingling with lights from below, glowing organisms rising up from the deep—blinking briefly, swimming away. He was in the arms of the sea. He would be saved. He had come this far.

He thought of his brother. He heard Paul's voice. He wasn't dreaming. The words flowed up from the night sea. His own words too. They were boys again at the edge of the sea. "Ready?" he heard himself say.

Neil was aiming a rock, standing on top of a rocky ledge. Paul stood beside him.

"Ready," Paul replied, mimicking the motion of a big-league pitcher.

They were ready.

At the sea's edge, between rock and tide pool, an elephant seal lay stranded in death. Waves struck the bleached and leathered carcass, sending ripples of movement through the animal's dead mass, suggesting life where there was no life. On the creature's back, a gaping wound opened to the gray sky, large as a window. A window open to death. The wind off the sea was pungent with extinction.

Paul's rock flew through the air. The putrid pool on the creature's back exploded in a splash of purple liquid, sending clouds of kelp flies to flight.

Neil flung next. On target. Then Paul once more. Then Neil. Shouts of morbid delight rose with each splash of stone, until their arms grew tired and the stones overflowed the wound. After a while, they left the dead animal, crossed a sandy stretch of beach, and ascended a trail up a sandstone bluff.

At the top of the cliff, they stopped and looked back. The creature had grown small in the distance. Seagulls, waddling like arrogant sailors, stood on the dead animal's back. They jousted with wings atop the carcass, and the winners dipped their heads.

Out beyond the beach, on a gray ocean speckled with whitecaps, a ship ran north under the overcast sky. Smoke curled back from its funnel. The air was cold. The wind blew hard from the water. Farther out to sea, Neil saw the gray sky breaking apart. Rays of sunlight streaked down, creating islands of light upon the ocean. He was looking for the boats. His father's boat. The Half Moon Bay boats returning to port from another day of fishing.

"Neil, what do you see out there? Do you see the boats?" Paul asked.

"No," he answered.

He looked at Paul. The wind moved a shock of hair on his brother's forehead. His nose was edged with snot. His brother was thinking hard again.

"It had a big heart."

"What did?" Neil answered.

"The seal. The elephant seal. Our rocks sank all the way to its heart. Had to."

"So?"

"So it had to have a big soul. Heart and soul. You've heard that. But I've never seen a picture of a seal in heaven. Flying around with wings, with all the angels and the people who got there."

"It didn't have a soul," Neil answered.

"How do you know? It had a heart."

"It just didn't."

Paul settled down and stared out at the gray water.

On the sea, the wind was opening and closing the breaks in the clouds.

"There," Paul said, pointing. "The boats."

Neil saw them too, far to the northwest, tiny specks

sailing into a shaft of light, coming their way. Fishing boats, running for home. The Half Moon Bay boats. Their father's boat.

"Neil, do you think we'll be fishermen?" Paul asked.

"I don't know," he said.

"Then what kind of men will we be?"

Neil looked again at the tiny boats. He saw the immensity of sky and water all around.

"Heroes," Neil shouted, laughing, hitting his brother on the arm, inviting chase. He ran away, ran on with Paul and the wind from the sea hard at his back.

Neil couldn't remember when the voices stopped talking, or when the two boys stopped running. Orion was low in the west. Constellations, stars, other worlds, had turned on the axis of the North Star like spokes on a wheel. An hour had passed. A million years had passed. He was on an ocean in a distant galaxy. He was a distant galaxy. A spoke on a heavenly helm. Turning.

Sometime later, a lifetime later, he saw them. They were coming. Happiness came to his heart. Eyes in the night, heading his way. Red and green lights on the night sea beneath the turning stars. Running lights below. Mast lights above. They were searching, coming straight for him. Henry Cabral had sent them.

He knew they wouldn't leave him. They were fishermen. His father was coming on the Maria B. *Cort Heinkel on the* Marina. *Ott Bergstrom on the* Norland. *Carmelo Denari and Nicki on the* Cefula. *He would be saved. He had come this far.*